STRICTLY PLEASURE

CARRIE ELKS

CHAPTER
ONE

I'm on fire.

Not literally, thank goodness. But my whole body is tingly and damp and the hair at the back of my neck is wet and sticking to my skin. I put my hand to my chest and feel a trail of sweat weaving its way down my cleavage. My bare cleavage.

Which means I'm naked.

I blink my eyes open and crane my head to find the source of the intense heat. He's laying behind me, his arm flung over my stomach, his chest curved against my back. His breathing is soft, his hair messed up, and I have no idea whether that's due to a poor night's sleep or me.

I feel that I need to point out something. I don't usually do this kind of thing. It's not that I look down upon people who have one-night stands. I'd love to be so carefree that I could sleep with somebody and walk away from them with a smile on my face, last night's clothes cladding my sated body.

But I just can't. I catch feelings. I feel hurt when they don't call. I overanalyze things so one-night stands are not good for me.

I lift his arm and manage to wiggle away from his still-slumbering body. I still feel like I'm about to combust, so I tiptoe naked to the bathroom and close the door as quietly as I can, my head pounding with a reminder that we drank way too many cocktails last night.

Although he drank more than me. There's some small comfort in that.

When I turn, I catch a glimpse of myself in the bathroom mirror.

I look terrible. My hair is a mess, there's a huge creased red spot on my cheek where I've been resting it against the pillow. A cocktail of emotions rush through me.

Horror. Embarrassment. The pure excruciating knowledge that I'm going to have to walk out and face the man currently sleeping like a baby in my bed.

Oh, did I tell you that I know him?

Liam Salinger. My best friend's brother-in-law and all around cocky rich guy.

I've known him for a few months. Since Ava – that's my best friend – got engaged to his brother, Myles. Who is lovely, by the way. And yes, some of that loveliness comes from the fact that he takes great care of Ava.

But back to Liam. How am I going to deal with this? I roll my eyes at my reflection, like it's her fault for getting me into this situation in the first place. And then I swallow and the sour taste in my mouth makes me wince.

To delay the inevitable confrontation, I brush my teeth. And shower. And as I wrap myself in a towel, with the vain hope that either he was a mirage in the first place, or he's had the good grace to leave while I've been skulking in here.

But no. He's still in my bed. In fact, he's made himself more at home. He's lying on his back right in the middle, one arm flung over his head, the bedsheet half-wrapped around his hips, revealing his admittedly fine looking chest.

If we were at his place, I'd walk out and not look back. But since he lives in New York and I live in West Virginia that's not happening. So he's the one who needs to leave.

"Liam," I whisper.

Nothing.

I say his name again, louder this time, and it results in a groan and him turning onto his side, facing away from me.

I'm not going to touch him. I just want him gone.

"For God's sake," I mutter and somehow that does the trick.

He lets out a low groan. I pull the white towel tightly around my chest. Why didn't I get dressed before I tried to wake him up?

He turns onto his back, stretching his arms above his head as though he has all the time in the world to LEAVE MY HOME!

I don't look at the way his chest muscles ripple. Okay, I do a bit.

Then his eyes open. He stares at the ceiling. Down at the bed. He blinks and his brows knit and if this was a documentary I'd find it fascinating. Man waking up and realizing he's not in his own bed.

But this isn't Netflix, it's my life and it's not funny at all.

His head turns in what feels like slow motion until those deep brown eyes land on me. His lips part but he says nothing for a moment. Just lets his gaze roam lazily over me.

"Sophie?" he croaks. "What's going on?"

"You're in my bed."

He looks down at the tiny flowers on my coverlet. "I can see that. Have I been here all night?"

"You don't remember?" I try to not sound annoyed.

Liam shakes his head slowly then winces. "Christ, what did I drink last night? Was it legal?"

"Mostly margaritas."

He lifts a brow. "I don't even like cocktails."

"You seemed to like them last night." I shrug because his choice of tipple isn't my top priority right now. "Um, you need to leave." I make a shooing motion with my hands in case he doesn't get it.

He puts his hand up, looking slightly more with it. "Wait a minute. Were you in the bed, too?"

"It's my bed," I tell him. "So yes, I was."

"And we…" He nods his head.

I take a deep breath. "Yes."

His eyes widen. "Did we use protection?"

Dear God, this man is going to kill me. "I'm covered. Now can you leave?"

"But we should talk."

"What about?"

"Was it okay?" he asks. "Was it good for you?"

My cheeks heat up. "Good for me as in did I…"

"Yeah. Did you?" His eyes don't leave mine.

I shake my head. That's the truth at least.

He sits up and runs his hands through his mussed up hair. Then he twists on the mattress and plants his feet onto my carpeted floor. The sheet still covers the important parts, thank God, because I don't think I could face that right now.

"Sophie," he says slowly. "You're lying."

My cheeks pink up. "What?"

"I always make sure a woman comes. Always. Multiple times."

Dear God, he's taking this as a personal failure. I just want him to go.

"Yes, you told me that at the bar."

He frowns. "I did? What else did I say?"

"That you never sleep with a woman more than once." I lift a brow because that's the truth. He was drunk and so was I and somehow we started talking about relationships.

He doesn't have them, apparently.

"So there you go," I say, my voice falsely chirpy in an attempt to end this once and for all. "We're one and done. Thank you and goodbye. I'm going to go get dressed in the bathroom. Please leave before I come back out. Your clothes are..." Where are his clothes? "Wherever you left them."

"Sophe..."

The way he says it makes my heart twist. Not Sophie. Just Sophe. "Please Liam, just go."

He looks almost relieved at that, and my chest contracts a little more. He wants an out. To extract himself without looking like a bad guy. And to be fair, I've given it to him.

We both went into this last night knowing the rules, even if some of them were broken.

"Okay." He nods. "Yeah, you go get dressed." He stands, the sheet falling away from his body and he looks completely unembarrassed at his nakedness.

I turn away so I'm not looking straight at him. "Can you do me a big favor?" I ask.

"Depends what it is."

"Well, I wasn't going to ask you for a second round." I lift a brow.

He huffs. I'm not sure if it's a laugh or an act of scorn. I can't see his face and actually I'm not sure I need to know.

"So what is it?" he asks.

"Can we keep this between us?" I ask him. "As in, let's not tell anybody at all."

"Sure." He sounds relieved. "Who would I tell anyway?"

"I don't want Ava and Myles to find out. I don't want things to get awkward."

"I won't tell them if you don't," he says.

"I definitely won't." There's a shuffling noise. "You can look now," he tells me. "I'm decent."

I turn my head and he's definitely not decent. Yes, he *is*

covered up, his black boxers clinging to his muscled thighs, covering the part of him I remember the most.

But he could be fully dressed and still be indecent. That's Liam Salinger for you.

"We're going to have to see each other again," he says. "When Ava has the baby. At the christening..." He scratches his stomach lazily, and I'm reminded of that animal quality again. He's completely at ease, completely unashamed.

Completely the opposite of me.

"I know that." I wince at the thought.

"So let's not make this awkward, okay?" he asks, dipping his head until our gazes meet.

"Okay," I agree. "No awkwardness."

He takes a final look at me before he grabs his jeans from the floor near my bedroom door, then walks out into the hallway, his bare feet padding against the tile.

"See you later, Sophie," he calls.

"Bye, Liam."

A minute later I hear the slam of the front door and I lean my head against the wall, mortification hitting me like a tsunami. Why did I do this? Why did I say what I said? Why didn't I go home last night when Ava and Myles did rather than drinking with the one man guaranteed to drive me insane?

I take a deep breath and peel myself off the wall, before walking to my dresser and grabbing my underwear. What's done is done. I have to accept it. At least he said it wouldn't be awkward. That's good, isn't it?

Spoiler alert. It gets awkward.

CHAPTER
TWO

SOPHIE

Two truths and a lie. Have you heard of that game? It's an icebreaker they seem to play at every corporate event I've ever been to. One of those excruciating 'getting to know you' kind of games where you have to tell two interesting facts about yourself, along with one complete lie, and everybody has to guess what the lie is.

The thing is, I suck at it. I can't tell a lie to save my life. I have a billion tells, from my eye twitching to my feet shifting like I'm dancing to *Saturday Night Fever*.

Maybe that's why I chose the profession I did. I'm expected to tell the truth. People rely on it.

The world can sometimes collapse because of it.

"And it's over to Sophie in our weather corner," Dan, the midday news anchor says, turning to his left where I'm standing in front of the green screen. He raises his brow expectantly.

"Hi Dan," I smile at him, the camera light blinking.

"It's my daughter's wedding this weekend," he says, steepling his fingers beneath his chin and putting on a serious expression. "Please tell me the weather is going to be fabulous for it."

I swallow. We haven't rehearsed this bit. We rarely do, because we've worked together for so long that our conversations flow.

"Um…" I've looked at those charts. I know the answer. "I'm sure the wedding will be fabulous no matter what the weather."

His smile falters. And this is the part of the job I hate. You wouldn't think it would be so difficult to be a meteorologist. Especially one whose main job is to present the weather on the local television station.

He blinks. "It's going to be glorious sunshine, right?"

"There should only be a few spots of rain," I say cheerily, trying to minimize the impact. "And late in the afternoon should be much better." Or at least by then it'll stop raining. That's something, right?

Dan nods and says nothing. But the expression on his face is worth a thousand words. He looks like I killed his favorite puppy. There's an awkward silence that's suddenly pierced by the producer shouting into my earpiece for me to move on.

"But let's get onto today's weather," I say, turning to the camera, trying to not wince at the volume of the screaming. "It's getting warm out there, folks. Already in the high seventies, and we're looking at hitting eighty-three by mid-afternoon." I click the button in my hand that changes the greenscreen behind me and talk through the slides I made this morning until I hear a shout in my earpiece to wrap it up.

As soon as the camera is back on Dan, he gives one of his trademark smiles that makes the heart of most women over the age of fifty flutter, and like the professional he is he thanks me and reminds the viewers that I'll be giving a full long term forecast in the next broadcast.

With the camera now firmly on the news desk, where they're talking about an influx of fireflies, and how that's preferable to last year's locust infestation, I pull out my earpiece and put it in the box, then grab my files and head back to my office.

Madison, our intern, looks up as I drop the files onto my desk and let out a big sigh. Our eyes catch and I can tell that she watched the airing. She hands me a coffee she must have bought from the shop at the front of the station.

"Don't look at Twitter," she advises me. "People think you've done some sort of rain dance to spoil Dan's daughter's wedding."

I grimace and take a mouthful of the latte. "Oops."

Just then my phone rings and an unknown number flashes up.

"Sophie West, WVFY," I say as soon as I accept the call.

"Miss West, my name's Sam Lawson. I work for Liam Salinger. He's asked me to liaise with you about a christening gift for your new godson."

Two emotions hit me at once. Elation about Charlie being my godson, because I'm so happy that Ava and Myles have chosen me to be his godmother. He's a bundle of gorgeousness and at three months he already has the best personality. Every time I see him I can't help but feel broody. His christening is in two weeks and I've been helping Ava arrange everything. It's going to be the best day.

The second emotion is annoyance. Which happens whenever I hear Liam Salinger's name.

He promised me that things wouldn't be awkward between us, but in the past ten months since that hugely embarrassing day he's done nothing but antagonize me. He enjoys it. I think he might live for it.

All I know is that I kind of want to smash his face in whenever I see him. And I'm not a violent person.

It's also not the thing you're supposed to do to your fellow godparent. I'm pretty sure the church would frown on it. So would Ava and Myles.

So although I want to groan as soon as I hear his name, I use my grownup voice and respond.

"Hi Sam," I say, immediately feeling sorry for her because she sounds nice even though she works for the devil.

"Hi Sophie," Sam replies, then pauses. "Is it okay to call you Sophie?"

"Of course," I say warmly. "And I've already bought Charlie a christening gift." It's perfect, too. I've arranged for an artist to paint a mural of Dandy the Lion in Charlie's new nursery. Ava has been agonizing over what to do to make the room perfect. The artist is a friend of a friend and I know he'll work with Ava to get it exactly how she wants it.

"Can I ask what you've bought?" Sam says, sounding awkward. "Just to make sure I don't duplicate anything." That's just so Liam, expecting his assistant to sort out his gift.

I pull my lip between my teeth. I want to tell her, I do. But Liam has this habit of one upping me anytime I do something nice. He has ever since that day… ugh. The one I don't like to think about.

It's like he gets a kick out of annoying me. Like when I hired a singer to serenade them on their honeymoon, and he had a mariachi band arrive at exactly the same time.

This time I'm not giving him the opportunity. "I tell you what," I say to Sam, who I still don't want to upset. "Tell him it's a big secret and I can't tell him because I don't want to spoil the surprise."

"He won't be happy," Sam says, clicking her tongue. "He really wants to know."

Of course he does.

"Tell him to call me if he has a problem. This isn't your fault," I tell her.

"I know," she agrees. "It'll be fine. He can throw a fit if he wants, it doesn't bother me. He's not even in New York at the moment."

"He's not?" I frown. "Where is he?"

"In Charleston. Not far from you."

My stomach tightens. Liam's here? I don't like that thought. I can deal with Liam Salinger at a distance. But knowing he's close?

Yeah, that's near impossible.

"Already? I didn't know he would be in town this early." I know he's coming for Charlie's christening, but I thought he'd come at the same time as the rest of his family, just for the weekend.

"It's a last-minute change of plan," Sam tells me. "Well, I'd better go. Thanks for taking my call."

"No problem. It was nice talking with you."

"You too. Have a great day."

She disconnects and I pick up my coffee. It's cooled considerably but I finish it anyway, and try not to think about Liam Salinger being so close. He'll probably be staying with Ava and Myles. They live in an amazing huge house on Virginia Street, which has a fully equipped guest house that Myles' brothers – including Liam – use whenever they're in town.

Luckily Liam isn't here very often. He's too busy building his empire to spend time in this little sleepy city in West Virginia. It must be boring to him, after the excitement of New York. Plus, there aren't models on every corner to hang on his arms.

No, I haven't been stalking his Instagram.

Okay, maybe a little.

I drop my cup in the trash can next to my desk and stand, rolling my neck. I need to clear my head and a walk around the block should help before I have to go in to update our webpage with the latest forecasts.

"You okay here for a minute?" I ask Madison, because although she's a great intern, she's only been here for a few months and is still learning how things work. "I'm going out to buy some lunch. You want anything?"

"I'm fine," she says, smiling. "Just running some forecasts for you to do the updates with later." She glances at the currently empty desk in the corner, where our boss, Michael sits. Luckily he's working the late shift, which means he doesn't come into the office until three.

It's ironic that every man in my life right now is a thorn in my side. Okay, not every man. Just Michael and Liam.

Charlie's a man and he's definitely not a thorn. Nor is my dad, or Myles come to think of it.

And as I walk out into the warm July sun, I find myself grimacing at the thought of Liam being in town. Because even though Charleston is the state capital, it's still small, and there's every likelihood I'll bump into him at some point.

Which is awkward as hell, because I told him a dirty lie and he believed it. I could live with that when he was hundreds of miles away. But when he's close I feel uncomfortable. Like I'm about to blurt out the truth at any minute.

The thought makes my stomach twist.

LIAM

"What do you mean she wouldn't tell you?" I frown as I hold the phone to my ear. On the other side of the boardroom table my brother lifts a brow. He has this sardonic way of looking at you. It's annoying actually.

It makes me feel like I'm ten years old again.

"She doesn't want you to know," my assistant, Sam, tells me. "Said to call her if you had a problem with that." Sam sounds way too happy about this whole situation. "I like her."

"I bet you do."

Sam's been my assistant for the last ten years. She's absolutely worth her weight in gold. She also doesn't suffer fools gladly. Including me.

I went straight onto Wall Street after leaving college, working in corporate finance for a large group of investors before striking out on my own. Now I run Salinger Enterprises – a small to medium venture capital company. I raise money through my clients – a group of extremely rich investors, then use it to finance start-up companies or, more often, turn around failing companies that I can see have a future if they were run right.

Myles, on the other hand, after dabbling in finance for a little while, became an editor at a New York publishing house. But since he met Ava and has moved permanently to Charleston, he's been working for me, looking for new investment opportunities here in West Virginia.

"I think it's the first time a woman hasn't come running when you clicked your fingers," she says, her voice full of amusement.

I roll my eyes because I have this unfair reputation as a playboy. I can't remember the last time I got to play with anything. I'm too damn busy for that. "Sophie's not a woman," I tell her. "She's a…" I narrow my eyes to think of the right word. And ignore the way Myles is staring at me now that he knows who I'm talking about. "She's a devil woman."

Sam chuckles. "I looked her up. She's the nicest woman in weather according to one of her fan pages."

"She has fan pages?" I frown. Why did I not know this?

"So many," Sam tells me. "A couple of them are quite disturbing."

"Oh Jesus." I wince. I can only imagine what they're like. "Anyway, back to the gift." Myles lifts his other eyebrow. He looks permanently annoyed now. "Any ideas?"

"Nope." She pops her 'p' just for the sheer hell of it. "A bottle of champagne?"

"Too lame."

"Something silver. Engraved. That he can keep."

"Do you think Sophie's buying something silver?"

Sam snorts. "I have no idea, Liam. Can't you just buy whatever you want?"

"If I buy the same thing as her she'll kill me." I still haven't forgotten the Mariachi incident. Just a damn coincidence, I swear, but it was like I'd arranged for a stripper at a board meeting. "Don't worry," I say. "I'll sort it out myself."

"That's what I like to hear," Sam says encouragingly. "You'll do great."

"Mmhmm."

"And if she gets angry, just show her some of the old Salinger charm. It works every time," she tells me encouragingly, even though she knows this isn't true. "Is there anything else or can I go now?"

"You can go. Have a good weekend. And Sam?"

"Yes?"

"Thank you for trying. I appreciate it." She's a good worker with a unique set of skills that helps the business a lot. She's also a single mom who never gets enough time for herself. I make a mental note to send her a gift card for a spa and a babysitter. She deserves it.

"Anytime, Liam. And good luck with the gift shopping."

When I put my cellphone on the table, Myles is still staring at me. I tip my head to the side and stare back. He's my eldest brother, but only by just over a year. But sometimes he feels about fifty years my senior.

We grew up as four brothers. Myles and I, followed by our brothers Eli and Holden. Like me, Holden lives in New York, and Eli plays hockey for the Razors, so he's currently in New England. Then when our dad married a third time he had two more sons – Lincoln and Brooks, who are a little younger than the rest of us.

Our final sibling is Francy. Francine if you want the full name. She's my dad's daughter with his current wife, Julia, and is not that much older than Charlie.

We have an eclectic family. Which brings me back to my older brother, Myles.

It galls him a little to be my employee, if only technically. But I kind of like it. It evens things up between us.

Not that he looks like my employee at the moment. His gaze has a touch of psychopath to it.

"What did I ask you?" he says, his teeth gritted.

I look at him carefully. "When?"

"Every time you and Sophie butt heads. What do I say to you?"

"Keep away from her?" I suggest helpfully. "Well I am. I'm just trying to find out what she's buying Charlie."

Myles rolls his eyes. "And what's with talking about my kid's gift in front of me? Isn't it supposed to be a surprise?"

"It *will* be a surprise," I tell him. Not least to me because I have no idea what to buy. "What's got you all grouchy, anyway?"

Fun fact, Myles is the grumpy one of the family. He can kill a human with a single stare. He has a bad case of resting asshole face which always makes people give him a wide berth.

Maybe that's why I've always been the easy going one. Trying to make up for Myles. He barks orders and walks away and I say please on his behalf.

It's how we've worked for the past forty years. It doesn't look like anything's changing, even though he's now married to the love of his life. And they've had a baby together.

"I'm not getting much sleep," Myles admits.

"That's usually a good thing," I tell him.

"So says the perpetual bachelor." Myles shakes his head. "I'm not getting much sleep because Charlie has colic and I'm trying to give Ava a break."

"That's too bad." I look at him carefully, wondering whether he's actually asking for help. "Do you want me to—"

"No!" He shakes his head quickly.

"You don't know what I was going to say," I point out.

"You were going to offer to babysit. And no thank you, I'm quite fond of my son."

"What do you think is going to happen if I'm in charge?" I smile. "I wasn't planning on taking him out on the town."

"I wouldn't put it past you," Myles mutters. I feel slightly offended, but I decide to not pursue it. He really does look tired.

"Shall we get back to business?" I suggest. That's the reason we're both here, after all. Myles has actually managed to find some promising companies. The opportunities here are potentially very profitable – more so than New York where everybody is fighting for the same businesses. So it looks like I'll be spending a lot more time in Charleston, which means I'll be spending more time with my nephew and Godson. Something that makes me happy.

"This one looks interesting," I tell him, pulling the piece of paper up to look at the numbers he's run, thankful to be able to talk business with my brother rather than about his wife's best friend who for some reason hates my guts.

Okay, I know the reason. I just don't want to think about it. Especially when I'm sitting in front of my brother.

"Yeah it does," he says nodding. "Let me talk you through it."

———

SOPHIE

I stop at my dad's house on my way home from work, carrying a brown bag full of fruit and vegetables because he always forgets to add them to his weekly grocery order. When he opens the front door and sees me standing on the step, his face bursts into a wide grin. He has flour on his cheeks and is wearing an old pink frilly apron.

"Come in, come in," he says, beckoning me inside. "I have some cakes in the oven."

"What are you cooking today?" I follow him to the kitchen which is filled with the aroma of baking and sugar. My stomach rumbles, reminding me I haven't eaten since this morning.

"Coffee and walnut cake, and some mini banana loafs." He glances at the brown bag I'm carrying. "What's in there?" he asks suspiciously.

"Things that won't make your teeth rot out of your mouth." I pull out the bananas and apples, along with the carrots and broccoli I bought from a vendor outside work.

"Hmm, these would be good in a cake," he says, lifting the carrots and turning them over. "Not sure about the broccoli, though."

"Maybe you could eat them without sugar," I suggest. "Like with a meal or something."

He shakes his head. "Where's the fun in that?"

The oven timer goes off and he grabs a pair of thick gloves, pulling the cake tins out and putting them on the side. This baking obsession is a fairly new thing. About two years old. He took it up as a way to keep busy after Mom died, but it kept growing. Now he bakes all week and runs a stall at the local farmer's market every Saturday.

They call him the Sugar King. It's a pretty good name actually.

"I saw you on the lunchtime news," he tells me, as he slowly loosens the first cake from the tin. "Shame about the weather for Dan's daughter's wedding."

"Yeah," I say. "I felt bad about that."

"Well your mom always said it was better to tell a hard truth than an easy lie." He turns the cake out and puts it on the cooling rack. "You did the right thing."

I give him a smile. "Thanks."

He nods. "Now tell me, how's your love life?"

He always asks me this, as though he's hoping the answer will change. It doesn't.

"I don't have time for one." I roll my eyes. "How's yours?"

"What makes you ask that? Your mom only died two years ago."

My heart does a little clench. We both miss her a lot. "I know, but she wouldn't have wanted you to be lonely."

He shifts his feet. "No need to worry about me."

"Well don't worry about me either," I tell him. We're completely understaffed at work. There's no money for more employees but there's also no way Michael and I – and Madison now – can provide a good weather service on our own without putting in the overtime.

"But you should still date. You're not getting any younger, honey."

Ouch. That's my dad, lacing the sweet with the sharp stabs. "Mmhmm," I say noncommittally because I'm done with dating right now. It goes in phases. I'll download an app, decide to throw myself into finding Mr. Right, then realize that the dating pool is actually a cesspit. So I'll take a break, forget about the pain, and do it all over again.

It was easy for Dad. He and mom met at a Carpenters concert. He was eighteen and she was seventeen and they'd kissed when "Close to You" came on. They were inseparable ever since.

When I was a kid I'd thought that would happen to me, too. That it was how life was supposed to go. You'd meet your soulmate in your teens, build up your career in your twenties, then start a family together. It had even started happening when I went to college. I met the guy I thought I'd spend the rest of my life with.

But it turned out he had different ideas.

I push that thought to the back of my mind. "Anyway," I say, passing dad an apple. "All the good ones are married now." The bad ones, too. I've had my fair share of being hit on by married men. Like when I was on vacation with Ava,

Myles, Lauren, and Liam. One guy tried to buy me a drink and his wife called the bar to check on him.

I was mortified. Liam, on the other hand, thought it was hilarious.

I wrinkle my nose at the memory.

"There's this fella at the market," Dad tells me. "Says he's thinking about getting divorced. You should come meet him on Saturday."

A shudder works through me. "It's okay, Lauren and I are taking Ava out for a spa day on Saturday before the christening on Sunday."

His face softens at the mention of Ava. "How is she? Did I tell you she brought her baby over to meet me?"

"You did. And she said you were amazing with him."

He beams. "Just practicing for when you give me grandchildren." He glances at Mom's picture again. "We both always wanted that."

I nod, trying not to feel guilty that I couldn't give her that before we lost her. "I know. Anyway, I should go. I have to be up at four tomorrow." Ready for the five a.m. newscast.

Dad kisses me on the cheek. "I'll see you on Sunday." Ava invited him to the christening. It's really sweet of her.

"Are you okay to get there on your own?" I ask him.

"Absolutely. I know you have to be there early."

"Okay then. I'll see you at the church." I give him what I hope is a severe look. "And try to eat something other than cake tonight."

He winks. "I'll try."

I wave goodbye and climb into my car, starting the engine. And when I get home to my apartment, about twenty minutes from my dad, I kick off my shoes, drop my behind into the comfy sofa that's followed me around since I spent way too much on it eight years ago, and let my head fall back.

I don't dare check my social media because people have been complaining about my forecast for Dan's daughter's wedding all day. It's amazing how invested they can get in an event they're not invited to. I also don't want to check my emails because I saw one flash up while I was at Dad's from Michael, my boss.

I still hate that word. We used to be co-workers until our old manager, left to go back to academia. I loved working for her – she was a true trailblazer for women meteorologists.

When she left she encouraged me to apply for her position. I was going to do it, too, but then I learned Michael had already put his resume in. And the thought of going up against him, but losing made me panic and not put my own application in at all.

I wish I hadn't been so scared. Especially since the changes he's made are crap.

Ugh.

I'm already bored of feeling sorry for myself, because actually I have a pretty good life. And although Michael aggravates me I mostly know how to handle him.

So I get up and shower then I make myself a quick dinner, before opening up my laptop to do the work I didn't have a chance to finish today, aware that all work and no play is definitely making Sophie a dull girl.

And my dad thinks I should be dating more. Ha. No chance.

CHAPTER
FOUR

LIAM

"That smells delicious. What is it?" Ava leans over the huge vat of ragu I have simmering on the stove top. My overbearing family should be arriving for Charlie's christening weekend soon and if I know my brothers they'll be hungry. Back when we were kids it was my job to feed them and it's a habit I haven't quite gotten out of.

"Making some meat sauce for Spaghetti Bolognese," I tell her. She's holding Charlie in her arms, and he's sleeping peacefully against her chest. Ava, on the other hand, looks anything but peaceful. Her hair is askew, her eyes have bags under them and she's still wearing her pajamas. "Go back to bed. I'll feed the family when they arrive. Put Charlie in his playpen here and I'll keep an eye on him," I tell her gently.

"Do I know you?" she asks, tipping her head to the side. "Because you look exactly like my annoying brother-in-law, except he's probably still in bed. With a beautiful woman he met on a night out."

"I'm not that bad," I say lightly, stroking Charlie's downy

scalp. I've literally never touched anything so soft as this kid. Never smelled anything as sweet either.

"Who's not that bad?" Myles asks, stumbling into the kitchen.

"Liam's cooking for your family," Ava says, stifling a yawn. "He's going to feed them when they arrive."

"You put celery in there?" Myles asks.

"Yep. And carrots."

"Good." He nods. "Tastes better that way." He grabs a spoon from the side and dips it into the pan, then lifts it to his lips.

"Careful, it's ho—"

Myles screams before I can finish the sentence. "I just burned my tongue." He sticks it out and it is a little red.

"Should have asked," I tell him.

"Should have warned me." He shakes his head. "Why are you cooking anyway?"

"Because somebody needs to feed the family when they get here," I tell him. "And you two are new parents with no sleep. So I thought I'd take care of it."

The truth is, I've been reading advice websites. I take my role as godfather seriously. All of them say the best thing you can do for new parents is to pick up the slack in the house.

They have a housekeeper so I can't clean the place. And to be fair, my cleaning skills aren't exactly great. But I can cook so that's what I'm doing.

And now I'm kind of regretting it because they both think it's weird.

I open my mouth to repeat my offer of looking after Charlie, but the kid gets in first, letting out an ear-piercing wail. Seriously, how can something so little scream so hard? Do they come with fully grown lungs?

"He's hungry," Ava murmurs. "I'm gonna give him the boob."

I try not to smirk. But Myles notices anyway.

"Not in here," he says, lifting a brow at me.

"I wasn't going to look," I point out. Not least because I'm not an asshole. Well, not a complete one.

"Sure. And the sun didn't rise this morning." Myles grabs a bottle of water from the refrigerator, pouring some into a glass. "Let's take it to the nursery," he suggests to Ava. "If we're in luck he'll go to sleep and we can catch a nap together." He kisses her cheek softly and she closes her eyes for a moment.

"Are you okay to stay here for when everybody arrives?" he asks.

"Yep." I keep stirring the sauce. "You guys go. And enjoy your… horizontal time."

"It's a fucking nap," Myles growls. "We're not all sex mad."

"Of course it is," I agree lightly. "Enjoy your fucking nap.

————

SOPHIE

I pull into Ava and Myles' driveway just after two. It's full of expensive shiny cars and I try to not get vehicle envy. Myles' family arrived at some point this morning, ready for the christening tomorrow, and of course they're all speed mad. I spot a Jaguar, a BMW, and two Mercedes. Even his mom drives an Audi. Like the house they're parked outside, they reek of money. Myles' dad is scarily rich, and his brothers are all successful in their own right.

I'd say Ava landed on her feet, but I think they're the ones lucky to have her. And she'd truly be just as happy if Myles was a poor fisherman.

That's just how she is.

I put my car into park and climb out, my heels scrunching

on the gravel. As I walk toward the house I shoot a text to Lauren, the third of our group of friends telling her I should be at hers in twenty minutes.

Because us girls have plans.

We've booked a spa day for the afternoon. Or rather, Myles has. When we told him we wanted to surprise Ava with some self-care he kind of took over and paid for us to have exclusive use of the place.

And yeah, he's relationship goals. He's ruining me and Lauren for anybody else.

As I walk up the stairs to Myles and Ava's house I take a moment to admire it. Built in 1899, it has nine bedrooms – enough for all his family – plus a huge guest bungalow that they offer to his brothers when they stay. The bathrooms are to die for – all marble surfaces and gold taps. I've only stayed over once – when Myles went away a few weeks ago and Ava wanted some help with Charlie – but it took a lot to drag me away.

When I knock on the door it opens almost instantly and I'm assailed by the loud sound of laughing and deep male conversation escaping from the hallway. Myles' brother Eli smiles at me. I've only met him once before – at Myles and Ava's wedding – but he's a nice guy and a successful ice hockey player.

"It's Sophie, right?" he asks.

I smile, pleased that he remembers. "That's right. I've come to steal Ava away."

"Oh yeah, Myles said you're going to a spa." He stands aside to let me in. "I think she's upstairs. Or maybe in the kitchen."

"I'll find her," I reassure him. "It's nice to see you again."

"You, too." He gives me the once over. I'm feeling pretty good today. I'm wearing a summer dress and a pair of heels because we're having a late lunch before our treatments.

And yeah, I'm also aware that a certain other brother of

Myles will also be here. And there's no way I want him to see me in a pair of sweats and a tank. Let's not make it *awkward,* right?

Ha.

Ava isn't in the kitchen, but Myles is, along with his mom and stepmoms, as well as his two youngest brothers. Like Eli, I've only met them once before at the wedding, but they remember me and greet me like a long lost friend. I get hugs from all of them.

"Your dress is beautiful," Linc, Myles' second-to-youngest brother tells me. "You heading out on the town or something?"

"She's going to the spa with Ava," Myles says, shaking his head at Linc.

"What about after?" Linc asks. "You want to do something after?"

"She's out of your league, Linc," Myles tells him. "And out of your age range, too."

"Age is just a number." Linc winks at me. Damn, Myles has good looking brothers. "Let's catch up tomorrow at the christening."

His words trail off and I feel goosebumps break out on my back and bare arms. And when I turn my head I'm not at all surprised to see who is standing there.

Looking stupidly attractive in a pair of jeans and a tight black t-shirt, Liam Salinger's dark brown eyes catch mine.

And my heart skips a beat.

"Sophie." He nods at me.

"Liam."

He says nothing for a moment but he also doesn't pull his gaze away either. My cheeks redden but I refuse to be the first to blink.

Then he runs his tongue along his bottom lip and I swear my body reacts to him.

Ignoring it, I lift a brow and he finally looks away. There's a smile playing at the corner of his mouth and I don't feel the victory I expected to feel.

It's aggravating.

"Is Ava ready?" I ask Myles, ignoring the way my heart is slamming against my chest.

"She's just finishing getting ready. I'll go get her," Myles tells me.

"Thank you."

"I hear you're off to the spa," Myles' mom says. "That sounds lovely."

"You can come if you'd like," I suggest. "We have the whole place to ourselves."

"Oh no." She shakes her head, but looks pleased at being invited. "I think the plan is to give Ava a break from all us Salingers."

There *are* a lot of them. Before her wedding, Ava sat down and patiently described Myles' family to me and Lauren. It's complicated, but basically his dad has been married four times, but nobody speaks of the first wife or knows where she is. So for all intents and purposes Linda, Myles' mom, is Rupert Salinger's first wife. Together they had four boys, Myles, Liam, Eli, and Holden. They divorced and he married Deandra – who's also here because for some reason she and Linda are as thick as thieves.

Deandra and Rupert had two boys. Lincoln and Brooks. And now Rupert is married to Julia and they have a little girl together.

And all of them are friends. And here right now.

Ava rushes into the kitchen, grinning when she sees me. She's wearing a navy dress with spaghetti straps and she looks beautiful and glowing. She'll complain that she still hasn't lost her baby weight, but I ignore her. She always looks amazing.

"Okay, I'm ready," she says breathlessly, then looks at Myles. "Are you sure you're okay with Charlie?" she asks him.

"It's all good." He kisses her softly. "Now go relax. We've got this."

She cups his cheeks and nods. Their eyes catch and something I can't quite understand goes on between them.

And then she pulls away and grabs her purse. We say goodbye, which involves more hugs, and then somehow I find myself in front of Liam again. He towers over me even when I'm in heels.

I wish he wasn't so good looking. And that we hadn't spent the night together. It would be much easier to ignore him then. At least he's only here for the christening. When he's in New York it's much easier to imagine him as being something close to the devil.

His full lips twitch. "Try to not make anybody cry live on air today."

So he knows about that.

"Can't promise anything," I say lightly, refusing to be ruffled by him. Because that's what he wants, to get a reaction.

Ava slides her arm through mine. "Stop upsetting my friends," she chides him. Then she turns to me. "Let's go."

And as we walk out of her beautiful, stupidly large house, and away from her stupidly handsome brother-in-law the tension in my body melts away.

Now I just need to get through tomorrow without killing him.

———

"Three glasses of champagne please," Lauren says when the waitress offers us drinks. "In fact, just bring the whole bottle."

"I'm not drinking," Ava reminds her.

"And I'm driving," I say to Lauren. "Sorry."

She shakes her head. "It's okay. I wasn't ordering for you. The drinks are for me." She drops her head into her hands. "I've had the morning from hell. Who breeds these bridezillas anyway? I swear I almost killed today's one."

Lauren owns a bakery in the historical district. She's known as the best cake designer in town. My dad's a mere beginner compared to her amazing creations, but this time of year is always the worst for her.

She only takes on two or three cakes per week. And she tells us the hardest work isn't in baking or decorating, it's in appeasing the bride and groom who can never agree on a thing.

In short, she has the patience of a saint.

While we eat a light meal, she regales us with the tales of today's wedding, in a beautiful pagoda overlooking the Kanawha River. We listen, rapt, because Lauren's descriptions of these events is like watching a reality TV show but better, because these people live in our city.

The three of us have been best friends since our college days. We were roommates freshman year, and from the moment we met it was pretty much a love match. After college we all ended up working here in Charleston, where Ava and I grew up, and I don't know what I'd do without them.

After eating we change and head into the steam room, sitting on the wooden slatted benches with towels wrapped around our bodies. Ava lets out a sigh and Lauren and I exchange a glance because she looks so tired.

"How's it going with Myles' brothers at your place?" Lauren asks her.

Ava sighs again. "I love them to death but they're so noisy," Ava tells her. "As soon as they arrived they woke

Charlie up. It's nice to see them all, but they just work better outside, you know? When they're inside it's a lot to take on."

I know exactly what she means. Like me, Ava's an only child. She grew up with just her mom whereas I had both parents, but we're used to silence. To sitting and reading without being disturbed. Being surrounded by the Salinger family is like turning up the volume of life about ten decibels.

"And is Liam looking as good as ever?" Lauren asks, sneaking a sly glance at me. She was there for our vacation and thought it was amusing how much Liam and I antagonized each other.

She doesn't know why we're so awkward though. Nor does Ava. I can't tell them. It's too embarrassing.

"He's actually being very sweet," Ava says. "He keeps offering to look after Charlie, and today he made a huge pot of meat sauce for everybody."

I blink. "Liam can cook?"

Ava's smile is soft. "He's a good guy underneath it all."

I snort. Which is a bit mean, but I can't help it.

"He is," she protests. "I know you two don't get along, but he isn't a bad guy."

"I still don't get why you don't like him," Lauren says.

"I don't know," I tell her, trying to work out how to change the subject. "We just clash I guess."

"You don't clash. You have UST," Lauren says.

I roll my eyes. "We do not."

Ava says nothing, just watching us talk.

"Yes you do," Lauren continues. "When we were on vacation he couldn't take his eyes off you. Remember how annoyed he got when he saw you talking to that other guy?"

"He wasn't annoyed," I tell her. "He laughed when he found out the guy was married." My cheeks heat up and it's got nothing to do with the steam room. It's just that the whole situation was embarrassing.

"Yeah, he was annoyed," Ava says softly. "You were at the bar so you didn't see."

I blink. He was? That's… strange.

"You two would make such a cute couple," Lauren says and this time I really do laugh.

"What?" Lauren asks. "Don't you think so?"

"Liam doesn't do relationships," I tell her, feeling on firmer ground

"He doesn't?" She looks at Ava. "He must have had girlfriends in the past."

Ava shrugs. "I think so. I don't know. He says he doesn't have time for relationships now."

"Sounds like somebody else I know," Lauren says pointedly, looking at me.

"If I did have time it definitely wouldn't be with him," I say. "He never sleeps with the same woman twice."

"What?" Ava frowns. "He said that to you? When?"

Oh shit. I'm skating dangerously close to *that night*. "Um, I don't know. It was a conversation in passing. It doesn't matter anyway." Because I wouldn't touch him with a ten foot pole.

"Poor Liam," Ava says, because she always looks for the best in people. "That's sad."

"I don't think he's sad about it," I say. "He seemed pretty impressed with himself."

"He didn't really have the best role models in life," Ava tells us, still looking thoughtful. "With their dad changing wives every few years and their mom still thinking the sun shines out of his ass, they all got affected by it."

"Myles isn't going around sleeping with a pile of different women," Lauren points out, beating me to it.

"No, but Myles swore off love until we got together," Ava says. "They're all a little messed up by their childhood, they just don't realize it."

The buzzer goes off, reminding us we've been sitting in the hot steam for too long. And I breathe – or at least try to – a sigh of relief. I don't want to talk about Liam anymore. I'll deal with him tomorrow at the christening and then he'll go home to New York and I probably won't see him again until Charlie's first birthday and that's not until next year. He can go back to his playboy ways and I can go back to normalcy.

That's just how I like it.

LIAM

"So you're going to be spending more time here in Charleston," Eli says to me, lifting his bottle to his mouth. "Wow." He glances at Holden. "You'll be the last man standing in New York."

Holden lifts his glass of whiskey. "It's okay. I'm too busy working to notice anyway." Holden is a doctor at Hamilton General in Manhattan. It's a minor miracle he managed to get time off for Charlie's christening.

We're sitting in the basement den of Myles' house. The air conditioning is on full blast, thanks to the still-warm evening. As soon as he'd bought the place Myles had this basement fully remodeled. Now it has a bar, a full size pool table, plus a mini-cinema complete with a game station, where Brooks and Linc are currently trying to smash the hell out of each other. At least it's on screen for once.

"What about your investments in New York?" Holden asks. "Who's going to be looking after those?"

"I've got a good team there," I tell him. "But I'll be splitting my time between both locations. I just want to make sure these initial investments here in West Virginia go smoothly."

"He doesn't trust me," Myles says, wryly.

"Not true. I trust you. I'm just a little more ruthless than you are." That's the strange thing about us. Myles looks like an asshole but inside he has a heart of gold. And when people meet me they think I'm the nicest guy but I don't have a heart at all.

"Maybe he has other reasons for being in Charleston," Eli murmurs.

"Like what?" Holden asks, as though I'm not sitting right in front of them.

"Like Ava's friend." Eli cocks a brow. "Did you see the way he was looking at her?"

Here we go. "Not interested," I say dryly. "Don't try to make something out of nothing," I tell him.

"She's pretty," Eli says, completely ignoring me. "And she has a body to die for."

"Did you see Linc trying to eat her up?" Holden laughs.

"Linc's a child." I'm trying to not get annoyed. Why can't we just talk about sports?

"I'm not a child," Linc shouts out. "You're just an old man."

Eli sniggers. "He's kind of got you there."

"Get outta here." I stand to grab another beer. I love my brothers to death, but they're annoying as hell sometimes. "Who wants another game of pool?"

"Not me," Eli says. "I'm heading to bed soon."

"Me too." Myles shrugs. "We have a big day tomorrow."

I put the beer back in the cooler, unopened. I didn't need it anyway. Myles is right, tomorrow is important. For him and Ava, but also for me. He's trusting me to be Charlie's godfather, I'm not going to let him down.

"Like I said," Linc mutters. "Old men." He looks over at us, his oldest four brothers. There is a gap between Holden, the youngest of the first set of us, and then Linc and Brooks who came later. But I was only trying to rile him when I called him a kid. He's in his twenties, after all, not so young these days.

"You coming?" I ask Holden and Eli. The three of us are sleeping in the guest bungalow. Linc and Brooks are sleeping in the house, along with all our parents and baby sister.

"Be out in a minute," Eli says, lifting his glass. "Just going to finish this first."

"Try to not make too much noise when you come in," I warn him.

"Yeah right." He grins. "Like you haven't kept me awake over the years."

Linc laughs, pausing his game. "Oh Liam, right there," he calls out, his voice falsetto. I shake my head at him.

"Oh Liam," Brooks joins in, fluttering his eyelids. "Nobody ever made me feel this good."

Ignoring their laughter, I walk out of the den and leave them behind. Myles is waiting at the top of the stairs for me, and he looks almost sorry for me when I reach him.

"They're a lot," he says, sounding almost sympathetic

"Yep." I can't help it if I always make sure the women I sleep with have a good time. Except that one time. I shake off that thought because it was an aberration. It's important to make it a mutually enjoyable event. Linc and Brooks could learn something from me.

Myles presses his lips together and nods. "I'll see you in the morning."

"You will. I hope you get some sleep tonight."

A smile ghosts his lips. "Me too."

He heads for the sweeping staircase that leads to the second floor and I head for the back door to the path that leads to the bungalow. The kitchen is dark and quiet – everybody except us brothers went to bed an hour or two ago. There's a full moon tonight and it lights my way as I reach the bungalow that'll be my home for the next few months.

The air is still warm, and the sound of locusts fill the air. For a moment I feel a sense of peace wash over me. Maybe that's another reason why I'm so keen to do business here. Because this city lets me breathe in a way that New York doesn't. It's full of foliage and insects and reminds me that life isn't all about chasing the next dollar.

Then I laugh and shake my head at myself because that's exactly what life's about. Maybe I should have drunk one less beer.

———

SOPHIE

Charlie is wide awake as I cradle him in my arms at the front of the church the next day. His wide blue eyes stare up at me, as though I have the answer to everything, and warmth rushes through me, because I want to protect him like I've never wanted to protect anything else.

I finish reciting the words the pastor tells me and then I pass Charlie to Liam. His whole demeanor softens as he takes his nephew. I'm starting to suspect some of the emotion of the ceremony may have cracked through his cocky exterior.

It doesn't stop me from hoping Charlie yaks on his shirt.

It's the pastor's turn next. He takes Charlie and dumps a handful of cold water on his head. Understandably, Charlie starts to wail. The pastor quickly hands him back to Ava, who kisses Charlie's head and hushes him softly.

And then it's over. Liam and I are officially godparents. The organ starts up, filling the stale air of the church with discordant music, and we all step down from the dais and join Ava and Myles' guests in the aisle.

It's a short walk from the church back to Myles and Ava's house where they're throwing a party, but there are cars for those who can't walk in the heat. Ava and Myles take one with Charlie, and their parents take another, urging my dad to join them, so he gives me a wave.

"Are you walking back to Ava's?" Lauren asks me. She's going to take a car because she wants to make sure the cake is ready. Whereas I want some air. Even hot, Charleston air.

"Yeah," I tell her. "I'll see you there." I step out of the church and shake the pastor's hand, thanking him for a lovely ceremony.

And then I pull off my sandals because there's no way I can walk in these heels. They look gorgeous but I'll end up breaking an ankle. Looping the straps in my fingers, I take a left at the end of the church path, following the crowd of people heading along Virginia Street.

"You know shoes aren't supposed to hurt," a male voice says. I glance to my left and see Liam there. He's towering over me since I'm barefoot.

"What?" I frown.

"They were specifically invented to protect feet," he continues.

I roll my eyes. "Thank you, Einstein."

He shrugs. "You see any guys take off their shoes because they're in so much pain?" he asks me, glancing down at my bare feet.

"Well no…"

He lifts a brow as though I just proved his case.

"But these shoes are pretty," I tell him. "It would make my heart hurt not to wear them."

He glances at the sandals in my hand. "Mhmm."

"And they make my legs look good."

"Your legs already look good."

I blink because that sounded like a compliment. "I'm

sorry?" I ask him, but he has that mask like expression on again.

And then he completely changes the subject.

"So what did you get him?" he asks me.

"What did I get who?"

"Charlie. For a christening gift."

I'd forgotten about that. "You'll see," I tell him.

"You can tell me now. I've already bought my gift." He looks pretty smug about it, too.

A feeling of horror washes over me. What if he's somehow gotten the same thing I have? "What is it?" I ask.

He looks at me from the corner of his eyes. "I'll tell you mine if you tell me yours."

"What are we, six?" I shake my head. "I'm not that interested anyway."

Liam sighs as though he's just trying to appease me. "I got a bespoke tree house for their yard. It's not something he can really enjoy until he's a bit bigger, but I thought he'll grow into it. It's got a ladder to climb up into it and a slide to get out." Liam shrugs.

"That's a beautiful gift," I say.

He blinks as though surprised. "Is it? I was worried it's a bit too... I don't know old."

"Old would be buying him his first car," I tell him.

Liam snorts. "Thought about it."

"I bet you did." A smile flits across my lips because that would be so Liam. And I take a minute to marvel that we're actually having a conversation without any snark involved. This would be a first since that fateful night.

"So now you can tell me what you bought," he says as we turn the corner onto Virginia Street.

I shrug. "I bought a mural by a local artist. She'll work with Ava to get exactly what she wants and then paint it on the wall of Charlie's nursery. I was lucky to get her, she's a friend of a friend of a friend. Highly sought after. And I know

Ava doesn't love Charlie's nursery yet, so hopefully this will get her there."

He opens his mouth to say something, but then a hand slaps his back and Linc joins us, out of breath because he's been running to catch up to us.

"I called your name when you left the church. Didn't you hear me?" Linc asks Liam. Then he looks at me. "Hi Sophie. You look fucking edible in that dress."

"Thank you," I say, stepping to the right so he can walk next to Liam. "You look pretty good yourself." He does, too. He and Brooks are a little taller and less muscled than their older brothers. Their hair is lighter, too. But all in all the Salinger brothers are annoyingly gorgeous.

Even when they're frowning like Liam is now.

"I meant to ask you," Linc says to me. "Do you have a ride home tonight? I'd be happy to drive you if you haven't."

I smile at him. "Thank you, but my friend Lauren is driving me home."

"Another time then."

"That sounds lovely." My cheeks redden a little because I'm not used to somebody blatantly flirting with me. Especially somebody who's years younger than I am. It's not as though I'm interested, but still.

"Did I tell you I've been watching your forecasts?" he asks me. "Every morning before I go to work."

"You do?" I ask him. "How? You don't get WVFY where you live, do you?"

"Nope, but I can live stream it on the internet." He shrugs. "I like to know what the weather's going to be like for Myles and Ava."

Liam makes a noise that sounds a little like he's suffocating.

"What?" Linc asks him, his voice lifting. "I just like to picture them happy."

"Sure you do." Liam shakes his head. "What are you

doing here anyway? Weren't you supposed to be greeting people as they arrive at the house?" he asks his little brother.

"Weren't you supposed to be, too?" Linc says back.

"I need the fresh air," Liam says sharply.

"So do I," Linc tells him.

"Excuse us for one moment, Sophie," Liam says, grabbing Linc's arm to stop him from walking. I shrug and carry on. The ground is getting hot and my bare feet are getting dirty and all I want to do is clean them off at Ava's house before I down a glass of champagne.

My mouth waters at the thought of it, right as Linc strides up to me. "Gotta go," he says. His face is neutral but there's something flashing in his eyes. "I'll catch you later, Sophie."

"Sure."

He speeds off and then a shadow comes over me. I know it's Liam without having to look.

"Try to not flirt with the children," he says.

My mouth drops open. "Did you seriously just say that?" The man is infuriating.

"I'm just trying to help," he says lightly.

"Who I flirt with has nothing to do with you," I tell him.

"You're my sister-in-law's best friend. I'm just trying to look after you. Lincoln's not what you need."

"And what do I need?" I ask him. "Since you're an expert on the subject."

I feel his eyes on my face, but there's no way I'm going to look at him right now. I'm annoyed and upset and there's no way I want him to know he's affected me.

"A man. Somebody who can give you the fairytale. The happy ever after. Not a kid like Linc."

I start to laugh. "What? Have I stepped onto a Disney set? What makes you think I want the fairytale?"

"Because it's written all over you. You scream long-term-commitment." His voice is annoyingly even.

"And you scream STDs," I huff back.

There's another coughing sound. Is he laughing? It sounded like he laughed, but I still don't dare look. We're only a hundred yards from Ava's house now. I seriously consider doing a sprint finish.

"I'm very careful about my sexual health, Sophie. I always use precautions and I get tested every three months."

"It's okay," I tell him, rolling my eyes. "We already had this talk."

I finally bring myself to look at him, and get a grim sense of satisfaction from the way the smile dissolves from his lips.

"Look," I say, before he can think of a smart comeback. "Can you just stop interfering in my love life, please? First the guy on vacation and now this."

"The guy on vacation was married. I did you a favor."

Ugh, he's right but I won't admit it to him. The memory of it is mortifying.

"I would have found out myself and walked away," I tell him. "I don't need your help and I don't want it, okay?" I don't know why I let him get to me every time. I'm annoyed at myself for thinking we could finally have a conversation without wanting to tear out each other's throats. Even more annoyed for thinking it was nice. "You promised me this wouldn't get awkward and it has." I sound emotional and I hate it. "That's not fair."

He looks at me for a moment, his brows knitting. Then he rubs his chin with the heel of his hand. "Okay," he says. "I hear you loud and clear."

Well that's good. We finish the walk in silence, and I've never been happier to be swallowed up by my group of friends and family, as they hug me and compliment my dress and tell me how well I did at the church.

And Liam walks into the house alone.

CHAPTER
SIX

SOPHIE

It's early in the evening and the party has started to wind down. I put my dad and Ava's mom in a cab and wave them off before turning around and walking back into the house.

I've kept these shoes on even though they're really killing me because I don't want to give Liam the satisfaction of seeing me barefoot again. Luckily, he's been mostly circulating with the guests. As always he's the center of the party, charming everybody he meets.

Occasionally our eyes have met and I've hastily pulled them away. I don't want him to think I'm watching him when I'm not.

Walking into the kitchen I find Ava scooting down filling the dishwasher. "Can I help?" I ask her.

She looks up smiling, though there are shadows beneath her eyes. I bet she just wants everybody to leave so she can catch some sleep. "I've got this," she says softly. "You're a guest, you shouldn't help clean."

"I'm your friend," I remind her. "Of course I should." I

start to round up some dirty glasses that are scattered around the countertops. As I hand them to her, the baby monitor on the kitchen window lights up. And Charlie lets out a low moan.

Ava sighs. She really does look tired. "Do you want me to get him?" I ask her.

"Would you?" She looks like I've just offered her one of my kidneys. "He's in the nursery. There's some milk I just warmed up for him." She walks over to the warmer and pulls out a bottle.

I take it from her, the plastic warm against my palm. "I've got this," I say because I want to help as much as I can. And feeding Charlie is one of my favorite things to do.

Since I'm going to the second floor I take my shoes off before hitting the carpeted stairs, then walk along the galleried hallway to Charlie's room. I can hear him snuffling as I push open the door.

And get the fright of my life, because somebody's in there already.

Liam Salinger is cradling Charlie against his broad chest. His tie and jacket long since disappeared, leaving him in a white shirt and dark pants. His shirt sleeves are rolled up, his collar unbuttoned far enough that I can see a hint of hair through the gap, and he's murmuring softly to Charlie in a way that would make most women weak.

A glance at the monitor tells me he's turned it off. Presumably to give Ava and Myles a break from listening to Charlie's cries. I was planning to do the same thing when I got up here.

"Hey hey," Liam whispers, not seeing me standing here. "It's okay, bud. I've got you."

Charlie snuffles loudly but it doesn't sound like a cry anymore.

"We're gonna give your mama a break, okay?" Liam continues. "She loves you but she's tired. You think you can get back to sleep for me?"

Charlie blinks, his beautiful blonde lashes sweeping down and then up. He's fascinated by Liam. Maybe I am a little too right now. Seeing him hold his nephew so tenderly makes my chest ache.

Charlie coos up at him and Liam winks. "That's it, buddy. I think we have a deal here." He sways for a minute more before walking Charlie back to his crib. But as he leans over to put him back on the mattress, Charlie lets out a piercing wail.

Liam immediately pulls him back against his chest. "I thought we had a deal?"

I clear my throat. "I think he might be hungry."

Liam startles, just like Charlie does when he wakes up suddenly. I bite down a smile. "I have some milk," I say, ignoring the weird tingle pulsing down my spine. "Ava said to feed him."

Liam holds his hand out for it. For a minute I think about asking to feed Charlie myself, because there's nothing more satisfying than that. But Liam was here first and I'm all about fairness.

A minute later, Liam is sitting in the rocking chair Ava bought when she furnished the nursery, Charlie cradled in his left arm while he holds the bottle with his right hand. Charlie's a noisy feeder, smacking his lips and making soft sounds as he drinks it down.

I lean against the door and watch. I'm waiting for Liam to tell me to leave or at least make an annoying comment about why I'm watching him like a creep. But he's too caught up in Charlie for that.

Before I can look away, Liam lifts his gaze to me.

"He's gorgeous, isn't he?"

I smile because this is something we can agree on. "He is. He's going to break a million hearts."

"I never thought Myles would have a kid," he continues, as though we're always having conversations like this. "But he sure makes beautiful ones."

"So does Ava."

He grins. "Touché." He blinks and then looks at me. "You think they'll have any more?"

"I'm not sure," I tell him. "Ava was worried that it might be too late to have one, let alone more." That's really how she and Myles got together. She decided to try for a baby alone because she was worried about her fertility. Then Myles – who she thought hated her – offered to be her donor.

One thing led to another and now they're a happy family.

"Imagine if he was a girl," Liam says, his brows knitting. "We'd have to lock her up in a tower to keep all the boys away."

"Boys like you?" I ask him.

He tips his head to the side. "Yeah, I guess so." His eyes don't leave mine. There's that silence again, except it doesn't feel quiet. It feels loud.

I go to apologize because that was rude. But he beats me to it.

"About that night," he says, his voice thick.

My heart hammers against my chest. "You don't need to say anything," I whisper. Mostly because I don't want to talk about it at all.

He opens his mouth to say something else but Charlie gurgles and a torrent of white comes out of his mouth, spraying all over Liam's shirt and even getting some on his chin. Liam's eyes widen, and for a moment I'm stuck between horror and abject amusement.

"Oh My God," I say, laughter bubbling up in my throat. "That's breast milk."

Liam splutters. "Christ! There's some on my lips."

I have to cover my own mouth because I don't think I can control myself right now. Seeing his horror at having his sister-in-law's regurgitated milk on his mouth is too delicious for words.

"Can you take him?" he whispers, standing. The top of his

shirt is plastered to his chest. I grab a cloth from the pile on the dresser and put it over my shoulder. I take another, passing it to Liam as I reach down and take a now sobbing Charlie from his arms.

"Shshsh," I whisper. "It's okay. There's more where that came from."

"I hope not," Liam says. He dabs his face with the cloth I gave him and throws it into the laundry basket near the door. I start to clean Charlie up, though luckily he seems to have gotten most of his spit up on Liam. There's only a few spots on the bib he's wearing. I take it off and use the dry part of it to pat him dry, then coo at him until he starts smiling.

"He's okay…" But my words trail off as I see Liam pulling his shirt off. He's not wearing an undershirt, so his bare chest is there in all of its glory.

And when I say glory I'm kind of underestimating it. Liam Salinger's chest is a thing of beauty. Defined but not overly built. A smattering of hair but not so much he looks like he's hailing from the seventies. Against my will, my gaze trails down to his stomach, where a thin line of hair leads to the waistband of his pants. They lay low on his hips, revealing the vee of his pelvis, and I swear the temperature has just risen by twenty degrees.

"Sophie," he says, his voice low.

"Yes?" I remind myself to breathe.

"He's just thrown up on you, too."

Horrified, I look down to see that Liam's telling the truth. It's not a blast of spit up like he got, just a little trail but it runs all the way down my left boob. When I glance up again Liam's eyes are trained on it.

"I'm not taking my dress off," I tell him.

His lips twitch. "I wasn't going to suggest you did." He walks over and grabs yet another cloth from the pile – no wonder Ava has so many of them – and passes it to me. But when I reach for it, Charlie starts to cry again, and I have to stroke his head to soothe him.

So Liam pats the spit up from my chest, his movement surprisingly gentle. He's so close I can smell his shower gel. Something masculine and musky. I can feel the warmth wafting from his bare chest, too.

My nipple hardens. He stops patting for a moment and mortification washes over me. I bring myself to look at him, but his eyes are trained on my chest.

Specifically my reaction to his touch.

I have no words. None at all. Charlie has quietened, too. It's just me, him, Liam, and my stupid nipple.

"Stop looking," I whisper.

"I can't," Liam replies, his gaze unwavering.

"Yes you can. It's just a nipple."

"To you it's just a nipple. But I'm a man, West. To me it's the fucking holy grail."

"Don't swear," I tell him, but I start to laugh anyway because what's the alternative? And the thing is, Liam Salinger is funny. Like laugh out loud make you all hot kind of funny.

He looks up and he's grinning, too.

"Can we pretend this didn't happen?" I ask him.

"Again?" He lifts a brow. "You're asking me to do a lot of pretending."

I pull my lip between my teeth. "I know. And I'm grateful for it."

Charlie feels heavier in my arms, and I realize he's gone to sleep.

"I'm going to put him in his crib," I tell Liam. "And then I'll clean myself up."

"Good idea." He watches silently as I carry Charlie over, making sure he's still clean from spit up. When he's laying quietly on his back I turn back toward Liam, and he's still not wearing a shirt. I mean of course he isn't.

It's not like he carries a spare one around with him.

He turns the monitor back on as I grab the empty bottle, and go to walk out of the nursery. But before I can go anywhere Liam gently grabs my wrist, stopping my progress.

I look at him, surprised. "What?" I ask quietly, because neither of us want to wake Charlie up.

He opens his lips then shakes his head. "It doesn't matter." He lets go of my arm and it immediately feels cool.

I frown. "Yes it does. What is it?" I'm intrigued now.

He reaches out to cup my face, the unexpected move making my breath catch in my throat. Then he leans down so close that for a moment I think he's going to kiss me.

But instead he runs his thumb over my jaw and presses his lips to my ear.

"I wish I'd made you come that night."

Then he turns on his heel and walks out of the room, and I watch him, too stunned to reply.

————

LIAM

I walk back to the party twenty minutes later, having gone back to the bungalow to clean up and put a new shirt on. Ava and Myles are upstairs with Charlie, and I'm pretty sure my uncle duties are done for the night.

"Linc's been bitching about you," Eli says, handing me a beer. "What've you done to upset him now?"

"Nothing," I tell my younger brother, taking the beer gratefully. Eli is the third brother in our family and a typical middle child. Out of all of us he's the most talented, too. As a professional hockey player, he can do things on the ice that most of us can't do on solid ground. "What time are you leaving?"

"Getting picked up at eight," he says. He has a meeting tomorrow. A promotional opportunity that he would be crazy to miss so he's not staying here tonight. "So you're really gonna spend more time here in sleepyville, huh?" he asks, surveying the land in front of us. The party has thinned out. People have either moved inside, because the insects in the summer can be hungry little bastards, or they've gone home.

"I'm getting attached to the locusts," I tell him. "Anyway, it's not so different to Misty Lakes and you always enjoy being there.

Misty Lakes is our dad's estate. He has a huge house there, and we've each built a cabin around the closest lake. Going there is like stepping back in time. I always feel like the kid I used to be as soon as we drive through the wrought iron gates.

It reminds me of when life was easier. When summers stretched forever. When I didn't have a whole bunch of people relying on me to pay their wages or fill their investment portfolios.

"Yeah, I like Misty Lakes, but I also like to live a bit," Eli says, lifting his beer to his mouth. "I thought you did, too. You're gonna get bored here within a week."

"I'll be too busy making money to get bored," I tell him.

He grins and punches me hard in the arm. "That's ma boy." He shakes his head. "I'm gonna miss seeing you go all Southern Gentleman while you're here."

I lift a brow. "I'm not a gentleman."

He laughs. "Damn right. So now that you're going to be spending more time here can I have your little black book?"

I shake my head at him. "I don't have a black book."

"Because *they* always call *you*." He lifts a brow. "I swear you got all the luck in the family."

"No, idiot. It's because I have a phone to store numbers in."

"Then just give me your phone, please."

I know he's teasing. And at any other time I'd be laughing along with him. I live a charmed life, I know that. I enjoy my job, I have a great family and friends. And I've never had a problem getting a woman.

Damn if my gaze doesn't sweep across the lawn at that thought. Until it lands on the one woman it shouldn't.

She's standing on the grass, her dark hair lifting in the breeze, revealing her soft, elegant neck and shoulders, her skin turned amber by the slowly setting sun. Her dress molds over her perfect curves and my dick twitches at the memory of her hard nipple.

If Charlie hadn't been there. If she didn't hate me. If I didn't have my damn rules... all of those scenarios run through my mind.

Because if it hadn't been for those, I would have run the pad of my thumb over it. I wanted to so badly.

If she was any other person, I'd walk over and charm her right now. And that's not a play. I want to make her smile. To watch her cheeks flush. To ask her questions and listen to the answers, because each one would help me to understand her.

To understand her needs and wants.

Because this is the thing my brothers don't get about me. I don't spend time with women because I want something from them. I spend time with them because I like giving. I like making them happy, I like giving them pleasure.

I like making love with them until they can't remember their names.

I never leave a woman unpleasured. Multiple times.

Never.

Until...

Christ, I need to stop thinking about this. I have rules for a reason. This way nobody gets hurt. And I wasn't kidding when I said that a woman like Sophie West reeks of needing commitment.

And you reek of STDs. I start to laugh at the memory of her reply because dammit she's funny. Then Eli gives me a weird look and I stop.

"Want a game of pool before you have to leave?" I ask him.

"Sure. Sounds good."

Leaving the lawn – and the woman I can't have – behind, I follow Eli down to Myles' basement and proceed to smash the hell out of him on the pool table.

And yeah, it makes me feel slightly better.

CHAPTER
SEVEN

SOPHIE

One good thing about working at a regional television station like WVFY is that everybody knows everybody. People have worked here for so long that they're more like family than colleagues. I always get a warm feeling when I walk through the main doors that lead to the reception area.

One of the bad things, however, is that you don't always get to choose your family. Or your co-workers for that matter. And I definitely didn't get to choose Michael Rimmer to be my boss.

He and I went out on a date. *Once.* We went straight from work to a steak restaurant in the historic district and he proceeded to make a note of everything he ordered, along with the exact cost and what a ten, fifteen, and twenty percent tip would look like. He got extremely upset when I refused to do the same.

I have no problem with splitting the bill on a date. But let's just split it fifty-fifty. If you're itemizing the extra Diet Coke you ordered you're probably not the man for me.

When he proceeded to tell me that whoever he married would have to accept that he played golf on Saturdays *and* Sundays without fail and that he would expect them to take care of the kids and visit his mom while he golfed, I noped right out of there.

I'm not sure he's ever forgiven me for that.

The best thing about him becoming my boss – and maybe the only good thing – is that he gets to decide who does what broadcasts, and he usually nabs the evening one. Which means he comes into work in the afternoon and I only have to put up with him for a couple of hours.

I've noticed that Madison is coming in earlier and earlier so she can do the same.

"Hey," I say, seeing them both in the office as I walk back from the lunchtime news. "You're early," I tell Michael, trying to not sound grumpy about it.

Michael lifts a brow. "We have a staff meeting in fifteen minutes."

Oh yeah. I'd forgotten about that. It's not a regular meeting. This one is to discuss our annual fundraiser. The WVFY Charity Auction and Ball. It's the pet project of our owner, Donald Regan, and since it's happening in two weeks he probably wants an update of where we're at with all the plans.

Michael's taking it very seriously this year because he's been given the role of emcee for the auction. He hasn't stopped talking about it.

I glance at Madison. "You want to grab some lunch to take into the meeting?" I ask her. At least we can dull the pain with calories.

"Yeah." She jumps up way too enthusiastically, joining me at my desk as I grab my bag.

"Don't be late," Michael warns. "I don't want the weather department getting a bad reputation."

"Too late for that," Madison mutters, low enough for him not to hear.

I bite down a smile. She's definitely settling in.

We walk to the coffee shop at the front of the building and get in line. Ahead of us I see some of the Sports Desk team having the same idea. Nobody loves an all staff meeting.

"Can I talk to you about something?" Madison says, shifting her feet.

"Sure."

"Michael wants to put me up for auction."

I blink. "He wants to what?"

"That's why he's in early. Because he wanted to talk to me. He says I'm the youngest and the prettiest so I should represent the weather department. He wants to auction off a dinner date with me." She frowns. "But I really don't want to."

Of course she doesn't. The urge to punch Michael in the mouth comes over me. Until Kathleen left, we'd all take turns hosting the lucky winner in the weather department for the day. Showing them how we forecast, letting them watch us as we do the news, and then setting them up to have a go in front of the green screen.

It was easy, and sometimes fun. But Michael's been muttering that we don't have enough time to do that this year. He's right, thanks to his terrible reorganization.

But to put our intern up for auction? That's so seedy and ugh.

I know why he's doing it. Because the news desk always does the same with their female anchor and they raise the most money every year. He's competitive and he likes to beat all the other departments.

"You don't have to do it," I tell her.

"He was really insistent," she tells me. "Said it would look good on my resume. And that my final report might depend on it."

"It won't," I reassure her. "Leave it to me."

"What will you do?" She looks up at me, hope in her eyes.

"I'll do it."

"You will?"

"Yep." We reach the front of the line and I nod at Madison to give her order first. I give mine with a controlled voice, because I'm beyond annoyed at Michael. Not just because it's sexist as hell in asking our young intern to go on a date with some rich businessman, but also because I'm supposed to be her boss, not him. I'm the one who does her reports and who will do the final one, too.

To try to bribe her with that stinks.

When our orders are ready, we carry them back to the elevator and take the car to the penthouse where the big meeting room is. We squeeze in next to the sports team, and I smile at Lisa, who's probably my closest friend here at work.

I've known her for ten years. She joined the sports team after she graduated from college. She was a mature student because she spent most of her late teens representing the US in gymnastic competitions, until she broke her neck during a dismount.

It took her a year to recover and she was told she'd never be able to compete again. Where most people would give up, Lisa pulled herself together and decided she wanted to be in sports reporting.

She's as strong as hell and can give the jocks in the sports department as good as they get. And though we're mostly work friends, I know she'd be there in a minute if I was in trouble.

And I would be for her, too.

"Look at him," she says shaking her head. "He thinks he's the shit."

I follow her gaze. Michael is sitting at the front next to WVFY's owner, Donald Regan. His eyes catch mine and I lift my brows at him.

I know your game, sunshine. And I'm going to beat you at it.

"Okay everybody, I think we're all here," Donald says. "So let's get to it. We're here to go through the arrangements for the charity ball. Our emcee for the night – Michael Rimmer – has kindly agreed to lead the meeting." He looks at my boss. "Michael, take it away."

I eat my bagel as Michael talks about the timings and reminds us we all need to wear dress formal clothes and to be ready to mingle with the guests. I kind of tune out because it's the same every year, and let's face it, I've been working here for longer than I care to remember. It's only when Madison elbows me in the waist that I blink and pay attention.

Michael talks through the lots that have been donated by our patrons. There are days on a yacht and vacations and artworks being offered. Everybody oohs and ahhs even though they're way out of our price range.

"And now to the WVFY teams," Michael says, and Madison shifts uncomfortably next to me. I shoot her a reassuring look.

"The news desk is giving away the chance to present the news, plus lunch with the beautiful Lorena." Michael smiles widely at her. "And of course the sports team have offered tickets to a college football game plus dinner. Well done. And now to the weather team…"

"I'd like to be the one up for auction," I call out.

Michael blinks. "It's okay, we have it covered, don't we, Madison?"

"Change of plan," I tell him. "I'll be doing it."

One thing about Michael is that he likes to get his own way, but he likes to kiss ass more. So when Donald nods approvingly he clears his throat and makes a note on his pad. "Okay," he says. "That's fine. Sophie West will be having dinner with the highest bidder."

Madison breathes a sigh of relief.

Lisa leans over to me. "You're really going to let him auction you off for dinner?" She has the same view as me on this. Maybe more so. She's worked hard to succeed in what's traditionally been a man's game and to be auctioned off because she's a woman feels wrong.

"No," I tell her. "I'll think of something else."

"You don't have much time. The auction's next weekend."

"I'll come up with something," I tell her resolutely. There's eight days until the charity ball, even with my stupid workload I should have time to make a plan.

"Good luck," she whispers as Michael glares over at me. "I think you'll need it."

———

LIAM

I pull my car into Myles' and Ava's driveway and park. The lights in the big house are blazing, so I climb out of the driver's seat and walk up there to let them know I'm home before I head back to the bungalow.

Home. The word makes me smile because this isn't my home. And yet there's a warmth to this house that's completely missing in my place in New York. I spent the flight here actually looking forward to seeing my brother and his family. Looking forward to spending time with my nephew and seeing how he's changed in the week that I've been gone.

I knock on the door and Ava opens it, smiling when she sees me. "How was your flight?" she asks me, stepping to the side to let me in.

"Not too bad." I lean down to kiss her cheek.

"And New York? Was that good, too?"

I follow her down the hallway to the kitchen, where Charlie's laying on a blanket watching the television. Well, not actually watching because the kid's only three months old. But his head is facing in that general direction as some animated dogs sing a tune that kind of makes my ears ache.

"Yep," I say. "All good." She doesn't want to hear the details. Meetings, spreadsheets, complaints, resolutions. I spent the last seven days running my ass off to get everything done.

I really need to duplicate myself.

"Is Myles home yet?" I ask her.

"No. He's still at the office. You want me to call him?" she asks.

"It's good. I'll catch up with him later. I just wanted to let you know I'm back safely in case you see the lights go on in the bungalow."

She grins at me. "I'm glad you are. I like knowing you're there."

This woman is heartwarming. No wonder my brother snapped her up.

"Oh," she says. "I have something to give you." She leans over the kitchen counter and rifles through some papers, pulling out a small envelope. "Your invitation to next week's ball."

I take it from her and pull the card out. It's embossed with gold. Expensive. "I'd forgotten all about that," I murmur.

"You can still come, can't you?"

I smile at her. "Of course." Myles thinks it'll be a great way to meet prospective investors. He's probably right. The venn diagram of people with money to invest and people who go to expensive charity auctions is a very tight one. It'll mean flying again next Friday because I have meetings in New York the day before, but it's do-able. I make a mental note to get my tux dry cleaned.

"Good. Because it'll be boring without you."

"Don't let Myles hear you say that," I tell her, but she's

right in some ways. I know how to have a good time, whereas he always finds it harder to relax. I spent most of our childhood being sociable enough for the both of us.

"Are you planning on bringing a date?" she asks.

I shake my head. "Nope."

"Oh that's right. Sophie said..." she trails off, looking alarmed. My chest immediately tightens.

Does she know about what happened between me and Sophie?

"What did Sophie say?" I ask.

"It doesn't matter," Ava says quickly.

"Yeah, it does." I look at her carefully. "What did she tell you?"

Ava swallows and I immediately feel like an asshole for cornering her. But Sophie and I made a pact. We wouldn't tell anybody.

Has she broken it?

Part of me is annoyed because it was her that insisted. But the other part is annoyed because I don't want Ava thinking badly of me. I value her opinion. She's more than a sister-in-law, she's a friend.

And I don't have many of those.

"She said that you don't spend more than one night with a woman," Ava said softly. "She didn't mean any harm by it. She was just explaining why you and she wouldn't be a good match."

I swallow hard. "She told you that?"

"Yeah." Ava looks embarrassed.

"I guess you think I'm some kind of Casanova, huh?" I shift my feet, feeling awkward.

"No." She shakes her head, sympathy softening her gaze. "I just thought it was... I don't know, sad I guess."

My chest loosens. "You don't need to worry. I don't feel sad."

"I just don't understand why you'd have that rule." She looks up at me.

This one's easy. "Because nobody gets hurt this way. Relationships always end in tears and I don't like it."

"Maybe you just haven't met the right woman," Ava suggests, with hope in her eyes. And I realize something. Myles hasn't told her about my past. I'm glad of that, because I don't need her to look at me differently.

"If she was the right woman I definitely wouldn't want to hurt her."

She still looks sad though. And I hate that. "Relax," I tell her. "I'm happy. I enjoy my life. And I make sure everybody around me enjoys it, too." That's what I like. That's what I'm good at.

"Okay." She smiles at me. "I'm glad you can come next Saturday anyway."

"Me too."

Charlie chooses that moment to start crying. Ava scoops him up and holds him against her chest and he immediately quietens.

An image flashes into my mind, of Sophie holding Charlie. The way she looked that day at the christening. So pretty. So happy.

Yeah, I wouldn't want to hurt her either. And I definitely wouldn't want to be hurt by her.

"I'm going to head back to the bungalow," I tell her, because I can see Charlie snuffling around her, and it feels like it's probably time for him to nurse. "You need anything before I go?"

"No, I'm good." She smiles at me. "Go relax. It's good to have you home."

———

Later that night, I'm sitting in front of my laptop replying to emails in an attempt to make a dent in my overfull inbox. My conversation with Ava is still playing on my mind. I'm not annoyed at Sophie for telling her about me – it's not exactly something I hide – but it's made me think about Sophie and that night again.

And I'm finding it impossible to get out of my mind.

I wasn't lying when I told her I wish I'd made her come. I also wish to hell that I remember that night. Damn those cocktails. I never usually drink like that but it had been Myles and Ava's pre-wedding party.

I guess I got a little bit emotional at the thought of my big brother settling down.

I remember some of the night. Spending time with Myles and our brothers, plus some of his New York friends who'd flown down for the occasion. Then we'd met up with Ava and her friends – a whole bunch of them because she's lived here for most of her life. And she's just one of those people who everybody loves.

Things get a little hazy after the party died down. I can remember my brothers going on to a nightclub and Myles refusing so I stayed with him. And then I remember getting him and Ava into a car before walking back into the bar where Sophie was trying to settle the tab.

I'd insisted on paying and she'd argued with me about it. And then we'd ordered another round of cocktails while we finished the argument. When I won, we ordered more and started talking about dating and how much harder it was in your thirties – or in my case forties. That's when I must have told her about my rule.

And then? Nothing. I can't remember going home with her and I can't remember sleeping with her. I only remember the next morning.

Somebody like Sophie deserves to be remembered.

I try to reply to another email but I can't concentrate. Sighing, I get up and pour myself some water and grab my phone.

I don't really want to talk about this with any of my brothers, but it's pulling at my brain. So I pull Eli's number up and he answers right after the first ring.

"Hey, you just caught me. I'm literally walking out to my car." Eli sounds out of breath and I realize he was playing tonight.

I'd completely forgot and feel bad because I always watch his games. I quickly type into my laptop so I can see the end result.

"Congratulations," I say.

"Cheers. So what's up?"

I swallow because I don't usually talk with Eli about stuff like this. It's more of a conversation I'd have with Myles.

But he's the last person who needs to know about my life with Sophie.

"Have you ever drank so much that you were unable to remember what happened the previous night?" I ask him.

"What?" Eli says, then lets out a chuckle before I hear the slam of a door. He must be in his car. "Did this happen to you?"

"Yeah," I tell him. "I keep trying to think about what happened and it's all blank. It's killing me. Do you have any idea how I can make myself remember?" If anybody knows, Eli does. He's constantly being assessed by doctors.

"The easiest way is to ask the people you were with," he tells me.

I frown. "I can't do that."

"Why not? Who was it?"

I swallow hard. "A woman."

Eli laughs louder this time. "Oh boy. And you can't ask this woman because…?

"I have my reasons. Do you have any suggestions or do

you just want to carry on laughing?" I sound testy, I know that. But this is bugging me.

"How long ago did this happen?" Eli asks, sounding almost sympathetic.

"A while ago." I don't want to tell him the exact date. He's not stupid, he could figure out who I'm talking about.

"So when you woke up in the morning where were you?"

My chest feels tight even after I exhale heavily. "In her bed."

"And what happened next?"

"She said she was going to get dressed in the bathroom and that I should leave before she came out." I frown. "I was feeling kind of rough."

"Dude," Eli says sharply. "This was all consensual, right?"

"Of course it was," I snap. "She told me we slept together, it wasn't good for her, and we would never be doing this again."

"It wasn't good for her," Eli repeats. "You mean you didn't make her…"

"That's what she said."

"Ho boy." He's quiet for a moment. "But you always make sure they have a good time. Liam's rule number one, she always comes first. That's what you told me when I came to you when we were younger."

I blanch because it's true. If a woman's going to offer me a night with her, I'm going to make sure it's good for her. No, not just good. Amazing. Unforgettable. I have a thing for making sure she walks away fully satisfied and then some.

I love women. That's why I'd never get into a full time relationship. They sure as hell deserve better than me.

When Eli was in his late teens he came to me for advice. And I took that seriously, telling him that women needed to be treated with respect. And yes, I know that sounds counter-intuitive coming from me, but I have nothing but respect for women.

I don't sleep with anybody without making sure they're on the same bandwidth as I am.

Which is why this whole thing with Sophie is driving me crazy. I lost control of the situation and I hate it.

"Look," Eli says, his voice pulling me out of my thoughts. "I think you gotta just put this thing behind you. Whoever she is has probably forgotten all about you already, right?"

"She definitely hasn't," I say.

"Wait. You've seen her again?"

I shift in my seat. "Not exactly. She's ah… a friend of a friend."

There's silence for a moment. "Do I know her?" Eli asks, his voice low.

I promised I wouldn't tell. But she also made a promise and didn't keep it. Plus I trust Eli like I don't trust anybody else.

"It's Sophie."

"Sophie, as in Ava's best friend?" His voice lifts. "Oh shit man."

"Right?"

He clears his throat. "That explains why she hates you."

"Thank you for that."

"Just saying what I see. You really know how to shit in your own backyard, don't you?"

"I drank too much and so did she," I remind him. "And it's done now."

"You're right. So you move on," he tells me. "Forget about it. Make sure the woman you sleep with next time gets double the fun."

"Sure."

"Dude, you're worrying me now," Eli says. I can hear a horn in the distance, and the low rumble of his engine. "This isn't like you. You're the fun guy. The life of the party. You don't brood like this."

"I know." He's right. I need to stop overthinking this.

Another horn blasts and I remember my brother's just won a game and is no doubt on his way to celebrate. "Listen, I have to go. Do me a favor and don't talk to anybody else about this."

"Of course I won't. I just wish I could make you feel better."

"You have," I tell him. "Seriously. Thank you for talking with me. I'll catch up with you soon."

"Okay, man. Have a good night."

"You too," I tell him, ending the call. Then I let out a long breath.

Eli is right. Enough is enough. I'm not going to worry about this anymore. I'm going to go to the event next week, spend some time with my brother and his wife, and find a way to get Sophie out of my system.

I already feel more like the old Liam. Hopefully he's back for good.

CHAPTER EIGHT

SOPHIE

The staff from WVFY arrive early to the Ambassador Hotel just as Michael and Donald asked us, to help set everything up before putting on our glad rags. Almost as soon as we come back down, the doors are open, the guests begin to arrive, and the orchestra starts up.

I glance at a table, trying to not feel smug as I see the list of auction lots. I changed mine without telling Michael. Luckily my friend runs the printing department and was able to reprint them with my new offering – so I'm relaxed and ready for the evening.

"You look gorgeous," Lorena, the evening news anchor says, kissing the air next to my cheek.

"Thank you. So do you." I smile at her.

I made a big effort tonight for a number of reasons. Firstly because Ava, Lauren, and I went shopping for dresses together and it was so much fun. I couldn't wait to wear this dress. It's a silver crossover halter neck dress that clings to my body like a limpet. It makes my bottom look a little bit big, but Ava assured me that it was perfect and to be honest I feel like a princess right now.

The second reason I wanted to make an effort because I'm going to be standing up on that stage. And even though I'm not going to be auctioning myself off exactly, I still want to look nice.

I sigh at the thought of the third reason. Because a certain man I spent a night with will be here. It's embarrassing because I shouldn't be dressing up for Liam.

Yes, after the christening it feels like there's been some kind of change between us, but I'm not at all sure how that makes me feel. Fundamentally things are still the same. I might find him attractive in a physical way, but emotionally he's a thousand miles away from the kind of guy that's right for me.

At least it's a beautiful evening. Through the windows at the end of the ballroom I can see the sun slowly sliding down the sky, casting an orange glow across the city, making the Kanawha River look like it's on fire.

Lisa joins Lorena and I as we stand and smile at the guests as they walk in. She looks radiant in a black satin sheath that shows off her perfect shoulders. Even though she gave up competitive gymnastics years ago she still has the best muscle definition I've ever seen.

Lorena clears her throat. "Have you organized your highest bidder?" she asks me, kissing the cheek of a man who looks delighted to see her.

"What do you mean?" I reply once he's moved on. "Won't the highest bidder be the person with the biggest wallet?"

Her smile wavers. "Oh honey, no. You need to hit somebody up, someone you don't mind having dinner with. My friend's boss is bidding for me. He has a lot of cash and he loves to give it away. I've already promised him the best night on the town."

"I'm not offering dinner," I tell her, relieved because I might have dodged a bullet.

"You're not?" She frowns. "I swear I saw that on the list."

"I had the list reprinted." Yes it was a waste of paper, but I paid for it myself.

Lisa is grinning at me. "Did you tell Michael yet?"

"Nope."

"So what are you auctioning if it isn't dinner?" Lorena asks.

"I'm going to give somebody a personalized weather forecast every day for three months. They tell me where they are and what they're doing that day and I'll tell them if they're going to get rained on or have beautiful sunshine."

It's a genius idea. And yes, it's more work than going out for dinner for a night because I'm going to make sure I do it right. But I'll do it on my time so it won't affect the team.

"Oh I love it." Lisa grins. "I would so bid on that."

"Do it," I tell her. "I'll give you the best forecast you've ever had."

I turn to see Ava and Lauren walking toward us. Ava is wearing the gorgeous red dress she chose when we went shopping last week. It's perfect for her, enhancing her new post-Charlie curves, her skin glowing and pearlescent against the deep ruby fabric.

"Look at you," she says breathlessly, hugging me tight. "Everybody's going to want a piece of your forecast."

"Will you bid on me if nobody else does?" I ask her, remembering Lorena's warning.

"Everybody's going to bid on you," she tells me. "Not because you look amazing – which you do by the way – but because they know what a great meteorologist you are."

"This is why I love you," I say. I give Lauren a hug next. She's as beautiful as Ava, wearing a midnight blue dress with a Bardot neckline and a cinched waist.

"You're gonna knock this out of the park," she whispers to me.

"Thank you." I'm feeling lucky to have them as my friends. Then I feel a weird sensation. My skin starts to prickle like it's suddenly gotten cold in here. I glance over Lauren's shoulder and see *him.*

Liam's standing with Myles, the Salinger brothers devastatingly handsome in their tuxedos. They look like they should be in a cologne ad, not laughing about something as they wait for Ava to join them.

Myles sees me and lifts his hand, smiling. I wave back as Lauren releases me and starts talking to Lisa, who apparently knows Lauren from the bakery she runs.

Against my will, my gaze shifts to the man who knows how to push every button I own. It clashes with his and my muscles tense. His gaze wanders lazily over my face, my shoulders, down to the dress I'm wearing, then just as slowly he lifts it back up until he catches my eyes.

There's something deliciously sensual about the way he doesn't look away. Just stares until my cheeks start to burn.

His dark hair is casually ruffled, his freshly-shaved jaw in contrast against the stiff collar and bow tie just beneath it. I've never met anybody as comfortable in his own skin as Liam Salinger. He could be wearing nothing but a thong right now and he wouldn't blink an eyelid.

His confidence is annoying. I wish my body didn't respond to his so much. It would be so much easier to deal with him then.

"Sophie?" Lisa says.

I blink and look at her.

"I'm going to head for the bathroom before we have to mingle," she repeats so I can hear her. "Are you coming?"

"Yes, good idea."

As I follow her I'm so aware that Liam is still watching me. I glance over my shoulder once more, and he isn't smiling anymore. There's a darkness to his eyes that I could get lost in if I wanted to.

"Watch the—oh shit!" Lisa calls out, as I slip on something on the floor. My arms flail like windmills as I feel gravity doing its thing, pulling me down toward the ground. Lisa lunges forward and wraps her crazily strong arms around my waist, catching me right before I hit the patch of what looks like spilled champagne that caused my stupidly high heels to lose their footing.

"Oh my God," she says. "I'm a fucking hero. I just saved you."

"Does that mean we have to get married now?" I ask her.

She grins. "Definitely."

We both start to laugh because it's such a ludicrous situation. She's swept me into her arms like I'm Scarlett and she's Rhett except she's only five feet six and definitely doesn't have a moustache.

She hauls me upright, and though my dress is wet at the hem it's barely visible.

"Okay?" she asks.

"I'm okay." I nod. Then I glance behind me – and Liam is still standing there watching.

But that dark look that shook me to my core is gone. Instead, he's laughing and so is Myles while Ava is shouting at both of them, though I can't hear what she's saying.

And it's weird, but I prefer this. Being around Liam is so much easier to deal with when he's not being dark and dangerous.

I can take the mocking, laughing Liam.

It's the one who looks like he wants to eat me instead of the three course charity banquet I find scary.

CHAPTER
NINE

SOPHIE

When I get back from powdering my nose, the hotel ballroom is filled with Charleston's finest, all dressed to the nines and making awkward small talk, waiting for the moment that the string quartet stops playing so they can actually sit down.

The staff members at WVFY haven't been allocated our own tables – which is just as well since each table of ten costs twenty thousand dollars. Instead, our job is to sit at a different table for each course and make sure everybody is having a good time. For the first course – carrot and coriander soup – I'm put with a table of old school Charleston grandees.

One of the men on my left takes pity on me and asks me what I do.

"I present the weather on WVFY," I tell him.

"Ah, you're on television," he says. "I don't watch that. Prefer the radio, always have."

"Ah, she'd be wasted on the radio," the man on my other side says. "Too pretty for that."

He's at least eighty and there's nothing lecherous in his words. He's just trying to be a gentleman, so I smile at him.

"I worked on the radio when I was a student," I tell him. "It's a lot harder to do a forecast when you don't have a map behind you."

"I wouldn't be looking at the map anyway," he says. Then the woman next to him slaps his arm. "Sorry, darling," he mumbles. She shakes her head then smiles at me.

"I think you're wonderful," she tells me. "You haven't steered me wrong yet. You were the only one who said it was going to rain last weekend, and you were right."

This isn't strictly true, but I take it anyway. And as I'm about to ask them if they're planning on bidding on the auction tonight I feel a tap on my shoulder.

"Can I have a word?" Michael asks. He looks annoyed. I can only imagine that he's seen the auction list.

"I'm busy," I tell him with a whisper, pointing at the table. As soon as he sees nine other pairs of eyes looking at him, he puts on an easy smile. All trace of annoyance disappears into the air.

"Hello," he says to them. "So sorry to interrupt you, I just need Sophie for a moment." He lifts a brow. "You don't mind, do you? It's to do with the auction."

"Of course we don't mind," the man on my right says, patting my hand. "You go ahead, dear. We'll finish our soup."

Michael lifts a brow at me, and I recognize that gesture. And now I'm the one annoyed because I really don't want to go with him, but I don't want to make a scene in front of our donors either.

I don't know what I was thinking really. Of course he was going to look at the list before the auction started.

"I'll be right back," I tell them, standing reluctantly.

"We'll make sure nobody steals your soup," the man says.

"Follow me." That's all Michael says for the next minute as we walk across the ballroom to the little area behind the stage where the production team is setting things up for the auction. Still not talking to me, Michael picks up one of the lists and shoves it toward me.

"What's this?" he asks.

"I don't know." I shrug, determined not to make a scene here either. I have to work with these people and they're all avidly watching us.

"Get back to work," Michael snaps at them. It's grimly satisfying to see there are people other than me who he doesn't lay on the charm for. When they start shuffling about again he turns back to me. "I asked you to be auctioned for a dinner," he tells me. "What's this nonsense about a personal weather forecast?"

I square my shoulders. "You asked me to be put up for auction and this is what I want to auction off. It's a much better prize than dinner. Somebody gets three months' worth of data just for them."

"And you think that's a good idea? Do you realize how much work that's going to take? WVFY is trying to make money, not pay for you to be somebody's weather slave."

"I'll do it on my own time," I say stubbornly.

"Just go out for dinner, Sophie," he hisses. He grabs a pen from his pocket and strikes a line through my auction lot, scribbling something above it.

"You can't do that," I protest. "Everybody has the paper on their tables."

"I'll explain you made a mistake."

I shake my head, furious. "No you won't. My auction is staying as it's printed."

"You'll make more money for charity if you just go out for dinner." He waves his hand toward the stage. "These guys don't give a shit about a forecast. They just want to take you out for dinner, have you look pretty, and maybe cop a feel or two on the way home."

God I hate him. And I'm so aware that the production

team is still listening in as he berates me. But I'm not going to get emotional this time, I'm just not.

Because that way he wins and I'm not going to let him.

"It stays," I say again.

"Maybe you can explain to the kids why we haven't raised the money we need then," he spits out.

"If I don't make enough on the auction I'll make a donation." There, that should do it.

But instead of conceding he starts to laugh. "You can't afford it. Jesus, Sophie, how stupid are you?"

I ignore his jibe because it's embarrassing. "Is that all you wanted to talk to me about?" I ask, my voice tight. "Or can I go back to dinner? My soup is going cold."

He shoots me an angry glance but says nothing. So I take the opportunity to pick my dress up a little and step over the wiring and boxes the production team has finished setting up.

There's no way I can keep working with this man without losing my mind. Tonight proves it.

My arm brushes one of the team, but I'm looking down at my feet because I'm not planning on tripping again. And by the time I get back to the table there's about two minutes left to eat my soup before we all have to rotate.

And I try to be sociable and make small talk, because this really is for a good cause. But inside I'm imagining the slow and painful demise of Michael Rimmer.

———

LIAM

Her arm brushes mine and for a moment I panic that she's going to see me, so I step back into the shadows to make sure she doesn't know I'm here. Watching that asshole talk down to her like she's an idiot has sent my blood pressure sky high, and when I look down my hands are curled into fists like I want to punch something.

Not something. *Somebody*.

This man who talked to Sophie like she was a piece of crap.

She'd be mortified if she knew I heard, that much is clear. I shouldn't be here at all. But when she walked past the table, that guy practically manhandling her, I excused myself and followed them.

Not that she needed my help because she can clearly hold her own. She gives as good as she gets, one of the things that I admire about her.

The asshole who was reaming her out goes to pass me, so I step out in front of him. He looks up, surprised, then puts on a fake smile.

"Excuse me," he says, trying to sidestep me.

I sidestep the same way he does, still blocking his way. The smile on his face wavers.

"Your name?" I ask, my voice low.

"I'm sorry?" He blinks, looking confused.

"What's your name?" I say slowly. There's no mistaking the annoyance in my voice. And the confusion on his face deepens.

He shifts his feet, not quite looking me in the eye. Like bullies everywhere he's actually scared of being confronted. "It's Michael Rimmer," he mumbles.

"And you work for WVFY?"

He nods.

"Well, Michael Rimmer," I say slowly, "Let's get one thing straight. If I ever hear you talking to Sophie like that again you can say goodbye to your job. And any chance of finding another."

He narrows his eyes. "Who are you to be telling me what to do?"

"A friend of your boss." I tell him. "Well actually your

boss' boss' boss." I lift a brow. "A very good friend." It's not really true. I know Donald to say hello to but not much more than that. But I know cowards like this man in front of me and a little threat usually does the trick.

I just want him to leave her the fuck alone.

There's a battle raging between his eyes as he tries to think the information through. For a moment I wonder if he's actually going to square up to me.

And part of me wants that.

The other part would hate that. Because Sophie would find out and she doesn't need to know about this. She's proud and she pretty much hates me. I can deal with that.

I just can't deal with the way she looked when she was being shouted at.

"Twenty minutes until the auction," somebody shouts out. "Mr. Rimmer, we need to go through a few things with you."

Michael lifts his hand to his face. It's actually shaking. "I need to go."

"Of course," I say smoothly. "Are we all clear?"

"I... ah..."

"Are. We. All. Clear?"

He nods rapidly. "Yes, absolutely."

"Good." I step back and it's a relief. Because my fists are still curled and my body is still on high alert. "Have a nice evening," I tell him, my voice deceptively casual.

He blinks. "Thank you. You, too."

I don't say anymore. Just turn on my heel and walk away from the mayhem of backstage, toward the table my brother paid an ungodly amount for. When I slide into my chair there's a waiter pouring coffee and I hold out my cup as he pours.

"Everything all right?" Myles asks me. "You were gone a while."

"Just talking business," I tell him, my expression neutral.

"Don't you ever take a night off?" Ava asks, shaking her head.

"Work always comes first," I murmur, lifting my coffee cup and taking a sip. From the corner of my eye I can see Sophie sitting at a table a few rows down. She's smiling and chatting, but her body is stiff.

I could relax you in three minutes, baby.

As though she can hear my thoughts, she lifts her head and her gaze catches mine. Her head tilts slightly, a lock of hair escaping from her elaborate updo. Her lips part and all I can think of is how good they'd feel. On my mouth, on my body. All fucking over.

We finish our entrees and the plates are taken away, but I'm so damn aware of her I couldn't tell you what I just ate. When they bring the desserts, I shake my head and gesture for the waiter to pour me more coffee instead, no cream, because I need to stay alert.

Sophie's at another table now. It's near the stage and full of the kind of guys who drink too much wine and spend too much time looking down her top. My jaw twitches as one of them slings his arm around the back of her chair, his fingers brushing the skin on the back of her neck.

"Do you think Sophie is all right?" I ask Ava.

"What do you mean?" she asks, looking over her shoulder.

"The table in front of the stage," I tell her, and she follows the direction of my stare. Sophie is talking to the man on her left, but the guy on the right is still stretching his arm behind her, his fingers brushing her bare shoulder.

I want to rip them out of his body.

And yes, I'm aware this kind of reaction isn't normal. Plus I have the sense not to actually do the deed. I'm not even sure if I'm capable of ripping an arm off. I mean, I go to the gym, but I imagine it's gonna need a lot of force.

"What's going to need force?" Ava asks me.

Alarmed, I turn to her. "Did I say that?"

"You mumbled something. I only heard force."

Thank God. "I was thinking about Star Wars," I tell her. "That Sophie could use the force right now."

She stares at me uncomprehendingly, then shakes her head. The wait staff are thankfully taking away the dessert plates, and Mr. Tickle has to pull his arm away to let them lean over. Sophie smoothly leans to one side and puts an elbow on the back of the chair to make it difficult for him to put his arm back.

Good girl.

"She seems fine to me," Ava says, sending a weird look my way.

"Ladies and Gentleman," a voice calls out over the PA. "Please take ten minutes to make yourselves comfortable, fill up your glasses, and shake the moths out of your wallets. We'll be beginning the auction as soon as you're drunk enough to overbid."

Everybody laughs. I don't, because I know that voice.

And yeah, I want to rip out that throat, too.

I'm not a neanderthal. I haven't gotten into fights as an adult. Even as a kid I preferred using charm to my fists. It was less painful and usually had better results. I don't understand this urge I have to get physical with these assholes. All I know is that I can't. It'll ruin any chance of having normal and pleasant interactions with Sophie in the future.

Mr. Tickle shifts his chair closer to Sophie's and whispers something in her ear. She shakes her head slightly and he shrugs, but it's enough to spark the annoyance in me again.

"Are you okay?" Ava asks, leaning across the table. "You look like you're overheating."

"I'm fine," I say, my teeth clenched. "Just need to send a message to my assistant."

Thank God Myles is too busy schmoozing the guy on his other side to notice my current reaction.

True story, Sam used to work for a private investigator until I headhunted her and made her an offer she couldn't refuse. It turns out she pretty much ran the business for him and knows all the tricks. Some of them I don't like to think about too much because I'm almost certain they fall into a gray area. Still, it's useful on occasions.

So when I tap her a message asking her to find out who the guys on table two are, I'm not at all surprised when she replies less than five minutes later with a full rundown of who bought the table – a law firm in Charleston – and who she thinks is at the table – mostly associates and their friends. No partners.

Basically, Moor and Rycroft LLP have sent the kids out to play.

I write myself a reminder to give Sam a week off for having to deal with my demands and put my phone away. Sophie is now standing, pointing at the stage and saying something to the guys who don't even bother to stand up like gentlemen should.

My body relaxes as soon as she walks away. Tomorrow I'm going to have a stern talk with myself because this weird reaction isn't normal. Maybe there was something in the soup. Or maybe I was right the first time. I'm going through some kind of existential crisis.

Maybe there's a more obvious explanation. Weird how the voice in my head sounds like Eli.

Maybe it's the old forbidden fruit. You want what you can't have. And if you can't have her, you don't want anybody else to, either.

Am I really that shallow? I frown because maybe I am.

The waiter is walking around the table refilling wine glasses. I shake my head because I'm really not feeling it right now. I need to keep my wits about me. Maybe even come to my senses.

It's amazing that nobody has noticed that I'm having a full

blown breakdown right now. Even Myles, who is usually attuned to everybody, has no idea that I'm seriously considering violence to protect a woman who doesn't need protecting and isn't mine to protect anyway.

But she's a friend. That's kind of yours.

Okay, I like that thought. It can stay. If she's my friend then maybe that's why I'm feeling this way.

Does she know she's your friend?

No, but I can remedy that. I'll talk to her. Explain that my one night rule still stands but it shouldn't stop us from being friends with each other. We can do what friends do. Go out and…

What do friends do?

I'll have to think about that later because the auction is about to begin. My jaw twitches as Michael comes out on stage, not a hair out of place, his tux and shirt perfectly smooth.

"Folks, it's that part of the night when we remember exactly why we're here," he says, smiling out at the crowd like he isn't a yank away from having his limbs ripped off. "So let's start by playing a little video about our chosen charity, Marie's Hope. The charity was founded in nineteen ninety-nine by the amazing Charles and Melissa Landry, the sister and brother–in-law of our owner, after they sadly lost their daughter Marie to Leukemia. The aim of Marie's Hope is to make every day a better one for children who are seriously ill, and I think you'll agree that the kids we've been able to help over the years, thanks to your donations, deserve every penny we raise."

He steps back and a video plays. A little kid comes on – a boy no more than five. He has a bald head and a tube coming out of his nose.

"I want to be an astronaut when I grow up," he says. "Like Buzz Lightyear."

There's something weird in my eye. Probably some dust. I

wipe it away.

"But I'm sick, so for now I just want to meet Buzz. In Disneyland. He trains kids like me to be superheroes. That's what I want to be, too."

Ava sniffles. Myles hands her his handkerchief. I notice his eyes are also glistening.

Benji – the kid in question – starts showing us his *Toy Story* collection. Then there's a voiceover, explaining that Benji did get to meet Buzz, along with photographs of this gorgeous, vibrant kid living his best life dressed like a Disney character.

The video stops. Michael walks forward and I don't feel like killing him anymore. "Would anybody like to know what happened to Benji?" he asks softly.

It's like the whole room is hypnotized. Yes, I want to know he's been cured. I want to know the kid is going to live his dream and become an astronaut.

Hell, I'll raise enough money to pay for him to do that.

"Please don't let him have passed," Ava whispers. Cold fingers of fear grab at my heart. I hadn't even thought about that.

And now I want to hit somebody all over again.

Michael claps his hands together. "I'm pleased to say that Benji is doing well. He wanted to be here tonight, but he's in the hospital undergoing an experimental treatment that's been funded by the charity. He's sent his best wishes and a promise that he'll be here next year, dressed as Buzz on the stage."

A sigh of relief ripples through the room. And the dust is still circulating, irritating my eyes. Ava glances at me as I wipe my eye again and I shrug at her.

She smiles back at me through her own tears.

"So without further ado, let's move onto the auction," Michael says. "Starting with lot one from our very own news desk. Tell me, good folks of Charleston, do you have what it takes to read the news?"

CHAPTER
TEN

SOPHIE

"You sure about this?" Michael still looks annoyed as I walk onto the stage. He's conveniently switched off his microphone so he can annoy me. "We'd raise a lot more money for kids like Benji if you let me auction you off for dinner."

"I'm sure," I tell him, even though I'm not. There was a moment back there while I was watching the video with Benji that I wondered whether I'm doing the right thing.

But people have told me they'll bid. I asked everybody at each table if they would like a daily forecast and they all thought it was a great idea.

Even the frat lawyer guys at table two.

"News and Sports raised a hundred thousand dollars between them," Michael says. "Let's see what you can do." Then he points at the front of the stage and I walk over, making sure I smile and look confident, because I want this to work.

I need it to.

"We're on lot ten of the auction, ladies and gentlemen,"

Michael says, having turned his mic back on. "Featuring Sophie West, everybody's favorite weather girl."

I keep smiling, even though I'm a meteorologist and not a weather girl and I know Michael said it to rile me.

"Now this one's a little different," Michael continues. "Instead of dinner with the girl of everybody's dreams, she's offering a three month personalized daily forecast for the lucky bidder." He lowers his voice. "Of course I'd prefer dinner but…"

Everybody laughs, so I laugh too. Then I turn and roll my eyes at him in what I hope is a cute Meg Ryan kind of way, though my intentions are definitely more deadly.

"So let's have our first bid. Shall we start at ten thousand?" he shouts out.

He started the other lots at twenty. I'm pretty sure nobody has missed that. And there's a pause that's way too long and I start to sweat underneath the blinding spotlight. Maybe I made a mistake.

"Ten," somebody calls out and I exhale heavily.

"Fifteen," another voice counters. It's hard to see anything standing here on stage. I blink to get acclimatized to the lights.

"Twenty." I recognize that voice. It's Ava's. I smile harder because I know she won't let me fail.

"Thirty." That voice is closer. From table two. The guy who was sitting next to me during dessert – the handsy one. He looks smug.

"Forty," Ava counters.

"Fifty." The lawyer smiles lazily. I squint and try to look in Ava's direction, shaking my head. I don't want her to bid anymore. Myles already spent a fortune on the table and I don't have the money to reimburse her if she goes over forty.

Handsy guy smiles at me. I start to reconcile myself to the fact I'll be giving him weather forecasts for the next three months.

At least it isn't dinner.

"Okay then, any more bids?" Michael says because the back and forth bidding has stopped. "I guess—"

"One hundred thousand."

A gasp goes through the crowd. I cover my eyes, trying to see who it is. Please don't let it be a jetsetter who flies to a different country every day. Forecasting that'll take up most of my free time.

"Do we have any takers for one hundred and ten?" Michael asks. He doesn't seem very excited by the high bid.

"Going once," he says. "Twice. And sold to the gentleman in the middle." Michael nods to one of the production staff who walks to the table where Ava and Myles are sitting.

Did Myles bid for me? That's incredibly sweet yet I'm going to owe him forever. I'll have to babysit until Charlie's thirty.

"Your name, sir?"

Even this part of the auction is over the top. The production assistant goes to the highest bidder with a microphone and they have a fun conversation with Michael.

"Liam Salinger."

I swear my heart misses a beat. I can't see more than shadows beyond the blinding lights, but I try anyway.

"Mr. Salinger," Michael says, which is a bit weird because he's called every other bidder by their first name. "Tell me, do you have a particular interest in meteorology?"

A wave of laughter ripples through the ballroom.

"I've always been a fan of the weather," Liam says. His voice is strangely soft, even though it's echoing from the sound system. "Ignore it at your peril. I think Noah's friends in the bible learned that the hard way."

"Indeed," Michael says, forced jollity lifting his tone. "So you'll be waking up every morning to the beautiful Sophie."

"To her forecasts, yes," Liam corrects. "And I'm very much looking forward to them."

"Let's see what Sophie has to say." Michael beckons me over. I lift my dress to avoid making a spectacular trip on stage and join him.

He smells of Sauvage and smarm.

"Congratulations, Sophie," he says, not quite meeting my eye. "How excited are you to be sending forecasts to Mr. Salinger every morning?"

I take a deep breath. "Hugely excited," I say, trying to ignore how weird my voice sounds through the speakers. I'm used to hearing it from the television, but I sound different here in this big room. "And I'd like to say a huge thank you to Mr. Salinger for donating so much money to such a wonderful cause. I'll do my best to make the sun shine on him every day."

The crowd laughs again, and Michael nods at me, which is my cue to leave the stage. I walk carefully down the steps, my satin dress still gathered in my hand. As soon as I reach the bottom I hear a voice.

"Sophie?"

I feel dizzy. I have to hold onto the back of a chair to stop myself from falling, before sliding my behind into the seat. "Yes?"

"Are you okay?" he asks. "You look a little sick."

"No, no, I'm fine." I don't look up. Mostly because I don't want him to see the pained look on my face. "Thank you for your bid. I appreciate it."

"I wasn't sure you would." He shifts his feet. From my vantage point I get a close up of the beautifully soft leather brogues he's wearing. I can't begin to imagine how much they cost.

"Why not?" I ask, still studying his feet.

"Because you don't like me."

I blink. "That's not true."

"So why won't you even look at me?" he asks me.

"I just…" I still can't believe he spent all that money.

"Sophie, please look at me." His voice is as soft as the leather of his shoes. And of course I look up. I'm not sure I could stop myself. It's like he's talking directly to my muscles, overriding my nervous system.

And when my eyes meet his I see genuine concern there.

"You don't have to send me daily weather forecasts," he tells me. "I just wanted to bid on something for the charity."

"It's a good charity," I tell him.

"Yeah. That video at the start..." he trails off. "Anyway, they asked me to see you to sort out the details, but let's call it quits." He lifts a brow at me and goes to walk away.

I stand up. "Liam," I call out to him. He stops mid walk and looks at me again.

"Yes?"

"Why did you bid on my lot? Why not somebody else's? There are some amazing ones tonight. You could have gotten a vacation on a yacht or a trip to the Bahamas."

He runs his thumb along his chin as though considering my question. Then he takes a step toward me and all logical thought goes out of my brain. I don't know when I started to find him so achingly attractive, but now that I do I can't get it out of my mind.

It's not just the way he looks at me. It's that he's different. Honest. I can hear Michael's voice in the background, schmoozing the audience and the difference between him and Liam couldn't be more stark.

Yes, he can be annoying. But I think more than anything it's because I can't control my responses to him. I'm used to being calm but whenever he's around I feel like I'm on a rollercoaster that's speeding out of control.

It's frightening. And exhilarating.

"I thought I could help a friend at the same time as supporting a charity," he says quietly. "I assumed you wouldn't want those lawyer guys to have the winning bid. And Ava already looked awkward so I took over."

"You bid way above the value of my lot."

His lip quirks. "If you say so."

"I'll do the forecasts for you," I tell him, because there's no way I'm letting him spend that much money and have nothing to show for it.

"I told you already you didn't have to."

"But I want to," I say. "It's for charity."

He pulls at his collar and my eyes immediately hone in on the dip at the bottom of his neck. His shirt is unbuttoned, his bow tie hanging loose.

"Okay then," he says. "How do we play this?"

"I just need an itinerary from you," I tell him. "You can ask your assistant to send it to me if you'd like. Then I'll give you a personalized forecast based on your location and plans."

"I'll send it to you," he says.

"That works."

"I won't always know where I'm going to be each week though. It'll mostly vary between here and New York, but I have to travel elsewhere sometimes."

"That's okay. You can just let me know when you know. Sunday evenings would be great for your weekly plans. That way I'll have enough time to do the forecast and send it to you each morning. There's no point in me sending it to you halfway through the day."

"And what will I do with this forecast?" he asks, a smile playing at his lips.

"Know whether to carry an umbrella I guess." I find myself smiling back at him. "Or whether to run outside or indoors on a treadmill."

His brows dip. "You think I need to start running?"

"I don't know." I try not to smile as he looks down to check his perfectly flat stomach. "The whole point is that the forecast is meant to help you make good decisions."

He starts to laugh.

"What?" I say, almost grinning because his laughter is contagious.

"If I knew a daily forecast from you would help me make good decisions I'd have paid for it long ago."

"I meant decisions about whether to be inside or outside," I tell him, rolling my eyes.

"I know that," he teases. "But maybe I like the idea of you being my decision guru."

"So we'll start on Monday," I tell him, because I don't think I can deal with him being sweet much longer. Annoying, yes. Even charming. But sweet…

That's too much.

"Sounds good." He nods. "I'll send you my itinerary on Sunday. Or at least what I think I'll be doing."

"Thank you." And it's weird, but knowing I'll have a detailed plan of his week makes me feel like there's a connection that shouldn't be there. Then something occurs to me. Something he said a few minutes ago.

"Liam, when you said you were bidding to help a friend, did you mean it?"

He looks surprised. "Of course I did."

"And I'm the friend?" I clarify. Because it wasn't long ago that we were at each other's throats.

"That would be the obvious conclusion."

"Okay then."

He tips his head to the side. "What does that mean?"

"Nothing." I shrug.

His eyes dip to my dress then back to my face. "I'll see you later," he tells me.

I'm still smiling as I turn around and walk back to the ballroom, where I'm supposed to spend the night talking with our donors and representing the station. Why is it that I like the sound of being Liam's friend?

It's only when I see Ava and Lauren waving at me across

the dancefloor that the smile slips. Because something else occurs to me.

You don't lie to friends.

And yet I lied to Liam once.

The thought pulls me out of my nice, woolly feelings. Because once he finds out about that I'm not sure he'll be so sweet.

CHAPTER
ELEVEN

LIAM

Sunday morning finds me in the sunniest of moods. I'm in Ava and Myles' kitchen, cooking them some brunch and listening to a nineties radio station. Myles is sitting in front of his laptop, Charlie against his chest in some kind of rubber chair that looks like a potty even though it isn't, and Ava is pulling weeds in their yard.

As I break some eggs into the pan, Will Smith comes on, "Getting' Jiggy Wit It".

"Bring it… uh uh uh…"

Charlie blinks, his head tipping to the side. He looks like he's ready for some fun so I join in the rap and tell him to *be on his mark and get ready, let's go…*

He gurgles as I point at him with the wooden spatula, still rapping the lyrics. I'm actually surprised I can remember them all. This song has to be more than twenty years old. Maybe more like twenty-five.

All I know is that one summer we'd played it on repeat while at Misty Lakes. In the days before smartphones and

WIFI, back when we thought we were going to rule the world.

Charlie's still watching, his mouth closing and opening almost like he's trying to join in.

And when I get to the chorus he gurgles louder. Almost hiccups.

"Wait," Myles says. "Shit, did he just laugh?"

"You just swore in front of your kid," I point out.

"Fu—." He shakes his head. "Sing it again."

"We're on the next verse now," I point out.

"Just keep rapping," Myles urges. Words I never thought would come from my brother's mouth.

I shrug and walk over to Charlie. We're almost at the next chorus. I sing the high summertime and tell him we're getting jiggy with it, and Charlie laughs again.

Myles starts to move in what I think is some kind of dance. Charlie's still laughing and it's completely intoxicating.

I feel like I'm the king of the world. No wonder Will loved singing this song.

When it comes to an end, Myles grabs his phone and opens Spotify, putting the song on once more. Then he pauses it. "Go get Ava," he tells me, his phone still trained on his son.

"You get her."

"I don't want to stop recording. In case it breaks the magic."

I think about teasing him but I know exactly what he means. We need to recreate this for her. So I run to the door and call her in. She stands from where she's weeding and walks inside, looking bemused.

"Just watch this," Myles says, putting Will back on again. And I do the same routine, the noises, the rap, the chorus, and Charlie laughs like he's about to wet himself.

"Oh my God," Ava says, grabbing her phone. "I need to record this, too."

For the next five minutes, we're all singing and dancing like loons to entertain a three-month-old baby who may either be laughing or hiccupping. And I don't care, because it feels good to be here. Good to share in this moment with the people I love.

Right up until the smoke alarm starts going crazy and I realize the eggs are burned to the bottom of the pan.

Luckily nothing else was burned and the pan wasn't Ava's favorite anyway. I remind myself to buy her a new one and then make the eggs in the microwave, serving up brunch on the breakfast bar.

"I could get used to this," Ava tells me. "I wish you could teach Myles to cook."

"I can cook," Myles protests.

"Yes, three things and that's all," she says, stuffing corn bread between her lips. "Did you make this from scratch?" she asks me.

"Yeah." I shrug, perplexed. It really is nothing. I'm always surprised that people are surprised that I know my way around a kitchen. Shouldn't everyone?

"Remind me again why I didn't marry you?"

"Because you met Myles first." I wink at her.

"And Liam will never be the settling down type," Myles adds.

Ava looks almost sad at that. "I guess not."

It doesn't take any of us long to empty our plates. Ava goes to clear the dishes but Myles and I shoo her off, and we load the dishwasher while she goes out to finish her yard work.

"So," Myles says as he tickles Charlie's chin. He's been laying in his bouncy chair like a champ, watching us as we eat. "A hundred thousand dollars for some weather forecasts."

I've been waiting for him to mention this.

"I really like the weather," I tell him, deadpan.

He narrows his gaze.

"What?" I ask him. Is it wrong that I enjoy riling him?

"Is there something I should know about you and Sophie?" he asks.

I burst out laughing. "Are you her dad?"

"No." He doesn't even crack a smile.

"Then no, there's nothing you need to know."

He looks thunderous and I take pity on him. There's a time to tease and a time to be straight with somebody. There's also a time when you don't want your brother to spontaneously combust.

"Listen, there really isn't anything to worry about," I say, trying to reassure him. "Sophie and I are friends. And I needed to make some charitable donations on behalf of the company. You know this."

"You hate each other," he points out.

"We don't," I tell him. "We've agreed to be friends. And you should be happy about this. You're the one who wants us to get along for Charlie's sake and now we do."

"And there's really nothing else going on?"

"No," I say honestly. "I donated to charity, she's providing a service. That's it. So stop looking so miserable and go dance with your son."

"Hmm," Myles says, then passes me a dirty plate. "Let's see how long the peace between you two lasts."

———

SOPHIE

From: LiamSalinger@SalingerEnterprises.com

To: SophieWest@WVFY.tv

Subject: You now know more about my movements than anybody else…

. . .

Sophie,

As promised, my itinerary is below. Do you need anything else? Let me know.

MONDAY – Meetings all day in Charleston
TUESDAY – AM as above. PM flying to New York.
WEDNESDAY – Meetings in New York. Dinner in the evening.
THURSDAY – Flying to Washington DC. Meetings in Capitol building.
FRIDAY – Meetings in DC. Coming back to West Virginia that evening.
WEEKEND – Planning on sleeping for 48 hours. Don't care if there's a biblical flood.

Have a good week,

Liam.

I smile at his weekend plans and make some notes on my pad. It's actually a slight pain that he's traveling so much – because I'm going to have to do forecasts for each area – but it sounds like it's going to be more painful for him. At least Saturday and Sunday should be easy, though. I already have to do the forecast for work and since he's doing nothing specific I can make it fairly generic.

His email is nice. Friendly. It makes me feel like this whole auction thing might work.

And then I think again about that stupid lie. I need to tell him. It was one thing covering up the truth when I thought he was annoying and hated me. But he said he wants to be friends.

And friends always tell the truth. Even if they know it's going to make them look terrible.

I look at my phone for five minutes before I get up the courage to reply. Via messenger rather than email because I don't want to use my work account for this.

> Hi, I hope it's okay to message. I wanted to check if you're free next weekend. I could buy you a coffee to thank you for your high bid. - Sophie

Two ticks come up and the next moment they're green. I feel a weird thrill knowing he's already read my message.

> Hey. Yeah, that could work. Did you get my email? I sent over my itinerary as requested. - Liam

Well that was easy. Maybe he won't be angry at me after all. I decide to worry about that next week.

> I got it. You'll have your first forecast tomorrow morning. I do have a couple of questions that should help me personalize it if that's okay? - Sophie

> Sure. Shoot. - Liam

> Your dinner plans for Wednesday - are you planning on dining in or out? - Sophie

> Not sure yet. I'm trying to impress a beautiful woman, so maybe outside? - Liam

A little spike of jealousy rushes through me. Which is stupid because why wouldn't he be trying to impress a woman? What he does with his love life has nothing to do with me.

And if we're going to be friends I'll have to get used to it. He's not exactly wanting for female attention.

> Sure. I'll check it out and let you know which to opt for. Hope you have a good trip. - Sophie

> Thank you. You have a good week, too. I'll see you over the weekend. Let me know which day works for you. - Liam

> I will. - Sophie

I hadn't expected this. To have to forecast weather for his dates. And if I'm being honest, I'm not sure I like it.

But the fact is, for the next three months I'm going to have to do it. He paid handsomely for the privilege of having personalized forecasts and I'm going to deliver them.

Even if he's whisking a model off to St. Lucia.

And I shouldn't be jealous. I know what he's like. It's not like he's dateable material. Whoever he's seeing on Wednesday night will have him for twenty-four hours at most.

I should feel sorry for her, not jealous that she'll have his undivided attention for one night.

And yet when I turn on my laptop to start working on his forecasts, all I can see are his warm brown eyes. And I hate that I want him to only look at me with them.

Because I can't fall for a man who will never give me what I want. That would be madness.

Surely my sense of self-preservation is better than that.

CHAPTER
TWELVE

SOPHIE

The next evening I'm walking out of the yoga studio with Ava and Lauren when my phone buzzes.

> Hi. I have a slight change of plan. I have to leave for Washington DC on Wednesday afternoon, so I'm moving dinner to tomorrow night. Will it still be okay to eat outside? - Liam

I know the answer to this. I ran the forecast for New York from Tuesday afternoon to Thursday and it's looking glorious.

> You'll be fine. The weather is looking great all week in New York. Have a good time. – Sophie :)

I add the smiley to let him know I'm not bothered at all about his dinner date. Then I turn off my phone and put it into my gym bag because I don't want to think about his date with another woman. Especially when it's a rare Monday night where all three of us have managed to make it to yoga. It used to be a weekly thing, but since Ava got pregnant with Charlie it's become more like monthly.

I miss getting together with my friends and I'm not going to spoil it by brooding about a man I shouldn't want.

"Okay," Lauren says, sitting down dramatically at our usual table in the café. "Has anybody else noticed how the rest of the class seem to be getting fitter while we just fall over every time we try to do a downward facing dog?"

"Speak for yourself," Ava says, smiling. "Anyway I have an excuse. I just had a baby."

"Charlie is almost four months old," Lauren points out. "At some point between now and eighteen years old that excuse is gonna sound stale."

"Never." Ava grins. "Oh hey, did I tell you he laughed this weekend?"

"He did?" I lean forward, excited. "Oh my God, did you video it?"

Ava excitedly gets her phone out and scrolls until she reaches the right video. "You're seriously going to die when you watch this." She turns the phone around so Lauren and I can see the screen as music blares out of the speaker.

"Will Smith?" Lauren says, lifting a brow. "Your son and I are going to have a talk about life choices…" Her voice fades away as Liam comes on the screen, rapping "Getting Jiggy Wit It" word-for-word as he dances around Ava's kitchen. Charlie lets out a watery gurgle, and then does it again, and Ava zooms the camera in on him as he watches his uncle with pure delight on his face.

"Oh Jesus, my ovaries just came out of deep freeze," Lauren mutters. "Can you stop with the hot guys and baby?"

"I can't help it." Ava shrugs. "It's the only way we can get

Charlie to laugh. I made Liam come over again this morning and it still works."

"I guess there won't be any more laughing for the rest of the week with Liam gone," I say before I think it through.

Ava looks at me, her brow raised. "What?"

"How do you know if Liam will be here or not?" Lauren asks.

I shake my head. "Because I'm doing his forecasts, remember? And I needed his itinerary. I know he's off to New York tomorrow."

"You two looked pretty cozy at the gala on Saturday," Lauren says, grimacing at the green smoothie the waiter just delivered. She's on some kind of detox which must be a living hell for her since she owns a bakery.

"We were just talking about the auction," I say. "It's part of my role to be nice to the donors."

Ava tips her head to the side but says nothing. This is probably awkward for her since Liam is her brother-in-law.

"We're friends," I tell them.

And of course they both burst out laughing.

"It's true." My protest barely registers through the volume of their giggles. "We agreed to stop annoying each other and be nice." I look pointedly at Ava. "Isn't this what you wanted?"

"Well yes, I guess." She smiles at me. "Although I was hoping Lauren was right and it was just unfulfilled sexual tension between you both."

"Oh I don't think Liam's anywhere near unfulfilled," I say. "He's got a date tomorrow night."

"He does?" Lauren asks. She looks at Ava. "Who's it with, do you know?"

"I try to know as little about my brother-in-law's love life as possible," Ava says dryly. "Especially now that I know his one night rule."

"Do *you* know?" Lauren asks me.

I shrug. "No idea. Just said he was taking her out for dinner and wanted to know whether he should book a table outside or inside."

"Do they have outside tables in New York?" Lauren wrinkles her nose. "Won't all those traffic fumes get in the food?"

"Myles and Liam know all the best places to eat," Ava says. "He'll probably take her to their favorite Italian place, it has this gorgeous courtyard that's to die for." Her eyes light up. "What I wouldn't give for some of their mushroom ravioli right now."

"I guess those Salingers know how to woo their women," Lauren says.

"They do." Ava sighs. "Myles is such a romantic."

Lauren and I exchange glances.

"Okay, so this part of the conversation is officially over," Lauren says, because neither of us want to imagine that. "How's work going?" she asks me. "Have you killed Michael yet?"

"Not yet." I grin. "I think he wants to kill me though. He's still annoyed at me for changing my auction lot." I'm riding on a high from that. And he's keeping his head down which is good.

We start talking about our plans for the weekend. I tell them about Madison's birthday on Friday – we're all heading out to a bar to celebrate. But I don't tell them about my plan to meet with Liam and confess the truth.

What I need to say is between him and me. I've made enough mistakes. I don't want them to know before he does.

"Will Michael be at Madison's birthday?" Lauren asks, wrinkling her nose.

"Unfortunately." I lift a brow. "She couldn't *not* invite him when the rest of the staff will be there." And maybe it'll be a chance for things between us to calm down. As much as I've enjoyed getting one over on him, we're both adults and need to work together.

"Ugh. Is there any way we can help?" Lauren asks. "Maybe we could put rat poison in his champagne."

"Or itching powder in his shorts," Ava says, wiggling her brows.

I smile because they're my people and they'd actually do those things for me if I asked. Which I won't because I'm in my thirties and not a kid.

"It's fine. I'm a big girl, I can deal with him for one night," I tell them. "He's been strangely hands off since the charity ball."

"That's because he knows you're worth something now," Lauren points out. "Although that's kind of a crock of shit because you were always worth so much more than him."

As I said, these women are my people. And that's why I love them.

———

It's almost nine-thirty the next evening when my phone rings. I'm sitting on the sofa in my apartment, wearing a pair of yoga shorts and a flimsy tank, my hair pulled back into a bun which is way more than messy. The television is on but silent, a Netflix documentary about a bank heist gone wrong flickering on the screen, subtitles telling me that apparently putting your gun down while you adjust your Scream mask isn't a good idea.

I also have my laptop balanced on my knees because I'm trying to multitask. When I see who's calling, I blink but answer it anyway, pausing the documentary so I don't miss a piece of important information.

"Hi Liam." I keep my voice light like I'm his friend. Because I'm supposed to be. It still feels a bit weird though.

"Sophie." His voice is low and gruff. The perfect pitch. I know a lot of people don't notice voices but I do. My mom had a thing about Neil Diamond when I was growing up and I couldn't understand her addiction to his growly low voice at all.

I do now though.

"Is everything okay?" I ask. Because it's Tuesday night. *Date night.* What's he doing calling me? "Don't tell me it started to rain on your dinner. I'm not offering you a refund."

He chuckles and I shift my seating position.

"No. It's glorious like you said it would be. My dinner date wanted to talk to you, that's all."

"I'm sorry what?"

He laughs again. The man is amazingly carefree. Who goes on a date and calls another woman, then encourages the two of them to talk? I'm seriously considering rescinding our friendship card.

"She wants to thank you for the forecast. I wouldn't have chosen this place if it hadn't been for your forecast."

"I thought the sun always shone on you," I say, because he really is the golden boy. And also because I don't want to talk to this woman he's dating. Not when I know what they'll be doing later.

No, I'm not jealous.

Okay maybe a little.

"You'd be surprised. Hang on..." There's a shuffling noise and I assume I'm being passed onto the date. I'm going to store this up for the next time I see Lauren and Ava. They're going to think it's the funniest thing even if I'm finding it mortifying.

"Hello? Sophie?" A smooth, feminine voice echoes into my ears. "How are you?"

"I'm good," I say. "How are you?" What's with this weird conversation? Should I be warning her that Liam is only good for one night? Isn't that what the sisterhood should do? I'm seriously contemplating it when she starts to talk again.

"I'm much better after spending the evening with my son," she says. "Thank you for helping him choose the perfect spot."

My mouth drops.

That's simultaneously sweet as heck and aggravating. He must have known I'd think the worse. And now instead of feeling jealous, I'm grumpy that I was worried about him having dinner with his mom.

"I'm glad you're having a good evening," I say, my voice warm because I really like his mom. "Was the food good?"

"Oh it was wonderful. Have you ever eaten here? It's called Arno's. In the West Village."

"No, I don't think I have." I know I haven't, but I'm trying to be polite here.

"You should come some time," she says, then her voice goes a little tinny. "You should bring Sophie here," she says, and I can only assume she's talking to Liam. "To say thank you for the forecasting."

I can't hear Liam's reply, but I hear his mom's laugh. And now I really want to know what he said.

But of course I can't ask.

"Liam's been telling me all about this prize he bid on," she says, her voice closer to the receiver now. "I think it's wonderful. So useful, too. I just wish he'd use it for something other than work. He has a yacht he could use in the right weather but he's always too busy for it."

Of course Liam Salinger has a yacht.

"That's a shame," I tell her. "All work and no play and all that."

"Yes, though I don't think anybody could describe Liam as a dull boy," she says wryly.

She's not wrong.

"Well I should probably let you get back to your evening," I say. "I'm so glad you're having a lovely time."

"Oh, there was one other thing. It's my birthday in a couple of weeks." She lowers her voice. "A big one. I'm not telling you the number but let's say it's not twenty-one. I'm having a party and I'd love for you to be there."

"My guess is thirty," I say. "And I'd love to come if I'm not working that weekend."

"You're so sweet. And for that you get a gilded invitation. It's at Misty Lakes, my ex-husband's estate. I'll ask my secretary to email you all the details if that's okay?"

"Of course." I'm touched that she's asked. And the fact is, I don't have much in my schedule for the next few weeks. "I'll do a forecast for you if you'd like."

"Oh I'd love that," she says. "You're so kind." There's a warmth in her voice that makes me feel like I'm snuggled in a blanket. "I can't wait to see you again. Oh, wait a minute, Liam's gesturing at me. I think he wants the phone. I'll speak to you soon, Sophie. You have a lovely evening."

"You, too," I tell her, then wait because I'm not sure if Liam wants to talk to me or get me off the phone.

"Sophie." Apparently he does.

"Liam," I say in as deep a voice as I can. A huff of a laugh rumbles down the line.

"Will you be up for a while?" he asks me. "I have a couple of itinerary changes to deal with. I'll tell you about them when I get back to my place."

I glance at the documentary I've paused. It's episode four of six. Of course I'm not going to bed until I know what happens. "Um sure. Yeah, I should be up for a couple more hours."

"Good. I'll speak to you then. Have a good evening."

"You, too," I say as he ends the call. There's a stupidly big goofy smile on my face. He didn't go on a date. And he wants to call me.

I could get used to being Liam's friend.

I wonder if that means I'll get a trip out on the yacht sometime.

———

LIAM

"You look tired," Mom says as I escort her into her building. The security guard tips his head at her as she presses the button for the elevator.

"I've been traveling since stupid o'clock this morning," I say. "Hopefully I'll catch up on some sleep this weekend."

"Make sure you do." She kisses my cheek as the elevator car arrives, the doors opening with a ping. "Thank you for a lovely evening. It's been so nice to see you."

"You're welcome. And likewise." I wink as she gets into the elevator. "Take it easy, old girl."

"Less of the old." She lifts a brow. "I'll see you at Misty Lakes in a couple of weeks." The doors close on her before I can reply, so I turn around and walk back out into the New York evening. It's hot and humid here, and even though we're on the upper west side, there are still a lot of people in the streets. My car is waiting and I climb into the back, directing the driver to my place in Tribeca.

My mom hates me living there, but it's kind of cool and convenient for working on Wall Street. It's less than a mile from my place to the office and most of the time I walk there, or occasionally make it part of my morning run.

It usually takes about twenty minutes in the car from my mom's apartment, but tonight traffic is unusually busy. There are some road closures too – things are constantly being torn down and rebuilt in New York City. It's one of the reasons I love it here.

There's always something going on.

And yet in the middle of the sultry Manhattan night, with horns blaring and pneumatic drills blasting I find myself wishing I was back in Charleston. Listening to the buzzing of the cicadas and watching the fireflies light up the leafy trees.

And my thoughts turn to Sophie.

I bring her contact details up on my phone. I've added a photograph – one of the ones from the christening. She's staring into the distance, a smile playing on her lips and I'm wondering what they taste like.

I wish I could remember.

I press the video button because I want to see her. It rings twice before she denies the call. Before I can press it again she calls me, but using voice only. For some reason that annoys me.

"What's with the rejection?" I ask her.

"You don't want to see me on the screen. I'm slobbing out."

"I do actually," I tell her.

"Why do you want to see me?" she asks.

So I can furiously beat myself off to your image later.

"Just want to see what slobbing out looks like in West Virginia," I say, ignoring that thought.

"Well for me it involves wearing shorts and a tank and not bothering to brush my hair."

It's like something's pinged in my brain. It's suddenly my life's mission to see those articles of clothing.

On her.

Obviously.

"Sounds good to me," I tell her. "Come on, let's video chat."

"No. Definitely not. Especially since I know you're all suited and booted for dinner with your mom."

"I'll take my clothes off if you want."

She starts to laugh. "Now there's an offer."

I wasn't joking, but it's not time to tell her that.

"Just show me your face," I tell her. "That's all I want to see."

"That's actually sweet," she says. "But I'm not wearing makeup."

"I hate makeup," I tell her honestly. "It's the devil's invention."

"No you don't. You think you do but you don't. What you like is the illusion of no makeup. But that actually takes more time than putting on makeup. It's all theater," she says. "Designed to entice you."

Well count me fucking enticed. "I've seen plenty of women with no makeup," I say. "I think I know what I'm talking about."

"You don't see women for more than one night," she points out. "So no you don't. You only see women on their best behavior. It's not until we've been dating somebody for months that we actually let them see what we're really like."

"Well I'm your friend," I tell her. "So you can be as make up free whenever you want to."

She lets out a breath. "Can you stop bouncing between sweet and asshole, please? Because that's more attractive than you think."

I blink. She's finding me attractive?

"Show me," I say. "And I'll give you an honest friend opinion on how enticing you look makeup free."

"You're not going to stop until I do, are you?"

"I guess I'll fall asleep eventually," I tell her. "But I'm intrigued. I really want to know. And maybe you do, too."

"Maybe…" she trails off. I tell myself to let it go, so I think about a subject change.

And then the video icon comes up.

I accept it with unseemly haste. The screen flickers and then there she is. Her hair pulled back with some tendrils escaping. But it's her face that I look at. There's not enough light for my liking – she must have a side lamp on – but I can still see those pretty eyes and her full pink mouth.

"You look incredible," I tell her, my voice hoarse.

"Shut up. You're my friend not my cheerleader." Her lashes sweep down. "You don't look so bad yourself."

Weird how much that pleases me.

"What are you doing right now?" I ask her.

"Talking to you."

I laugh. "Before I called. What were you doing then?"

"I'm watching this documentary about a bank robbery gone wrong while I'm doing some work." She looks almost embarrassed. "Where are you?" she asks.

"In the car going back to my place."

"You're not driving?"

"Nope. Had some wine with my mom. Anyway, it's easier to be driven than to drive in Manhattan."

"I get that. The last time I went to New York I almost got run over."

My chest tightens. "You did? Where?"

"In Times Square." She looks almost embarrassed. "I was distracted by this huge poster of McDreamy. I guess that tells you how long ago it was."

"McDreamy? Who's that?"

Her mouth drops open. "You don't know who McDreamy is? Seriously?" She sounds appalled.

"Is it some kind of McDonald's ice cream?"

She collapses into a fit of giggles. And I laugh too because her amusement is infectious.

"McDreamy is a character in *Grey's Anatomy*," she says once she gotten control of herself. A lock of hair has fallen out of her bun and she sweeps it back. "Played by Patrick Dempsey. Don't tell me you've never watched it."

"Never," I admit. "Don't hate me."

"We need to rectify this. You need to be educated on the

show. It's a huge gaping hole in your repertoire. How do you get girls if you don't know who McDreamy is?"

"I've no idea," I say honestly. "Educate me now."

"Oh it's going to take longer than a car ride back to your place. You need to watch the show. You need to feel all the emotions. Have your heart pulled apart by Meredith and Derek. Have it put back again by Cristina being your person. Scream out loud because George…" She trails off, but I can't take my eyes off her face. It's animated. Alive. Beautiful. "I can't spoil it for you. You need to experience it yourself."

"How many episodes are there?" I ask.

"Um, there's like eighteen seasons."

I lift a brow. "How many episodes per season?"

"I don't know. Around twenty or twenty-five."

I do the math. "You're talking around four hundred episodes."

"I guess." She pulls her bottom lip between her teeth. I can't take my eyes off it. "It's worth it though."

"Okay then. Let's do it."

She tips her head to the side, her mouth curling up. "What?"

"If I'm going to watch all those episodes, I want to do it with you. We'll buddy watch it."

"When?" There's a smile playing on her lips.

"Tomorrow night?"

"How do you know I'm not doing something tomorrow night?" she asks me.

"Are you?" My voice comes out rougher than I expect.

"No. Apparently I'm watching season one of *Grey's Anatomy* with you."

I remind myself to cancel tomorrow night's business meeting in DC. "Good. Let's video call at the same time. That way I can ask you any questions I might have."

"You're not going to be one of those annoying people who talks through the show, are you?" she asks me skeptically.

"No. I just want to see you while we watch."

She blushes. "You do?"

"Yeah I do. Is that okay?"

"Yes it's okay." She nods. "I think."

Good. Well I'm glad we've settled that.

CHAPTER
THIRTEEN

SOPHIE

It's Friday and we're all frantically trying to get everything done before we all head out to celebrate Madison's birthday. A few of us have gotten together and bought her an afternoon at a beauty salon – where she is right now being pampered and getting ready – so I'm trying to do her work and mine.

It doesn't stop me from getting distracted when I see an email pop up on my screen though.

From: LiamSalinger@SalingerEnterprises.com
   To: SophieWest@WVFY.tv
   Subject: Thoughts on Meredith and Derek…

Sophie,

I'm sitting in a boardroom listening to the most boring presentation, so I thought I'd give you my verdict on the series so far. (By the way, how did we manage to get through six episodes in two nights. Are you as tired as I am? Thank God it's Friday.)

THE GOOD

- The opening scene. Après-sofa sex. I approve.

- Stolen elevator kisses with somebody you shouldn't be kissing. I also approve.

- Car sex. Yup.

- McDreamy (that's Derek's nickname, right? Not a brand of ice cream.) – the man has game despite the hair. Good for him.

THE BAD

- Severed penises. Well one of them. In a stomach. Should I say more?

- The way Meredith and Izzy treat George when they walk in on him in the shower. It's emasculating (see severed penises).

- The gore factor. (See severed penises).

- The fact that I never want to go into a hospital again because I might get seen by an intern the day after they've drunk until they've vomited their stomach up.

Okay, I need to go. Apparently, they want me to make a decision on something. Did you still want to meet up this weekend? I propose we watch more then.

Liam

From: SophieWest@WVFY.tv

To: LiamSalinger@SalingerEnterprises.com
Subject: Sex isn't everything…

Liam,

Seriously, the only things you like about *Grey's Anatomy* is the sex? What about the emotions, the relationships, the sheer agony of losing a patient you've bonded with?

And also, you may not like McDreamy so much after episode nine. Just saying.

Sophie

P.S – Yes to this weekend. Does tomorrow night work? You're very welcome to come to my place.

I send it and sigh because tomorrow night I'm going to have to tell him everything. And I don't really want to because I'm actually enjoying spending time with him. I like being his friend. He makes me laugh and says nice things and makes me feel pretty.

I hate the idea of spoiling that.

But what else can I do? I only have myself to blame. If I'd told him the truth earlier I wouldn't be feeling sick at the thought of it now.

From: LiamSalinger@SalingerEnterprises.com

To: SophieWest@WVFY.tv
SUBJECT: NO SPOILERS!!

You're seriously going to leave me hanging there? You're a cruel woman. And also I think I might have just spent an obscene amount of money on a company I didn't want.

See you on Saturday. Message me with a time.

Liam

From: SophieWest@WVFY.tv
     To: LiamSalinger@SalingerEnterprises.com
     SUBJECT: Stop emailing me jackass!

Before you go broke.

Sophie

I'm smiling goofily at my phone when Michael sweeps into the office. "I need you to work tomorrow," he says.

I look up from my phone. "You're supposed to be taking this weekend. You sent the roster around last week."

"Well now I have to be elsewhere tomorrow," he says, talking slowly as though I'm not able to hear him. "So you need to do it."

"I can't. I already have plans." I look him straight in the eye. His jaw is tight, his gaze narrow. He's wearing a white shirt and gray pants, and if it wasn't for his personality he'd probably be considered attractive.

Okay, he is attractive. But not to me. That wore off along with my teenage bad skin and the urge to wear Livestrong bracelets.

"Why are you being difficult?" he asks. "If you want to be part of the team you have to sacrifice sometimes."

"Because I'm doing something with a friend and I don't like letting friends down." I shrug. "I'm sorry but you're going to need to rearrange your plans."

He doesn't walk away. Instead, he shuffles his feet and looks at his hands. "My mom's in the hospital," he says quietly. "I need to visit."

All the fight goes out of me. "Oh God, I'm sorry."

He nods but says nothing.

"Of course I can do it," I tell him. "I just need to rearrange a couple of things."

"Thank you. I appreciate it."

"I hope she feels better soon. Is there anything you need?" I ask him. The memories of my own mom's sickness hits me right in the gut. I even find myself putting my hand on top of his.

He shakes his head quickly. "Just doing the forecasts will be good."

"All day?"

"I'm afraid so. Last one is at nine."

"Okay. I'll be here."

He walks out and I grab my phone, quickly tapping out a message to Liam.

> I've just been told I need to work tomorrow until late, so I'll need to take a raincheck. I'm sorry. – Sophie

It's weird how disappointed I feel. I barely have time to

think about that before a reply flashes up on my screen. I guess he still isn't paying attention to his meeting.

> What time will you be finished? – Liam

> Not until after the nighttime news. At around ten. Way too late. – Sophie

> You'll still need to eat, right? I'll pick you up from the station. I'll cook for you. – Liam

A little thrill washes through me.

> You don't need to do that. I'm sure you've got better things to do than feed me. – Sophie

> I don't actually. And I want to feed you. I'll see you tomorrow. – Liam

The typing icon disappears and I assume he's in another meeting. Or the same one that he emailed me from. Either way, I don't want to cost him any more money so I put my phone away and turn to my laptop. I have work to do before I need to head to the bar.

And now I'll need to work tomorrow, too. But the sting of it lessens knowing I'll see Liam tomorrow night.

I don't want to think about why it lessens. Or why seeing him sends a thrill through my body like I've just touched an electrified fence.

And I really don't want to think about the fact that I'd decided tomorrow was the night I'd tell him the truth. Because this lovely détente we have between us could implode once he knows everything.

I'm not sure I'm ready for that.

———

Madison is loving being the center of attention. Her dark hair is flowing down her back, her nails painted a yellow color that looks great against her skin, and her eyes can't quite focus because she's had way too much to drink.

I'm going to put her in a cab in a minute. She'll thank me for it tomorrow. It's almost eleven anyway, and I have to go home myself. Neither Madison or Michael will be in tomorrow and it's going to be a long day.

And a long evening, because I'll be seeing Liam. The thought sends a shiver down my spine.

In the corner I see Michael, who's just walked in after the evening news. He's with Dan and a few others who must have finished for the night. I guess he's leaving tomorrow to see his mom.

"One more round," Madison says. "On me. Let's make it shots."

This is my cue to get her home.

It takes me almost twenty minutes but I manage to get her outside and hail a cab. I lean in through the passenger door and give the driver directions on how to get to her place. Luckily, he's one of our regular taxi drivers at the station and he promises to look after her. She lives with her parents in a gorgeous ranch house in the mountains just outside the city. I slip him a fifty because I'm not sure she'll be able to open her purse when they get there, let alone find her wallet.

"Call me when you're in the house," I tell her.

"Sure." She pats my face. "You're such a great boss, Sophie." She leans back and closes her eyes. I turn to Rob, the driver. "Can you make sure she gets inside safely?"

"Always." He nods. He has two daughters in college. He gets it.

"Thank you." I close the door and watch him drive off, then I turn to walk back into the bar, but I see Dan and Michael walking out, although they don't see me. I guess they really only stayed for one quick drink.

"Okay then," Dan says, his voice full of alcohol-fueled jollity. "I'll see you at the golf course tomorrow. Eight o'clock tee-off. Don't be late."

"I'll be there," Michael tells him.

I freeze. So he's not rushing to Baltimore to see his mom tomorrow.

He's playing golf, the rat bastard.

"Michael?" I call out.

He turns slowly, blinking when he sees me standing there. His face blanches and then he marches over to me and grabs my elbow, steering me down the sidewalk toward the alley at the side of the bar. "Please don't make a scene," he mutters.

"How's your mom?" I ask him.

He lets out a heavy sigh. "Actually, she's not well. She has a cold."

"You let me think she was really sick." I'm so pissed with him it isn't funny.

"I didn't say that," he points out.

I frown, because I can't remember exactly what he said. I do remember some things though. "You lied," I tell him. "You said you were going to the hospital to visit her."

"No I didn't," he says, his voice almost patient. "I said she was sick and I needed to visit her. Both are true. I'm just not doing it."

My mouth drops open. "You knew that's what I'd think. You knew it was the only way I'd agree to work tomorrow. I can't believe you'd do that."

"This golf meeting is important," he tells me. "It'll benefit you, too."

"How exactly?" I ask, my voice scathing.

"Because someone from the Network is coming down. A friend of Dan's. He said they might have some plans for the weather desk. I want to find out what they are, and maybe you should, too."

He means somebody from NTV – the national television

network that WVFY is part of. They provide the national shows that everybody loves and talks about. We kind of fill in the blanks with news, weather and sport. Most local television stations are affiliated to or directly owned by a national network. We have a friendly rivalry with WVAT over in Huntingdon who are affiliated to BTV – Broadcast Television.

"Why would they be interfering with the weather desk?" I frown.

There's a look of sympathy on his face that I don't like at all. "You understand the station is losing money, right? They're looking at every department for savings, including us. They don't have to have a weather team, they could just buy in the forecasts." He lifts a brow. "Everybody is expendable."

"I haven't heard that," I tell him, shocked that we're losing so much money.

"Because you don't go to management meetings. Everything is on the line, Sophie, including your job." He puts a hand on my shoulder. "But don't worry, I'm on your side."

I shake my head because I know that's not true. Michael is only ever on one side – his own. But I believe him about the rest. It makes sense.

"I need to go," I tell him, because I don't like the way he's looking at me. As though I've already lost my job and can't pay my rent.

"Sophie…"

"It's fine." I pull away from his touch. And I turn my head because I don't want him to see my expression. "I have to be in work early tomorrow. Have a good time at the golf club."

CHAPTER
FOURTEEN

SOPHIE

It's Saturday and I haven't stopped moving since I arrived at the station this morning. There's a parade going on in town so I've been doing hourly updates on our social media platforms to reassure people that the clouds they're seeing above are only cumulus. The little fluffy clouds we used to draw in the sky when we were kids. It isn't going to rain on anybody's parade today.

I also had to spend longer on my makeup than usual, thanks to the shadows beneath my eyes after my late night. I dab the concealer on as Adam from production rushes in and asks me if I'm ready to do the solo forecast for the website.

One of us records these each day. It's an in depth look at the weather for today and beyond, which lasts around five minutes but usually takes half an hour to record. They squeeze me in around recorded news interviews whenever there's a long enough break in the studio schedule. I finish off my under eye concealer and check the rest of my appearance.

It's a sad fact that television cameras pick up every little imperfection. If your hair isn't perfectly styled or your dress has wrinkles you can bet your life that viewers will notice and be tweeting about it before you're even off air. It got worse when they introduced high-definition television a decade ago. There was a scramble for face lifts like you wouldn't believe.

When everything's ready, I follow Adam into the studio and fix my microphone pack to my leg, where the viewer won't see it. I fluff my skirt over it then walk to the green screen. There's a little piece of paper taped to the floor that says 'weather' which is my cue of where to stand. Unlike when I'm presenting live during the news, I don't have to wait for the anchor to pass over to me, so I wait for Adam's cue then smile as the camera starts to roll.

"Hello, I'm Sophie West and you're watching WVFY weather..." The auto prompt screen rolls in front of me. I've written all these words, just as I created and loaded the graphics that will be superimposed onto the green screen behind me.

"As the evening draws to a close there'll be more cloud accumulation," I say, pointing at the green screen. Once upon a time we used to use sticky clouds to show where they'd be, but now I just have to hope to God I'm pointing in the right direction. "But don't worry, they'll be burned away by the sun first thing in the morning... oh shit." My pointer clatters to the floor and I roll my eyes. "Sorry," I say to Adam, leaning down to pick it up.

"S'okay. We'll edit some photographs in here. Go again from 'As The Evening'..."

The teleprompter rolls back up and I smooth my skirt and touch my hair. In my earpiece somebody tells me to add some more powder to my nose, so I walk over and do that before heading back to my spot in front of the screen.

In all, it takes three attempts to get the five minute record-ing. That really isn't impressive, I prefer hitting it out of the park with the first try. But once Adam says we're all good I head back to the office. The afternoon flies by as I respond to social media posts and questions. Then I go outside before the evening news and take an obligatory 'isn't this weather lovely' photo and post it, wishing everybody following me on Twitter a great evening.

I also have to delete about ten DMs from guys who want to meet up, want to bend me over in front of the green screen, and one who insists that it's going to rain because his penis is bendy today.

Yep, it's a glamorous job.

By the time the late evening news comes around I'm lagging. It takes even longer than usual to make myself look perky. When I first joined the station we had makeup artists and hair stylists but they disappeared about ten years ago in an attempt to control costs. Right now I'd give my left arm to have one of them use their magic on me.

"Twenty minutes until live." I don't recognize the guy who shouts into the make-up room. Not that it surprises me, they use the new people on weekends, trying them out to see if they'll make the week day cut. This one looks like he's barely out of high school.

When we're all in position, Adam talks us through the show. It's been a slow news day so there's a big report from today's parade plus a story about a house cat who keeps jumping in cabs and hitching a ride all over town. It's the story they'd drop if breaking news came in, but one that we need as a filler on a day like today.

Just before the green recording light goes on, I look up at the glass window where the production team sits. And I see Liam.

He's wearing jeans and a t-shirt, talking to the news editor, that trademark grin pulling at his lips.

And my stomach does a little somersault.

I gave his name to security earlier but I expected him to be waiting for me in the lobby, not to be watching me live. And as the light switches from red to green I find myself looking up again. He's looking straight at me this time, and mouths 'hi.'

I mouth hello back but look away because I can't let him distract me. And then Lorena introduces the team and I look at the camera and smile, before she launches into the headline news.

It's fifteen minutes until my first forecast and I spend most of it surreptitiously looking up at the window. A couple of times our gazes meet and I feel it all over my body.

He's taking me to his house tonight. He's cooking for me tonight.

And if he wants more? My heart slams against my ribcage at that thought.

"After the break we'll be hearing all about the weather for tomorrow," Lorena says. "Is it going to be as glorious as today, Sophie?"

"You betcha," I say smiling.

The camera is back on Lorena. She tips her head to the side and looks directly at it. "Don't go anywhere. We'll be right back."

———

"A very good night to you from all of us here at WVFY Weekend Evening News," Lorena says twenty minutes later. I'm still standing on my spot because the camera will pan out at the end, showing the studio and presenters before going back to our affiliate programming. I put a smile on my face as the closing music starts up, and Dan leans over to talk to Ray on the sports desk, the two of them laughing softly about something.

And then it's over and I breathe a sigh of relief because I didn't mess up either of my forecasts.

Dan puts his hand on my shoulder as we head out of the studio. "You did good tonight."

I smile at him, thankful that my blooper about his daughter's wedding weather is now history. "Thank you."

He veers off to the right when we're in the hallway, heading straight for the men's room. I head to the left to grab my things from the office when Liam appears in front of me.

"Hey." He looks completely relaxed in his jeans and a black t-shirt.

"Hey yourself," I tell him, feeling a little giddy. "Did you enjoy the news?"

"Best thing I've seen all week." He glances down at my clothes. And yeah, I dressed carefully this evening. On top I'm wearing a red jersey crossover blouse that makes my boobs look good because I knew I was seeing him. It goes perfectly with a black skirt that lands just above my knees. "You ready to go?" he asks.

"I just need to grab my bag and make sure tomorrow morning's forecast is loaded on the website," I tell him. "Do you want to meet in the car?" I left mine at home this morning and took an Uber to work, knowing I wouldn't need it this evening.

He shakes his head. "I can wait."

So he joins me in the office, watching patiently as I load up the back end of our website and check that everything is ready for go live in the morning.

That's when I realize I've forgotten to take off my battery pack. The box is digging into my thighs. Without thinking, I stand and put my foot on the seat of the chair, unclipping the strap that's hooking the mic pack around my leg.

When I glance to my left Liam is watching my every movement, his eyes dark. Then he lifts his gaze to mine.

And I feel breathless.

"I'm ready if you are," I tell him.

"I am."

We're on the road toward his place when I remember that I'm not just going to his place for a meal. I'm going because I need to tell him something.

Something that might make him hate me for good. I shift in my seat and look over at him. He's staring at the road, his hands loose on the wheel, his profile illuminated by the almost-full moon.

"Liam?"

His eyes flicker to me then return to the road. "Yeah?"

"There's something I need to tell you. As soon as we get to your place." There, I've made it known. Now I can't back out. And it's the right thing to do.

"What is it?" he asks, genuinely curious.

I pick at an imaginary piece of lint on my skirt. "Just something you need to know."

"Do you have a boyfriend?"

I blink. "No."

"An STD?" He lifts a brow and I actually laugh.

"No, it's not that."

"Then just come out with it."

"I can't." I shake my head. "I need you to not be driving." Mostly because I'm scared he might crash. But also because I need to look at him when I say it.

It might be the last chance I get to look at him.

"Well it's a good thing we're almost home then," he says, taking a left onto Virginia Street. It's less than a minute before he pulls into Ava and Myles' driveway, then takes a left toward the guest bungalow that has its own parking area. He shuts off the engine and turns to look at me, concern furrowing his brow.

"Are you okay?" he asks. "You look a little peaky."

No, I'm not okay. And before I can think it through I finally blurt out the truth.

"I lied to you all those months ago. We never slept together."

LIAM

"What?" I blink, looking straight at her. Sophie shifts uncomfortably in the passenger seat. She's looking up at me with those pretty brown eyes.

Taking a deep breath, she starts to explain. "I'm an idiot. And once I said it I couldn't take it back. Mostly because I thought you'd never let me hear the end of it if I did." She glances down at her hands. "And maybe there was some self-preservation in there, too. I thought that if you thought you'd slept with me you wouldn't be interested in me anymore."

I run my tongue along my bottom lip. "You don't want me to be interested in you?"

She exhales heavily. "No, that's not it. I didn't want to be interested in *you*. There was this chemistry there from the start…"

"You could say that." It was more like fireworks. I remember the first time I saw her, talking to Ava, wearing a flirty white dress that ended mid-thigh. My eyes had immediately been drawn to her, and I'd asked Myles who she was.

And of course, he warned me off right away.

"Let's go inside," I say. "Best not to be talking about this out here." Not when Myles and Ava's house is right next to the bungalow. I'm pretty sure she doesn't want them hearing this.

She nods, and I don't like how vulnerable she looks. Like she's afraid I'm going to turn on her and scream or something. "Sophe," I say softly. "It's okay."

"You don't know that."

"I know you," I tell her. "We're friends, aren't we? Let's go inside and you can explain."

This time her breath is ragged. Her eyes reflect the light of the moon, full of tears. Before I can say another word, one of them escapes, rolling down her cheek.

And I'm horrified.

"Baby." I pull her against me, my arms wrapping around her. "How long have you been worrying about this?"

She sniffs against my chest. "A while."

"Then stop worrying for Christ sake. Everybody tells lies occasionally. And more than anybody I know you have a good explanation." I kiss the top of her head, and the smell of her shampoo fills my senses.

And of course I get hard.

Shifting back so she doesn't feel it, I cup her cheeks, feeling the wetness of her tears on my fingers. "It's okay," I tell her again.

"I hate lies. I've always hated lies." She sniffles. "Ever since we learned about George Washington and that cherry tree in kindergarten."

"What story is that?" I ask, frowning.

"The one where he chops down a tree as a kid and then his dad asks him about it and he says he can never tell a lie." Her lips wobble. I'm still cupping her face, staring down at her.

"I've never heard that," I tell her. "Did that really happen?"

"No." Her voice wobbles. "That's the stupid thing. It's a myth told to kids to try to stop them from lying. I only found out it wasn't true when I went to Mount Vernon in eighth grade."

I'm trying not to laugh because she looks genuinely upset. "So somebody told a lie about George Washington not telling a lie, and that lie has made you always tell the truth?"

"You're teasing me," she says. "But I still hate lying. I can't remember telling a fib this big to anybody else."

"Then I'm honored." And I am in a weird way. Especially since she's coming clean now.

She told a lie because she was afraid of the chemistry. Which means she feels it, too.

A light flickers on in Ava and Myles' hallway. "Come on, let's get inside." She lets me take her hand and I lead her up the steps, still holding on to her while I use the other to slide the key into the lock. And then I pull her into the house, closing the door behind her. Myles and Ava had better mind their own damn business, because I need to concentrate on cheering her up.

"Can I use your bathroom?" she asks. "I need to wash my face. Tidy myself up."

"Yeah, of course. I'll start dinner." I gesture for her to walk ahead of me, but she still looks so unsure. It's unlike her to be so reticent, so upset. And yeah, I want to know more about this lie, because let's face it, it changes everything, but more than anything I want her to smile again.

"It's okay," I tell her.

She frowns and shakes her head. "No it isn't. But thank you for pretending it is anyway."

———

SOPHIE

I was such an idiot to blurt it out like that. I stare at my reflection, the thick makeup I put on at the studio is smudged and I look absolutely terrible. I run the faucet and wash my face before squeezing my eyes shut for a moment.

I have to walk out there. I have to explain.

I can't just throw that information at him and then hide away.

When I walk into the kitchen, he's stirring a pot of sauce. He looks up as I enter.

I take a deep breath. "That morning when we woke up

together," I say, needing to get this out before I start to think twice about it. "You assumed we had sex and I was about to deny it, but then I realized that it was the answer to all my prayers."

"Pretending to have sex with me was the answer to your prayers?" he asks, his brow furrowing.

I shake my head. "That's not what I mean. It was just that you were so insistent about only sleeping with a woman for one night. And I thought about how much easier life would be if that had actually happened. We could walk away and forget about all the tension between us."

"Tension?" A smile plays at his lips.

"Chemistry," I say and his smile widens. "Aren't you angry with me for lying?" I ask him.

"Would you prefer if I was?"

I don't know the answer to this. I just wasn't expecting him to be so cool about it. I've been angsting over this for months. I hate myself for misleading him. And now here he is, completely nonchalant.

I don't understand it.

He pours a glass of wine and passes it to me. So he's not throwing me out, I guess. Then the oven beeps and he slides some crusty bread into it.

"It kind of makes sense," he says, his eyes on mine.

"What makes you say that?" I ask him.

"Because I'm extremely attracted to you."

Oh. My heart does a flip in my chest. "So you're not attracted to a woman once you sleep with her?"

He shakes his head. "Not like this, no."

"Like what?" I ask him. "Can you explain it."

He stirs the sauce and checks the bread, before pulling a salad he must have made earlier out of the refrigerator. And when he finally turns to me there's an intense expression on his face.

"I want you like I've never wanted another woman in my life."

"Oh!" I'm a mixture of embarrassed, gratified, and completely shocked. "Seriously?"

"Did my bidding on your lot not give it away? What about video calling you every night so I can watch you smile as we watch *Grey's Anatomy*? Did that not make you think that I might be a little attracted to you?"

"You said you wanted to be friends," I point out.

"I do. I do want to be friends." And isn't that the weird thing? "I just don't know how to do this. I don't know how to be your friend and be attracted to you. But I'm trying, Sophie. I really am."

I nod. "I know you are. I like this side of you. But I don't know which side of you is real," I confess. "The Liam who treats me like a queen, or the Liam who knows how to press every button I have and enjoys it."

"Can't they both be real?" he asks.

His eyes catch mine. There's an honesty in them that slays me.

"I think maybe they can," I say softly. "But can I ask you a question?"

He nods. "Shoot."

"Why won't you sleep with a woman more than once?"

CHAPTER
FIFTEEN

I swallow hard. This is where she finds out that I'm a piece of shit. And even though she's being vulnerable in front of me I just can't reciprocate. So I give her the sanitized version. "Because I don't want to hurt anybody. Or be hurt. And no relationship lasts. Watching my dad go through life like a bulldozer taught me that."

She pulls her lip between her teeth. "So you'd rather be alone? Isn't that sad?"

The sauce is almost boiling. I switch it to low and grab another pan to heat up the water. It's good to have something to do while we have this conversation because I'm so tempted to walk over to her. To pull her against me and shut out this feeling.

The painful emotions I've spent most of my adult life avoiding.

"I don't mind being alone. I have a good life," I say lightly, taking the fresh pasta I bought from the farmer's market today from the pack.

"Of course you mind being alone. We all mind being alone. We're social creatures. We were built to fall in love, to have families, to build relationships."

"But if you know you're shit at something, sometimes it's better to avoid it altogether."

"You're not shit at sex," she tells me.

"How would you know?" I ask, my voice low.

"Because you do it a lot."

I laugh. "Not as much as you might think." The water has begun boiling and I slide the pasta inside, then grab some plates and silverware. "Can you lay those out?" I ask her, passing her the fork and spoon. "We'll eat in here if that's okay with you."

"That works."

The oven beeps and I pull out the bread, slicing it on a board before sliding it over. I test a piece of pasta and it's perfect, so I drain the pot and add it to the sauce, stirring it lightly to make sure it's all coated.

And when I plate it up, I'm satisfied. The sauce is made of roasted peppers and tomatoes, with some nduja sausage cooked and chopped into tiny pieces. It has a zing to eat, but it's also hugely aromatic. When I pass Sophie her plate, her eyes widen and I like the way she looks surprised.

"You made this from scratch?" she asks me.

"Yep."

She forks a piece of pasta and lifts it to her lips, sliding it inside. Her eyes widen as she swallows, then forks up a second then a third.

"This is so good," she tells me between bites. Within five minutes the whole thing is gone. And I think I might have found the perfect woman.

After dinner I pour her another glass of wine – drinking water for myself because I'll need to drive her home – and we slump on the overstuffed sofa in the living room. I pick up the remote and cue up the next episode of Grey's, and Sophie kind of nestles against me. I find myself putting my arm around her so we can both feel comfortable.

Her head rests against my shoulder and I smell the shampoo she uses. It's flowery and sweet. There's a tendril falling against my hand and I rub it between my fingers.

"This is nice," she murmurs, as Derek tiptoes out of Meredith's house.

Yeah it is. Real nice. And then a memory hits me. Of the morning after I didn't sleep with Sophie. The one that kind of changed everything between us. I'd been standing naked in front of her, she was wrapped in a towel. And she'd said something that hit me to the core.

"Hey," I say. "If we didn't sleep together why did you tell me I didn't make you come?" I ask her.

She lifts her head to look up at me surprised. "Well you didn't," she says. "That bit wasn't a lie."

"But I would've. If I'd have had sex with you."

She shakes her head but says nothing.

"What?" I ask, a little offended. "I would have. A gentleman always makes sure a lady comes first."

"Yeah, well sisters do it for themselves these days. A guy has never made me orgasm, not without me helping him."

"What?" I frown. "That can't be true." Can it? How the hell didn't her previous boyfriends knock themselves out to make her happy? Jesus, I'd be burying my face between her legs until she was screaming my name.

"Of course it is," she says, looking almost prim except for the dirty words coming out of her mouth. "Men seem to think that women should be multi orgasmic. But the fact is it takes a lot of work."

"I know that," I say. "But it's the kind of work a guy should love. Nothing's better than seeing a woman lose herself to pleasure."

"Maybe they're faking," she says, smirking.

"Nope." I shake my head. "It's easy to tell if they are."

She shifts in my arms, but I don't release her. I like the contact too much. "Have you seen *When Harry Met Sally*?" she asks me. "That's how easy it is for a woman to fake it."

"Nah," I say. "A man can feel when a woman comes. There are tells. Not just the clenching, though that's fucking delicious. You guys get all blushed and breathless. And then sleepy."

She pulls her lip between her teeth. She's looking a little flushed right now. "I've never met a guy I haven't had to help along with my own fingers."

"You've met me," I say. I look into her eyes and see how interested she is. With one arm still around her, I use the other to caress her face, cupping it softly as I tip her head until we're so close I can feel her breath.

"Never let a man treat you as anything but a princess," I tell her, my voice rough. "You deserve so much more than what you've been given."

Her lips part but she doesn't say anything. Just sighs softly. She's all soft and pliant in my arms. The television flickers in the background but this woman has all my attention.

Her lips part as she stares at me. "What do you do to make sure a woman's always satisfied?"

My lip quirks. "It's not exactly rocket science. Kiss them. Touch them. Work out what parts of their bodies react when I give them my attention."

"Like her breasts?" Her eyes are a little glassy. Her breath is faster. She's turned on and so am I.

"Sometimes," I say. "But not always. Every woman has different erogenous zones."

"What if you can't find their zones?" Her brows knit.

"I always find them," I tell her. "They're always there."

"Show me," she whispers.

I blink. "What?"

"Show me how you find them."

I'm stupidly hard. I'm not sure I've ever heard anything sexier in my life. "You want me to touch you?" I whisper.

She nods.

"What if I end up making you come?" I ask, my dick twitching at the thought.

Her face flushes.

Christ, I want her.

"I'd be okay with that," she whispers.

My lip quirks. "Yeah. I would, too." I run my thumb along her bottom lip then push it inside. Her eyes widen but she sucks and damn if her tongue doesn't flutter against me.

It doesn't take much imagination to picture her doing that to my cock. My heart slams against my chest.

"Can I kiss you?" I ask, because kissing is so underrated when it comes to arousal. That's why most porn is crap. Too much anatomy and not enough sensuality. The way to a woman's pleasure begins at the mouth.

"Yes," she whispers, and a thrill rushes through me. I want nothing more than to taste this woman.

To show her exactly how easily she can come with the right guy.

Still cupping her jaw, I move her in my arms until she's almost sitting on my lap. I spread my legs so she can fit between them, then press my lips against her ear. "You're fucking beautiful," I whisper, truth shining in every word. "Every inch of you is perfect." I slide my hand down her neck, over her shoulder, trailing my fingers down her side. She squirms against my cock and it feels amazing. I kiss her ear, then her throat, before turning her head so my lips are a breath away from hers. Her back is against my chest, her head angled perfectly, her chest rising and falling rapidly as I slide my arm around her waist.

"Such pretty lips," I whisper, because orgasms need communication, too. "I want them around my cock sometime."

Her breath hitches. "I want that, too."

"But not tonight," I tell her. "Tonight's all about you." I glance down at her mouth. Her bottom lip is trembling. She's ready for me. Like a peach about to fall from the tree. I slide my hand inside her shirt, my rough fingers touching her smooth, warm skin, and she gasps softly.

And then I kiss her. Softly at first, my thumb caressing her jaw, my other hand stroking her stomach. Her mouth is warm and welcoming, opening up to let me in, and I slide my tongue against hers until she lets out a moan. Her breath is coming in gasps, and I haven't even touched her where it counts.

Oh the things I want to do to her. They're messing with my brain. I slide my hand up further, my fingers feathering the curve of her breasts and she gasps into my mouth.

Christ she's responsive. What kind of idiots haven't wanted her pleasure? Haven't taken the time to learn exactly what gets her off? I tighten my grip on her jaw and she kisses me back enthusiastically.

"This okay?" I ask her, because consent is everything.

"More than okay," she says, lifting her arm behind her to slide her fingers into my hair. Her nails scratch my scalp and pleasure suffuses me.

My girl likes a little power play? Okay then, bring it on.

I lift her off my lap and lay her back onto the sofa, my eyes feasting on her perfect body as I pull back from her. She's still wearing her shoes – uncomfortable looking heels with a strap that circles her ankles. Hot as fuck, especially if they were wrapped around my hips, but I want her to relax.

So I unfasten them and slide them off. Her feet flex and I rub my thumbs against them, smoothing away the tension in her muscles. Then I move my hands up, savoring the feel of her legs, taking my time to smooth my thumbs against every inch of her, until I reach the back of her knees.

And she starts to laugh. "That tickles."

I grin because I love her laugh. "It does?" I ask her. "How ticklish are you?"

She wrinkles her nose. "Pretty ticklish. But don't go there, I hate being tickled."

"Noted." I nod, filing that information away for another day. Because there's nothing I want more than to hear her scream with laughter.

The same way I want to make her scream my name in pleasure tonight.

I push the hem of her skirt up until it's wrinkled over her thighs, and massage my way up her legs. I want her to get used to my touch. To relax under it.

To not be afraid of me.

I want her to welcome me. To beg me. I want her to need this the way I do. And from the way she's looking at me, her eyes hooded, her lips swollen, I think she does.

Fuck I hope she does.

"Can I take off your blouse?" I ask her. She nods, her gaze never leaving mine. There's something more than desire there. Something deeper.

It's trust. She trusts me to make her feel good. And it makes my heart do a weird clenching thing.

Releasing her thighs, I lean over her, kissing her softly. "You're doing so well," I tell her, and she practically beams at me.

She likes being praised? That's hot as hell. "Such a good girl," I tell her and she moans. I kiss her hard because I can't not kiss her.

I *need* to.

Like I need oxygen.

Her hands wrap around my neck as she kisses me back, her mouth demanding and needy. I slowly edge her top up her body a little at a time as we kiss, then gently tug it off to reveal her smooth stomach and perfect breasts behind a lacy half cup bra.

I kiss her throat and her chest, then the swell of her breasts. She watches me silently as I move my mouth to her nipple, sucking at it through the lace.

"Oh!"

I suck harder and she arches her back. I slide my hand behind her but don't stop my ministrations to her perfect tits.

Nudging her bra cup down, I make contact with her bare nipple, scraping my teeth across it before lashing it with my tongue. Her fingers tangle in my hair as I do the same to her other nipple. I'm an equal opportunities kind of guy. And I'm quickly becoming addicted to the taste of her skin.

I reach around her back with my other hand, releasing her bra and sliding it down her shoulders. She has to lift her body up from the sofa to help me, her stomach tense and her back arched. I throw it to the side and kiss my way down her stomach.

Her legs part before I can even reach the waistband, her skirt hitching up until it's covering nothing. Her panties are lace, too, matching the bra I discarded.

"Do you wear lingerie every time you present the weather?" I ask her.

"Yes. I like pretty underwear."

I file that little piece of information away in my head, too. "I'm going to get a hard on every time I watch you talk about cumulostratus or whatever it is," I tell her, sliding my hand up her thigh. My fingers graze her panties and damn, they're wet.

"That for me?" I say, sliding my fingers along them.

"Yes," she breathes.

And I can't help it. I need to inhale her in. So I push her skirt up over her hips and slide my cheeks along her thighs until my nose hits her.

She smells perfect. I'm so hard it hurts. And because I'm an impatient motherfucker I don't bother pulling them off, I just push them to the side and slide my tongue along the neediest part of her.

"Liam!" she squeaks. I smile against her and lick again. She almost bucks off the sofa. I lift one hand up to steady her stomach as I carry on worshipping her core.

I slide two fingers from my other hand inside her, capturing her clit between my teeth, sucking and licking this perfect woman until I feel her tightening around me. Her breath is escaping in huffs, her fingers coiled into my hair, her hips moving as much as she can to the rhythm of my sucking while my hand holds her down.

"Oh, OH!"

I lift my head up and she blinks at the sudden lack of contact.

"You pretending now?" I ask her hoarsely.

"No." She shakes her head rapidly. "Please don't stop. I'm so close."

Yeah, I know she is. Her flushed face and wide eyes make me feel like some kind of God. Then I dip my head back down, revelling in the essence of this perfect woman, and twist my fingers until I know she's at the edge. Her thighs tighten around my head, her nails scrape my scalp, her aching cries fill the room.

And then she lifts her back off the sofa and lets out a long, high-pitched cry. "Liam…"

And fuck if I'm not almost coming, too. I try to commit this moment to memory because I'll need to jerk off furiously to it later.

I need to remember how she smells, how she tastes. How she feels when she abandons herself to pleasure. I need to commit everything to memory because my life has never felt more perfect than it does right now, buried in this woman.

But I, more than most, should know that something this perfect never lasts.

CHAPTER
SIXTEEN

SOPHIE

I feel like I'm in some kind of drugged stupor, except it's a person I'm intoxicated by, not an illegal substance. It's only when Liam lifts his head and my hands are still tangled in his hair that I realize I didn't do a single thing to help this along.

He made me orgasm without any assistance at all.

And yes, maybe it's shameful to reach my late thirties without having a purely male-induced orgasm, but I don't really care because now that I've had it I want more.

Just not yet, though. Right now I want sleep.

Liam smiles softly, his eyes flickering over my face like he's trying to figure out if I'm okay. I smile back at him, finally releasing my death hold on his head, and he climbs up over me, cupping my face with the hand that hadn't been squeezed to death by my pleasure.

"You okay?"

"Yeah," I breathe. "Just trying to work out how to use my muscles."

He laughs and it does something to me. "Can I kiss you again?" he asks.

"What's with all the questions?" I mutter. "You just made me see stars, I think you can kiss me."

"I wasn't sure if you'd be okay with tasting yourself."

Oh. Of course. His lips are glistening. "I guess it depends how I taste," I say softly.

"Like fucking heaven."

It's weird how much I like that. How much I liked him telling me I was a good girl and that I was perfect. I know they're all lines he uses to make a woman feel good. But they worked on me.

Is that sad?

The honest truth is I'm too wrung out to care, in the best of ways. "Kiss me," I whisper, and his smile is so winning it hurts. Then he presses his mouth softly against mine as he strokes my hair. "So damn beautiful," he murmurs.

And yeah, that works. I taste myself and it isn't terrible. I like that he likes it.

I like that he likes me. Even if it's just as a friend. And tomorrow I'll think it through but tonight I just need to sleep.

"Let's get you to bed," he says, noticing my flickering eyes.

"Too tired to get in the car," I mutter. "I'll sleep on the sofa."

He chuckles. "You can sleep in my bed."

Before I can protest – and let's face it, I wasn't really going to protest *that* much – he slides his hand beneath me and lifts me into his arms. My body rushes through the air and for a moment it feels like I'm on a rollercoaster ride, but then I wrap my arms around him and I'm safe.

Safe.

That isn't a word I'd use to describe Liam Salinger. Dangerous, yes. Edgy, for sure. But never safe.

He carries me down the hallway to his bedroom, kicking open the door and laying me on his white comforter. And before I can say anything, he pulls the zipper on my skirt down, peeling it away from my body and folding it neatly. I lift my hips so he can slide my panties down, too, and then I'm naked before him, spread out on his comforter.

His eyes rake over me as he adjusts himself, and I realize that only one of us got pleasure tonight. Concerned, I reach for him. "Let me help you with that…"

My fingers curl around the outline of him. He's hard as steel and my heart races. But then he puts his hand over mine, pausing for a moment before he pulls them both away.

"You're exhausted," he tells me. "And I'm okay. Whatever guys have told you about blue balls, they're lying. It doesn't hurt, it does go away, and it won't affect our fertility."

I laugh because I heard all of those growing up. He walks over to his closet and pulls it open, grabbing a t-shirt that he carries over to me. "It'll swamp you, but it's soft and comfortable," he tells me. "I have a spare toothbrush if you want it."

"I should…"

"I'll grab it and bring it out here."

And that's what he does. He makes me comfortable, then gets me clean, and then pulls the covers down and encourages me to nestle into his mattress. When my head hits the pillow he presses his lips against my brow and kisses me softly.

"Sleep," he urges. "I'm just gonna take a shower then I'll join you."

I nod. "Don't be long." But before he even makes it to the bathroom my eyes have already closed.

———

LIAM

• • •

Bright rays of sunshine penetrate my sleep, piercing my eyelids and making me groan. I try to fight it for a moment, way too comfortable in my slumber, but the sun wins out and finally I open my eyes.

Then I remember last night and I reach for Sophie.

But she's not there.

Turning onto my side, I frown as I inspect her side of the bed. There's still a dent in the pillow but the covers are neatly tucked over the mattress in a way only Sophie could have made it.

"You in the bathroom?" I call out. No reply comes back. I groan and climb out of bed, running my hands over my messed up hair. I cross the floor in three strides, but the light in the bathroom is out.

Where the hell is she?

The bungalow isn't big and it takes me less than a minute to realize that she isn't here. The clothes I stripped off of her are all gone.

And she did the goddamned dishes, too. I think that's what kills me. She stood in the kitchen and made sure everything was pristine before tiptoeing out without a goodbye.

Just as I'm about to grab my phone and call her, I notice movement coming from Ava and Myles' kitchen. Did she go over there?

Not bothering to shower, I pull on yesterday's clothes and run my hands through my messed up hair in a vain attempt to get it under control. Then I wrench open the door and stomp across the lawn and the driveway to the main house, walking through the open doors that lead into the kitchen.

Myles and Ava look up, surprised. Charlie kicks in his bouncy chair.

"Hi," I say, looking around to see if Sophie's here.

"Hi," Myles says, looking confused.

"Everything okay?" Ava asks. "You look tired."

"No he doesn't. He looks like he just dragged his sorry ass out of bed," Myles says, lifting a brow at me. "Which I'm assuming he just did. Not that I'm jealous."

"Myles was up most of the night," Ava says, smiling at me apologetically. "He's a bit cranky."

"I was also staring at your place a lot," Myles says. "Did you have a good evening?" His words are pointed. I try to assess the situation. Sophie clearly isn't here. And from the way Ava is looking at me – like I'm still her favorite brother-in-law – she has no idea that Sophie was at my place last night.

Myles, on the other hand, looks like he wants to kill me. And I'm not sure if he saw something he shouldn't or if he's just tired like Ava said.

Either way, it feels like a strategic retreat is in order. "I need some sugar," I lie. "That's why I'm here. Can I borrow some?"

"What do you need sugar for?" Myles snaps.

"For my breakfast," I tell him. He doesn't move so I walk over to the cupboard where they keep the baking supplies and pull out the paper pack of sugar. Then I pour some into a bowl and put it back.

"There," I say. "That wasn't hard, was it?"

"So that's all you wanted?" Myles asks.

"Yup." I nod. "Gotta go. Lots to do today."

"Like what?" Ava asks, interested.

"Actually, I need to talk to you," Myles says, ignoring Ava's question. "In my office."

I start to laugh. Then Ava joins in.

"What's so funny?" Myles asks.

"You sound like a school principal," Ava says. "Or Liam's boss. And I know for a fact you're neither."

"Let's talk tomorrow," I tell him. "At work. I need to go right now."

"But…" he protests.

"Myles," Ava says, putting her hand on his. "Liam's right. Whatever work thing you need to discuss can wait until tomorrow." She smiles softly at him and I watch my grumpy-ass faced older brother practically melt in front of her.

"Okay," he agrees softly. "Tomorrow."

"Great. Glad we got that sorted." I start to back out. "See you guys later. Have a great Sunday." And then I carry the sugar I have no need for back to the house that's empty of the one person I need to talk to.

I put the bowl down and stomp into my bathroom, planning to shower, brush my teeth, and get dressed.

And then I'm going to find Sophie and figure out why she left without saying a word. Because I'm pissed as hell about that.

———

SOPHIE

Watching Lauren deal with the Sunday morning rush is like watching an artist at work. With the help of only three members of staff she manages to serve around eighty people, including those coming in for their regular weekend orders. Every seat in the Camelia Bakery is full, with a line of people waiting outside the door.

It's not an ideal time to turn up to have a heart-to-heart with the only friend I can confide in, so I sit on one of the counter stools drinking a large mug of coffee and stuffing my face with one – okay two – of her delicious donuts, as she rushes around the room like a whirlwind.

The second time she passes me she puts a hand on my shoulder. "It'll quiet down in ten minutes," she tells me."

I look skeptically at the full room. "Are you sure you don't want me to come back later?" I ask.

"Nope. Stay right there," she says, topping up my coffee cup. "I need to know why you walked in here looking like you didn't go home last night."

Ten minutes later, the line is gone and there are a couple of tables free. The frantic activity has dwindled, everybody has their coffee and pastries, and there's a happy Sunday morning buzz in the place. Lauren pours herself a cup of coffee and sits in the now-empty stool next to mine.

"Hey." She smiles as she takes a sip.

"Hey."

Lauren is one of my very favorite people. She, Ava, and I have known each other for most of our lives. We met on our first day of college and never looked back. They know me better than anybody else in my life.

"So who is he?"

I blink. "What makes you think it's a he?"

She smiles. "Well let's see. You're wearing a skirt and a blouse that are crumpled as heck. And because I tuned into the evening news last night, I happen to know you were wearing that same skirt and blouse yesterday. By the way, great broadcast."

"Thanks." I give her a small smile.

"So?"

I swallow hard. It's embarrassing to admit, but I'm also in desperate need of somebody to talk to. There's no way I can confide in Ava about this. She's too close to the situation and I'd hate for her to have split loyalties.

"I spent the night at Liam's," I say quickly.

"Oh." Lauren's eyes widen. "As in..." She wiggles her brows. "*Spent the night?*"

I take a sip of coffee to give me courage. "As in we didn't do *that*, but we did some other stuff and then I slept in his bed. With him."

"But I thought you two didn't get along."

"We don't." I frown. "Well we didn't, but we do now I guess. He's been really sweet to me since he won the auction." I tell her about our messaging and watching *Grey's Anatomy* together and then about last night.

And yeah, I admit that I lied to him. She's particularly interested in all the details of that first night when nothing happened but I pretended it did.

"No way," she hisses. "I can't believe you didn't tell me. I need details. All of them."

"There aren't many," I point out. "Nothing happened, remember?"

She folds her arms across her chest. "But he slept in your bed all night. Naked." Her eyes widen. "Is he as impressive as I think he is?"

"Yep."

"Oh." She sighs. "I can't believe you lied to him. Or that he believed it. You're such a terrible liar," she says.

"I know." I look down at my plate, now empty save for some donut crumbs. "But this felt different. Like, I don't know, self-preservation I guess."

"Why self-preservation?" she asks, sounding confused.

"I think I've always been attracted to him," I admit. "But he's the kind of guy who would break my heart, not one that would ever settle down. So it was easier to tell a lie and know he would never be interested in me than, I don't know."

"What makes you think he can hurt you?" she asks me. "Surely that would only happen if you let him get too close."

"I have kind of," I admit. "I really like spending time with him. He's funny and he's charming and he's as into *Grey's Anatomy* as I am."

"So you're friends then." She nods, as though she understands. I'm glad somebody does.

"Well yeah."

"With a few benefits." She wiggles her brows.

"I guess. But he's not the kind of guy who wants more than one night. That's why I left so early this morning, to spare us both the embarrassment of him explaining it was all a mistake."

"You're still going to have to face him though," Lauren points out. "Even if you weren't both Charlie's godparents there's a small matter of his daily forecast for the next two and a half months."

His daily forecast? My mouth falls open. I haven't sent him one today. I did most of the work yesterday but I'd planned to take another look at the weather systems first thing this morning. I'll have to message him and ask if it's okay for me to send it in an hour.

When I pull my phone out of my bag the battery is completely dead. Lauren has some charger cords behind the counter – left by customers who never returned for them – and it takes me a couple of tries to find the one I need. She plugs it into the socket on the side of the counter and I watch as the little loading bar comes up on the screen and my phone finally comes to life.

An alert tells me I have five missed calls and two voice-mails. And then some messages flash up in quick succession. All from Liam.

> Is everything okay? I woke up and you were gone.

> Can you just call me to let me know you're okay, please?

> I'm outside your house. Can you let me in?

> Sophie, answer the door.

Okay you're not here. WHERE ARE YOU?

This is not okay. I'm worried about you. CALL
ME, WEST!

Are you pissed at me?

I'm five minutes away from going back to talk
to Ava. I'm not kidding.

And I'm going to tell her EVERYTHING.

Okay not everything. But please let me know
you're okay.

"Um, those are not the messages of a man who's not interested," Lauren says. I almost jump when I realize she's reading them over my shoulder.

"He's just annoyed I left without waking him. I probably hurt his ego."

Lauren lifts a brow. "Don't you think you should call him and put him out of his misery?"

"Yeah, I better." I pull his number up, guilt pulling at my stomach. I shouldn't have left like that, the same way I shouldn't have lied. This man just makes me panic every time.

I don't know how to deal with it.

"Actually, don't bother," she says, her gaze fixed on the front of the bakery. I turn around to see him standing in the doorway, his angry gaze fixed on me. A shiver snakes down my spine because even furious, Liam Salinger is glorious.

The mouth that kissed me all over last night is pulled into a thin line as he walks toward me. He's dressed in jeans and a gray t-shirt – pretty much the same kind of outfit most guys in the bakery are wearing – and yet he stands out so much.

Every female in the shop turns to look at him.

"Sophie," he says as he stops dead in front of me. "Do you ever check your goddamned phone?"

"I just checked it," I tell him. "Sorry, I didn't mean to worry you."

"I wasn't worried until you didn't pick up. And you weren't at home. I've driven around half of fucking Charleston looking for you. I even went into the television station." He shifts his feet. "Your boss is a prick, by the way."

Lauren's eyes switch from Liam to me and back again like she's watching a tennis match.

"My phone died," I admit. "I wasn't planning on being out all night."

He looks pointedly at Lauren, who's listening like we're her favorite audiobook. She smiles easily at him. "It's okay," she tells him. "I know everything."

"Of course you do," he says. "And I hope you told her it's not nice to run out on somebody without telling them goodbye first."

She nods. "I did. And I told her she should have sent over your weather report by now."

I widen my eyes at her. The traitor. "Lauren…"

"Well you should have. But now Liam's here so you can give it to him in person."

I look up at him. His eyes are softer now. There are little gold flecks in the brown of his irises. "It's going to be sunny today," I say. "Some cloud coverage this afternoon but nothing that will develop into anything."

He nods. "That's good. We won't get wet then."

"We?" I frown.

"You're going to spend the day with me."

"Oh!" Lauren looks like she's going to combust. "That's so lovely."

"I can't," I tell him. "I have things to do."

"Like what?" Lauren asks. I make a note to have a good talk with her later. She's not helping.

And she's supposed to be *my* friend.

"I have to go visit my dad. And then I have to get groceries. Plus, I have a pile of laundry I didn't get to last week." I look up at Liam. "And don't tell me I can leave it until another day because I have literally nothing to wear."

"I wasn't going to suggest that," he says easily. "I was going to offer to help."

I swallow a laugh. "You want to help me with my chores?"

He shrugs. "Why not?"

Um, because you're Liam Salinger, the hugely wealthy CEO of a massively profitable company who must have people to do all those things for you?

"Maybe he wants to see your panties," Lauren says helpfully. "As he loads them in the washer."

I shoot her a withering look. We're definitely having that talk later. And then I rifle through my purse because even though she's annoying me I don't want to leave without paying. I pass her a twenty and tell her to keep the change, then I walk out of the bakery, Liam following me every step of the way.

When we're outside I let out a long breath. "You really don't have to do this," I tell him. "I wasn't lying when I said I had a hundred chores to do."

"I wasn't lying either. I want to do them with you." He looks around. "I assume your car isn't here."

"Why do you think that?"

"Because you came here by taxi. I called all the companies. Gave them a description."

I blink. "That's a bit… stalkerish."

"I really was worried by then. And I wasn't lying about calling Ava either." He shows me his phone and the last call on it.

"What did you tell her?" I widen my eyes.

"That we were supposed to meet up to discuss next

week's forecasts." He shrugs. "You should probably call her and tell her you're okay."

Yeah, I should. The last thing she needs is to be worrying about me.

I shoot her a message, and reluctantly follow Liam to his car, sliding into the comfortable passenger seat. Was it really only last night when I was sitting here as he drove me back from the station?

It feels like a lifetime ago.

"So where do you want to start?" he asks.

"I need to drop by my dad's. You can stay in the car, though."

He starts up the engine. "That would be rude. I've met your dad before. I should come in and say hi."

I turn my head to look at him. "Why would you want to do that?"

"Because I like your dad," he says, as though it's a stupid question.

Well okay then. If he wants to see him, then let him. No skin off my nose. Maybe a day with me doing chores is what he needs to see I'm not that exciting. I give him my dad's address, the briefest of directions, and within five minutes we're pulling up outside his house.

The curtains are still closed. It's weird because Dad's always an early riser. He loves sitting with a coffee in the early morning sunshine.

And he'd never let his curtains stay closed. He'd worry too much about the neighbors' opinions for that.

"Are you okay?" Liam asks.

I shake my head. "I think there's something wrong." Pulling at the handle, I climb out of the car. Liam walks beside me up the steps, and then I knock on the door.

No answer.

"Oh shit."

"What's wrong?" Liam asks.

"He's always up at this time." My hands shake as I find his spare key in my bag. "He has a heart problem." My fingers are trembling as I try but fail to slide it into the lock. Liam gently takes the key from me and opens the door easily.

"There's probably a simple explanation," he says as we walk inside. "Mr. West?" he calls out. He's holding my hand. I don't know when he grabbed it, but it feels nice.

"Dad?" I shout, rushing down the hallway, Liam still holding onto me. "Are you okay?" I wrench open his bedroom door, my stomach twisted as I steel myself for the worst.

"Sophie?" Dad sits up. His chest is bare and from the fact his pajama pants are strewn across the floor I can only assume his bottom half is, too.

And so is the woman next to him.

"Dad?" I blink. "I… ah…"

Liam tugs my hand. "Sophie wanted to make sure you were okay. And it looks like you are."

I'm frozen to the spot, staring at my dad, who stares, horrified, back.

The woman next to him smiles at me. "Are you Frank's girl?" She has a strong Charleston accent. She also has pink hair, which I'm kind of jealous of.

"Um yeah," I say, my face flaming. "Sophie."

"It's lovely to meet you." She doesn't look at all embarrassed, unlike Dad and me. "I'm Jenny. From the market. I run the crystal stall a few down from your dad."

"Crystals. Right." I nod. Dad hates anything new age. Then there's silence again and it takes Liam's mouth against my ear for me to actually start to think clearly.

"We should go now," he whispers. "Call your dad later, okay?"

I nod but don't move.

"Mr. West, I'm glad you're okay. It was a pleasure to see you again," Liam says. "Jenny, it was nice to meet you."

"Likewise," she says, beaming.

"Um yeah. Dad, I'll call you later."

He nods, looking distinctly gray. Liam tugs at my hand, but I don't move.

"Step backward," he urges, whispering in my ear. "Come on, you can do this."

I let him pull me this time. When we get into the hallway he closes my dad's bedroom door then puts his arm around my shoulders, steering me to the front door.

"You're doing great," he murmurs. "One foot in front of the other."

It's only when we get outside, walking back down my dad's path, that the mortification hits me. "Oh God," I say, pulling my hand from his so I can cover my face with my palms. "Tell me that didn't happen."

"What didn't happen?" he says, a huge grin on his lips.

I cover my face with my hands and let out a groan.

"Come on," he says. "Let's get back in the car." He opens the door and lets me climb in, then walks around to the driver's side. When he slides into his seat he turns to look at me.

"I'm absolutely mortified you saw that," I tell him. Hell, I'm mortified that *I* saw that.

"I've seen so much worse," he tells me. "My dad has had a lot of girlfriends. And I have five brothers. You really don't want to know what I've walked in on."

I will myself to look at him. There's so much sweetness in his expression that it makes my chest feel weird. "My dad hasn't had a girlfriend since my mom died," I tell him.

"Well he has one now. How do you feel about that?" He turns on the engine.

"I don't know." I frown. "She seems nice, doesn't she?"

He laughs. "She can hold a conversation in an embarrassing moment, which is more than you and your dad can do." He pulls away from my dad's house. "It'll be okay," he tells me. "You'll laugh about this one day."

"Promise?"

His smile turns soft. "Yes. Now let's get back to your place. We have a date with the laundry basket."

CHAPTER
SEVENTEEN

LIAM

So here's the thing. I don't have a lot of time in my life for laundry, but right now I wouldn't want to be anywhere but here, loading Sophie's washer with her clothes, covering them with suds and hitting the start button.

And yeah, I've touched her underwear. No, I didn't smell them.

But I might have thought about it.

After we got home, she showered and put on these cute little shorts that mold to her ass and a t-shirt that kind of hangs over them, with 'Forecasters Do It Wetter' emblazoned across her breasts. Her hair is up in one of those messy bun type things that I swear girls do just to make us hard.

And she hasn't put on any make up, of which I approve heartily.

"Oh God, not so much soap," she calls out, reaching out to stop my hand. I blink because I've been staring at 'Wetter' on her t-shirt for a few seconds too long while pouring in the washing powder.

"Sorry. Want me to scrape them out?" I ask, frowning at the white layer on top of her clothes.

She sighs. "No, it's fine. But if I have a rash next week it's all your fault."

I think she's over the whole seeing her dad naked with another woman in his bed thing, which is good. For a moment there I thought she was going to faint. And yeah, I was half looking forward to catching her in my arms, but honestly I think she would've ended up getting embarrassed and pushed me away.

The thing is, I don't want her to push me away. I'm having way too much fun with her. She's a friend. She's hot. I know what she looks like when she comes.

And I like that.

She hits the start button and the machine turns on. I can hear water pouring into the drum.

"How long does it take?" I ask her.

"About an hour. I put it on the eco setting," she tells me. "Better for the environment."

"You care about the environment?" I'm not ribbing her, I'm just interested.

"Of course. I'm a meteorologist. I see every little change in our weather system. Things are getting bad, we all need to try to make things a little better."

I nod, but I'm distracted by the way her nose wrinkles when she's being earnest. It causes three little furrows at the top that I want to smooth out.

"Liam?"

"Uhuh?"

She lets out a sigh. "You need to stop looking like that."

"Like what?" I'm genuinely confused. "This is the way I look. I'm not sure I can change it, not without extensive surgery anyway."

Sophie rolls her eyes. "I meant your expression. Stop looking at me like… I don't know."

"Like I know your orgasm face?" I suggest.

She blinks and I kind of like that. "That's not what I was going to say."

"But I do, don't I?" And if I'm being honest, I'm kind of obsessed about it. It's one of the reasons I was pissed this morning. I was hoping to see it again.

Maybe multiple times.

"I don't have an orgasm face," she says testily.

"Yeah you do."

"No I don't." She frowns. "And why are we talking about this, anyway? I thought what happened last night would stay in last night."

"You're getting last night confused with Vegas," I tell her patiently. She lets out what sounds like a strangled groan.

"Seriously, Liam. Last night…"

"Was good?"

Her face softens. "It was lovely. And you were lovely. But can we move on now?" She slides the pack of detergent back on the shelf of her laundry room. Not that it's really a room, more of a closet really. Just the washer, the dryer, and us.

"I was lovely?" I ask. "That doesn't sound like high praise."

She starts to laugh. "Is that what you want? Praise? Okay then. You were amazing. The best. Now can we stop talking about it?"

"What if I don't want to stop talking about it?" I ask her.

For a moment she says nothing. Those little lines appear again. "Liam, you're the one with rules. One night, no repeats. We had our night and I'm really hoping we can stay friends. That's what I want. I like you. I like spending time with you." She lets out a long breath. "I don't want to mess things up." She puts her hand on my chest and pushes me out of the laundry room. I step backward and she steps forward, like we're in some kind of dance. Then she reaches behind and pulls the door closed, but I still don't move.

"We didn't have sex," I point out.

She's not wearing any shoes and I'm towering above her. I have to drop my head and she has to incline hers just so we can make eye contact.

"I know. I was there," she tells me.

"So technically that wasn't our one night."

She blinks. "Did I ever tell you that my uncle was an alcoholic?" she asks me.

I lift a brow at the change in conversation. "Um, no."

"He had rules, too. All kinds of ones. And when they got in the way he'd push them gently until he got what he wanted. No drinking before six but it was five? No worries, it's six somewhere, right? That's what you're doing. Pushing at the rules. Seeing what breaks. But the thing is, Liam, you'll end up breaking me."

It's like she just punched me in the gut. "I'd never hurt you," I tell her.

"You'd try not to. But you will. I'm not cut out for one night stands. I'm not the kind of girl who can walk away from people I care for. You and I, we'll have to see each other for Charlie's birthdays and holidays. And if I see you there with another woman knowing that she's having what I had with you at least for one night." Her voice cracks. "I'm sorry, it just won't work."

"Okay," I say, my voice tight.

"Okay?" Her brows lift. "Okay, as in let's move on and forget this conversation so tonight we can watch the next episode of Grey's and you can hate on McDreamy?"

I shake my head. "No, not that. Okay as in I understand. You need more. You fucking deserve more. And I want to give you more." The tightness in my chest is almost painful, but that's okay. It's a reminder that I'm still alive because right now I feel like I could be floating away.

"What do you mean?"

I put my fingers beneath her chin, reveling in the softness

of her skin. Then I lean down until our eyes are inches from each other. She doesn't move, doesn't breathe, just looks at me. "Let me prove that I can give you more," I say. "That I can be the kind of guy who deserves you."

"Liam…" She blinks, her thick lashes sweeping down. "I don't think you can do that."

"People can change."

"I know they can. But for themselves, not because they want somebody else. I don't want you to change for me. I want you to do it for *you*."

The pressure in my chest is unexpected. There's so much sweetness in her expression that it takes everything I have not to drop my head down further until my mouth takes hers.

And I think she'd kiss me back. Despite the protests of rejection if I kissed her, Sophie would kiss me back.

I know how to seduce. I know how to make her melt. I know how to make her come.

But I don't want those things. I want to make her fall for me.

And isn't that the kicker? The one thing I do my best to never do yet now here I am, desperate for it.

My brothers would laugh like hell if they could see me right now.

I step back, putting some much needed space between us, ignoring the voice in my head that tells me I'm making a huge mistake.

"Right," I tell her. "I get it."

"I'm sorry." She attempts a smile, but it's wavering. "I hope we can still be friends."

I nod. "Friends. Of course."

This time her smile is true. "Thank you for being so understanding."

"Oh, I understand," I tell her. "Look, I should go now. I have to do a few things."

"Okay." She nods, her eyes shiny. "That's fine."

"But we'll still watch Grey's together soon, okay?"

"Sure. I'd like that," she says softly.

Not as much as I will, I'm certain. But I have bigger things to deal with now.

———

"I need your help," I say to Myles and Ava as I walk into their living room. They're snuggled up on the sofa together, Charlie's monitor on the fireplace.

"Is everything okay?" Ava asks. "You look weird."

I do? I frown. "This is my thinking face. I have a lot on my mind."

Myles sniggers and I give him a pointed look. If I could go anywhere but here for advice I would. But let's face it, as much as I love Eli and all of my other brothers, they're single as fuck.

Myles is the only one who's actually settled down. And to be honest, that's a minor miracle because he's one grumpy-assed son of a bitch.

"Take a seat," Ava says, pointing to the leather chair by the fireplace. "Would you like a drink?"

"No, I'm good." I sit on the chair and lean forward, looking at their surprised faces. "So here it is. I think I'm in love with Sophie."

"I fucking knew it," Myles says, jumping up. He looks genuinely pissed. "I told you to leave her alone. I told you not to mess with her. Of all the damn people in the world…"

"Myles," Ava says, reaching for his arm to pull him back down. "Did you hear what he just said?"

"That he's messing with Sophie? Oh yeah, I heard." He glares at me. "Christ, man, can't you keep it in your pants for a minute?"

I smirk because I did keep it in my pants. And for longer than a minute.

"Liam said he's in love with her," Ava says to him. Then she smiles at me. "I'm so happy for you both."

"Wait. What?" Myles frowns. "In love? *You?*"

I nod and he looks at me like he has no idea who I am.

"And she loves you, too?" Ava's eyes are dancing. I think she's already picturing what to wear to the wedding.

"Ah, no." I shake my head. "She doesn't want me. Or at least the me I used to be." I run my thumb along my jaw, thinking. "Or that I still am but don't want to be. Anyway, she's not interested in being anything other than friends."

"Thank God." Myles tips his head back on the sofa. "Finally a woman with some sense when it comes to you."

"I resent that," I tell him. "I'm a catch."

"You are," Ava agrees. "So what exactly did Sophie say?"

I fill them in on most of the details. Not everything because I'm a gentleman and some things should remain private. But there's enough for them to understand the situation, and by the time I finish Myles looks stunned and Ava just looks sad.

"She's the first woman who rejected you, that's all," Myles tells me. "You don't want her, you just want to prove that you can have her if you want."

I shake my head. "No. I've been rejected before. I know how that feels. And it doesn't feel like there's some kind of pneumatic drill going off in your ribcage."

"You make it sound so romantic," Ava says, smirking.

"I didn't realize you could physically feel love before now." I frown. Or that it was fucking painful.

"Oh you can for sure," Ava tells me. "I felt it for Myles long before I realized what it was."

He looks at her, his expression filling with warmth. "I felt it for you, too, babe."

"Can we bring this back to me," I ask. "I need your help."

"What do you want us to do?" Myles says. "Force her to fall in love with you?"

"No. I want to know how you got Ava to fall for you. I mean, she's way out of your league, right?"

Ava sniggers. "That's true," she agrees. "I am."

"Well, it helps if there's some attraction there," Myles says.

"She's attracted to me," I tell them. "That's not a problem. It's the rest I need your help with."

Myles lets out a sigh. "Can't you just forget about her? Do us all a favor."

"No, I can't."

Ava runs her finger over her bottom lip. "The thing is, there's no real way to make somebody fall in love with you. And you wouldn't want to make them do that anyway. All you can do is be yourself and if they want you, they'll let you know."

That tightening feeling happens in my chest again. "But she doesn't want me. She said so."

Ava shakes her head. "She said she didn't want to be a notch on your bedpost. But you're telling us she wouldn't be that."

I'm not sure where she's going here, but I'm listening anyway.

"So what she really needs is to believe in you. The falling in love will happen naturally if she does."

"Okay," I say, my eyes trained on her. "How do I get her to believe me?"

She shrugs. "I've no idea."

"Jesus." I throw my hands up in the air. "You two are no help."

"Sorry," Ava says.

"But not that sorry," Myles adds, leaning forward to grab the television remote from the coffee table. "Now it's time to be silent and catch up on *Bridgerton*," he tells me.

I decide to leave because being addicted to one television

show is enough for any man. "Thanks for everything, guys," I tell them. "You've been great."

"You don't need our help," Ava says, smiling at my annoyance. "You're a catch, Liam. You just need to realize it."

"No he's not," Myles mutters, turning up the volume. "He's a pain in the ass."

CHAPTER
EIGHTEEN

I'm in the office bright and early on Monday, even though I had to work on Saturday. There's not enough of us for me to take a day off. Something is going to have to give because at this rate we're all going to collapse of overwork.

I open my laptop and sigh. Maybe I'm just grumpy because I haven't heard from Liam since he emailed me last night with his itinerary for the week. He didn't add anything cute to the email, didn't mention watching anything together either. Just a simple email and that was it.

I should be happy, shouldn't I? I told him this couldn't work. And yet I'm not. I'm annoyed because maybe I wanted him to fight for me.

And yes, I know that's game playing and I don't like playing games. I'll have a severe word with myself later.

From checking his itinerary I know he's going to New York this morning. I sent him his daily forecast an hour ago but he hasn't replied to that either.

Before I can brood on it anymore, Michael rushes in, a

triumphant smile on his face. "You know what this is?" he asks, holding a sheaf of papers in his hand.

"Your next bestseller," I say, lifting a brow.

"You know I don't like books." He shakes his head. "Anyway, it's a request for bids from the network. They want regional weather hubs and they're asking *us* to submit a proposal." He lifts a brow. "I told you it would be worth me going to that golf course."

"They want what?" I ask.

"The network wants eight weather hubs across the country. Then when there's a weather event they'll call on one of the hubs to take lead and cover it for all the stations in the local area as well as nationally." He slaps the report on my desk. "It's a great opportunity. I'd like you to write up our submission."

I look at the thickness of the sheaf in front of me and try to not sigh. "I'm not sure I'll have time," I tell him. "I'm already covering two jobs." *And sometimes three when you can't be bothered to call off your golf games.*

He says nothing, just stands there. I keep my gaze stubbornly on the papers because I don't want to look him in the eye.

Ugh, I hate him.

Finally, he clears his throat. "I'm trying to help us all here. You know how easy it would be for the station to buy in the weather forecast. If we get awarded the regional hub contract we'll have additional funding. Which means we can have extra staff. So please get this done." He lifts a brow.

I grudgingly nod. Part of me knows he's right. We have to prove we're adding value to the station. And having regional hubs makes great sense. No point in every station in the local area sending a meteorologist out to report on a tornado or hurricane when one can do it for everybody.

And as I read the report I find myself getting excited. This is a real chance for change in the department. And if we get the contract I'll be the person who won it for us. Michael won't be able to hide that. It might even mean a promotion.

But it also means I'll have to work on it in the evenings, because my days are already overly full with running forecasts, updating the website, and appearing on air. But maybe that's a good thing because I won't have time to brood about my conversation with Liam yesterday.

Or about how he made me feel when he touched me all over.

There's a part of me that wants to feel that again, if only for one night. He made me feel safe and yet in complete danger. It's an intoxicating combination.

But my heart tells me that one night would only make me feel worse. Because once he was gone I'd feel more alone than I've ever felt. And I'm old enough to know that sometimes the things you want are bad for you.

It doesn't mean I didn't touch myself last night as I thought about him. Or that I keep checking my phone to see if he's replied to my forecast yet.

He hasn't, by the way.

I'd brood on it more, but the morning runs away with me. By the time I've updated the website with current forecasts, I have to run for the lunchtime news, getting a dirty look from the producer because I've just managed to put my mic pack on before the intro music begins.

And once I finished that, I had to stay behind to record some spots for the website and our social media accounts. So by the time I get back to the office I'm desperate for lunch, or at least a coffee to keep me going.

But there's a crowd of people around my desk.

"What's going on?" I ask.

"Did you order lunch?" Lisa asks. She doesn't even work in this office, the sports team has a room a few doors down the hallway. It's full of merchandise for the local teams and when you walk in there you take your life in your hands because the odds are good you'll get hit in the head by a flying baseball or basketball or occasionally a hockey puck.

"No, are you guys planning to order some?" I ask. It's not often we all pool together and get lunch delivered, but maybe it's somebody's birthday and I've forgotten.

"I don't think we need to," Ray, an ex-baseball player, says. *Is there anybody in the sports office or are they all here?* "I was hoping you might plan on sharing."

He steps back and that's when I see the platters covering my desk. There are five of them, all silver with those domed lids, though I notice a couple of them are askew and I suspect the sports team of looking to see what's inside.

They're literally ruled by their stomachs.

"I didn't order this," I say, frowning because it looks expensive. And then I see the napkins with *The Ambassador Hotel* emblazoned in gold lettering against a backdrop of white and a cold wave of fear washes over me.

"Did somebody order this on the station's account?" I ask. I know how much a buffet like this from the Ambassador costs. We only order from them when we have important people visiting. And I know for a fact that I'll end up in trouble if my name is against this order.

Of course my thoughts immediately turn to Michael. Is he trying to get me in trouble with the station bosses?

"Who knows, but it's here so we might as well dig in," Ray says, lifting a dome up. Crushed ice covers the platter, and nestled between the shards is the most expensive array of shellfish you'd ever want to see.

"Fuck. I love lobster," Lisa breathes.

"Don't touch anything," I tell them, batting Ray's hand away. "There's been a mistake."

He looks like he's on the verge of tears.

"I need to send this back before we get billed," I say.

Ray's lip wobbles as he traces the point of a lobster claw. "But it's so pretty…"

"This isn't on the company tab," Lisa announces. As I turn to look at her, I spot Ray steal a shrimp from the corner of my eye.

"Seriously?" I ask him, my eyes narrowing. "You thought I wouldn't notice?"

"If they take it back they're just going to throw it away," he points out, not unreasonably. "That would be an unheavenly waste."

"Who's L?" Lisa asks.

I keep my eyes on Ray. "I've no idea."

"The invoice says, 'I wasn't sure what you wanted for lunch so I ordered you a bit of everything'. Then there's an L."

Ray's hand creeps out again. I don't bother to stop him this time. "It's from a friend," I manage to rasp out, knowing exactly who L is. What the hell is Liam thinking, sending me all this food?

It's like a dam has burst. Once everybody realizes I'm not going to be fired for the food order, they're grabbing at the lids, oohing and aahing at the food laid out on them.

I don't have time for this. But I'm also confused. Why is Liam sending me lunch?

"Leave me something," I tell the sports team. "I just need to make a call." I grab my phone and walk out of the office, the sound of chewing and gobbling filling my ears. When I get out into the hallway it's thankfully empty so I bring up Liam's number.

He answers after the first ring.

"Sophie," he says, and just hearing his voice sends a thrill through me. This isn't healthy. I'm not a lovesick teenager. I shouldn't respond like this, I'm in my late thirties.

"You sent me lunch."

"Was it okay?" he asks. "I need to find out what you like. I thought about ordering pasta but it can be messy to eat in the office."

"You could have sent me a sandwich like any normal person," I tell him. "Or not sent me anything at all." I rub my brow with my fingertips. I think I'm getting a headache.

"But I want to get on your right side," he says smoothly.

"Why?" I'm genuinely confused.

"Because I need to watch that episode of Grey's tonight. And I want to watch it with you," he tells me.

Oh. "Don't you have a hot date to go to while you're in New York?" I ask, because I'm a masochist that way.

Liam's silent for a minute. Then I hear some muffled tones as though he's talking to somebody. "I'll be there in a moment," I hear him say. Then there's a sound like a door closing.

"Sorry," he says, "I was supposed to be in a meeting five minutes ago."

"You're a busy man," I say softly. "I'll let you go." But I don't hang up. Yet.

My office door opens and Ray walks out carrying a platter. Yep, a platter. He must have moved all the food around because this one has a variety on it. Shellfish and pastries and some of those vegetables with dips. He winks at me and pops a carrot stick into his mouth before he disappears into the sports office.

"Don't go anywhere," Liam says. "We need to get one thing straight. I'm not going on any dates. I'm not seeing anybody else. The only woman I'm interested in is you." His voice is low and gritty.

My throat constricts. "I thought we talked about this."

"Yes, we did. And you let me know that you don't believe in me. So I have some work to do. And I know that some lobster and fruit doesn't prove anything. But I wanted to let you know I was thinking of you. And make sure you're thinking of me, too."

"Liam…"

"You don't need to say or do anything right now," he says,

as though he can read my mind. Which is good because I'm literally stumped for what to say. "This is about me. I need to prove to you that I'm not the guy you think I am. I need to show you that I want more."

"More?"

"Of you," he breathes. "So much more."

There's some more muffled voices. He lets out a soft 'fuck'. "Baby, I need to go."

Somewhere deep inside, my feminist self raises its head. I should tell him I'm not his baby. It's shameful but I'm too full of excitement to actually listen to the sensible voice in my brain.

He called me baby. I kind of want to shout it out.

"Grey's tonight. Please," he says hurriedly.

"Okay," I breathe.

"Thank you. I'll talk to you later. Have a good afternoon."

"I will, and you. Oh and Liam?"

"Yes?"

I'm kind of disappointed he doesn't call me baby again. "Thank you for lunch."

CHAPTER
NINETEEN

LIAM

I walk into a boardroom full of angry faces. "Hello everybody, apologies for my lateness."

Richard Dawlish, one of my top investors, gives me a sickly smile. "Hey, we're just glad you're in the state for once. We thought we'd lost you."

They've clearly made him their spokesman during my absence. Which is fine because I can deal with people like Richard in my sleep. He's motivated by one thing and that's money.

And I've made him a rich man over the years.

Right now he's pissed with me because he thinks I've been neglecting our business. But he hasn't quite got the concept of the internet, or the fact that most investments can be monitored over the web.

"I had some concerns keeping me in Charleston," I say lightly. "But I'm all yours now." I pour myself a coffee and take a seat. "Did you get the report I sent over the weekend."

"Well yes," Richard says. "But we prefer to see you face to face. We have a lot of money invested in you."

"Not in me, Richard. In companies I find," I remind him. Because nobody is buying me. "Did you have any concerns with the report?"

He looks down at the paper in front of him, pausing as he tries to find any fault with it. "The Flashman investment isn't paying out as quick as we'd like."

My phone flashes and a message pops up on it. It's from Sophie. And yes I should be assuaging Richard, but I'm way more entertained by the picture she sent of her eating the cake I sent. She's captioned it "Are you trying to rot my teeth?"

My lip curls. "The Flashman investment is paying out exactly as planned. A little faster, actually," I say. "Don't forget that summer is a slow time for winter sports equipment. By next quarter we should be seeing a significant profit." I look at the others around the table who are silently nodding. "Does anybody else have any concerns?"

"The thing is, Liam, we invest with you because you're based here in Manhattan. When we need you, you're here. Or you have been." Richard clears his throat and looks around at the table, but nobody catches his eye. "But now we have to wait days to see you and ask you questions."

"I'm always at the other end of a phone line," I remind him. "All you have to do is press a button and I'm there." I look over at Rachel Cline, one of my earliest investors. I've turned her multi million fortune into a billion dollar one. "Rachel, did I not talk with you on Friday night when you needed to liquidize some of your investment?"

"Well yes, you did," she agrees.

"And the money was in your account on Saturday morning?"

"Yes, it was."

"Do you think it would have been there any faster if I'd have been in the office?"

Her expression softens. "No, I don't think it would."

I let my gaze roll over everyone at the table. "I understand that change can cause anxiety. But there are so many opportunities in Charleston right now. Your New York investments are still being taken care of, but I can offer you more this way. More opportunities, higher returns, and a lot less risk." I lift a brow. "Look at what we did with Smith and Carson." That's the publishing house that Ava now runs. "There's no way in hell we can get that kind of return for your money in New York."

A few of the people around the table nod their heads.

"But if you're uncomfortable with that I understand. Say the word and I'll have your investments returned to you. I have a long list of people who would like to be part of the future we have to offer here."

That's no word of a lie. A day doesn't go by without someone asking if I'm taking on new clients. Many of them are hugely prestigious. But I have a sense of loyalty and these are the people who have been with me from the start.

"I'm okay with you looking at Charleston," Rachel says.

"Yep," Sydney Clark, the man next to her agrees. One by one they all give me the assent.

"Richard?" I ask. His jaw is ticking. He's a self-made man. He knows the value of every dollar. He's also proud as hell.

He lets out a long breath. "It would just be nice to see you in New York more often."

"Noted." I nod. "And I miss you, too."

Laughter breaks out across the room, the atmosphere diffusing. Even Richard manages to crack a smile. With their grievances aired, I go on to talk about the companies we're working with right now, giving them a rundown of where we're at.

By the time we finish the meeting everything is calm. We stand and talk, while Sam arranges for fresh coffee and pastries.

The irony that I can persuade these hard-faced investors to trust me when I can't persuade the woman I love to do the same doesn't evade me. I wish I could talk her around as easily.

But I'm not daunted. I can rise to the challenge.

Because I want her more than I've wanted anybody else.

"Do you have any dinner plans?" Rachel asks, touching my elbow. She's almost eighty but her dinner parties are legendary.

"Actually, yes," I tell her. "I'm eating dinner with my girl." Virtually, at least.

"You have a girlfriend?" She smiles at me. "How wonderful. I didn't know that. What's her name?"

"Sophie," I tell her. "And to be honest, she's not my girlfriend yet. But I want her to be."

Her eyes twinkle. "Oh my. A woman who can resist your charms. No wonder you want her. It's like that Groucho Marx saying. What is it?" She frowns. "Oh yes. 'I'd never belong to any club that would have me as a member.' Isn't that it?"

I laugh. "Sounds about right. She has high standards." And I'm not sure I can meet them.

"Of course she does, dear." Rachel pats my arm. And then squeezes my bicep, her eyes widening. "But you'll win her. I know you will."

———

SOPHIE

I'm trying so hard to keep my eyes on the television screen, but every now and then I sneak a peek at my phone, just to check that he's still there.

And he is. He's set up his phone on his knees, I think, though it's hard to tell from this angle. If I'm being really honest, I'm a little too distracted by the fact he's bare-chested, propped up on some pillows on his bed, his finger tapping his chin as we watch the last episode of the first season together.

"Jimmy and the twins," he repeats, his lip curling upward. "Good name for the male anatomy."

"You haven't heard that one before?" I ask, smiling because he's smiling. And yep, that makes me a sap, but this is the best part of my day.

Until now I've felt like I've been barely surviving. With trying to do two peoples' work and getting my head around the submission Michael wants me to write, my brain feels constantly full. I should be working now, but I promised I'd do this with him.

And I'm so glad I did. There's something about Liam Salinger that calms me, which is crazy if you think about it. I've spent most of the time I've known him riled up by his presence. But now all I actually wish is that he was here with me watching the show.

"Nope. I know some others though. Johnson, Wang, Baloney pony…"

"Wait!" I shout out. "Baloney pony? That can't be a real phrase."

"Look it up. You want me to keep going?" he asks. "I've got more."

"Just watch the show, Salinger." I smirk and pull my eyes away from him. I've got my own phone balanced in my hand so he can only see my face and shoulders. Like him, I've changed out of my work clothes and into something more comfortable. But for me it's an old t-shirt and a pair of yoga shorts as I lay on the sofa, the flickering of the television lighting up my face.

"I'd rather watch you," he says, his voice low. It sends a shiver down my spine.

"I thought we talked about this," I tell him, but it doesn't stop me from feeling thrilled. I like that he likes me.

I just don't like that he could hurt me if I let him.

"Yeah, but that was before you decided to lay on the sofa."

I lift a brow. "I'm not allowed to lay on my own sofa now?"

"You can lay anywhere you want. It's just that I keep remembering the last time we were on a sofa together."

Oh. I start to blush. "That was… nice."

He winces. "Ouch. Damned with faint praise again."

"Shut up," I say again, but I don't really mean it. I just don't know how to navigate this thing. I've never been so attracted to a man in my life. Especially not one I know is bad for me. The memory of his lips on mine as his fingers worked their magic makes me start to feel hot.

I shift on the sofa, feeling my cheeks begin to burn.

"Sophie…" His voice is low. "Are you remembering it, too?"

"Yeah. I am."

There's no smile on his face anymore. Just an intense look that I recognize from last Saturday. Maybe before that, too. Liam Salinger does good sex face, and I hate that.

I can only imagine how intensely he makes love. My thighs clench tightly.

He clicks his remote and it pauses for the both of us since we're on buddy watch. George freezes on my screen and it occurs to me that neither of us have been paying attention for the last few minutes. We'll have to rewind when we turn it back on.

"Let me look at you," he says.

"You are."

"Properly. Pull the phone back. I want to see all of you."

Heat pools in my stomach. I pull it back and he hums approvingly.

"You look amazing, West."

"It's just an old cropped t-shirt and shorts."

"No, baby. It's your body. You could be wearing a potato sack and you'd be the most beautiful woman I know."

How am I supposed to fight against a man who says things like that? There's an inevitability to this. A thread that's tied us together since we met and it's only getting stronger. I've tried to break it, to cut it, but it keeps on coming back.

I'm falling for this man I shouldn't want.

I lift my hand to push my hair out of my face and he actually moans.

"Christ your stomach. Every time I look at it I remember kissing my way down to your sweet pussy. You know how often I think about it?" he asks me. "Every single fucking second. If I was there right now…"

"What would you do?" I ask, my voice gritty. I know I should stop this. I'm playing with fire. Maybe even leading him on.

But I can't help myself.

"If I was there right now? I'd be behind you, your soft rounded ass against my hard cock. I'd want you to know how turned on I am. I'd want you to know that you own me. And I'd want you to know that I own you, too."

He does. And it scares me. I let out a squeak.

"I'd push my hands inside that t-shirt. And I know you're not wearing a bra, so I'd tease you by tracing the outline of your breasts. I'd do it until your breath is coming in gasps and you're begging me to touch your nipples."

They're already hard, pushing against my t-shirt. I'm almost certain he knows that.

"And then what?"

"I'd turn you around so you're straddling me. Then I'd worship your tits until you don't remember your name. You'd know mine, though, because you'd be moaning it out loud."

"Liam…"

He runs his hand down his bare stomach, his fingers tracing the ridges. "Yeah," he says. "Like that. I'd keep kissing and sucking and scraping my teeth against you, then I'd kiss my way down your sweet stomach to your thighs. I'd be able to smell you, and it'd make me even harder than I already am." He slides his hand under the waistband of what I think are sweatpants, and although I can't see what he's doing, I know.

He's touching himself. And I don't think I've ever seen anything as glorious as that.

"I want to see you," I tell him. "I want to see you touch yourself."

He squeezes his eyes shut for a minute, like he's trying to maintain control. "Yeah?"

"Yes," I whisper. "I want to see your cock." I can't believe I just said that. And yet I love the way it makes his lips part.

He pushes his waistband down his taut hips, but I can't see anything more because of the angle of his phone.

"Your phone," I whisper. "You need to change the angle."

He chuckles. "My good girl has a little bad in her."

Yeah, I do. I remain silent as he moves the phone so I can see him in all his glory. It's thick and veined and glistening at the tip.

"Oh…" I whisper. "It's beautiful."

He laughs again. "Beautiful? Seriously?"

"Yeah." I nod, still staring at him. "It's perfect, Liam."

"You're crazy."

"Touch yourself," I tell him, because I need to see it in action.

"You sure?"

I'm absolutely certain. "Touch yourself until you come."

"Jesus, Sophie." He does as instructed, fisting himself, moving his hand up and down slowly as I watch, enraptured. His thumb slides over his tip, and all I can think about is that it should be my tongue.

I want to worship it like the deity it is.

"I wish I was there," I tell him.

"What would you do?" His voice is tighter. Almost strangled.

"I'd take my clothes off so you could look at my body," I say, my cheeks pinking because I'm not used to talking like this. "Then I'd crawl down the bed, my hair trailing along your stomach, until my mouth is hovering just above you."

"Jesus…" he manages.

"Then slowly, so slow it drives you crazy, I'd slide my lips over your head, then trail my tongue over that glistening tip."

Okay so maybe this is easier than I thought it would be. And it's turning me on, too.

He grunts, as though he doesn't have the words any more. I feel powerful, as though I could bring him to his knees.

"I'd have to curl my hand around you, too," I whisper. "Because you're too big to swallow. Though I'd try."

He almost splutters. For a minute I wonder if he's choking.

But no. Just turned on. So am I, for that matter. Maybe it's a good thing there's hundreds of miles between us because my willpower is non-existent when it comes to him.

"I'd move my head up and down. And you'd thread your fingers through my hair, guiding me because you know that I like to please you. And because you're so turned on, you'd start to fuck my face, using my mouth like you own it."

He's fisting himself harder now, the tip of him swollen and red.

"And I'd be so turned on, too," I whisper. "Because I love the taste of you. The silkiness of your skin beneath my tongue. The hardness of your cock as you hit the back of my throat." I slide my hands down my nipples. They're so sensitive I gasp.

"And then I'd open my legs and trail my fingers between my thighs. Touching myself because you make me so needy."

"Touch yourself now." It's harsh. A command.

I do as I'm told.

"Are you wet?" he asks.

I slide my yoga shorts down because they're way too tight to do this with them on. And then I touch myself.

"So wet," I whisper.

"For me."

"Always for you," I tell him. "Always."

"Slide a finger inside yourself."

"I already have," I admit.

"Such a sweet little pussy. So tight." His breath is ragged. "Tell me it's mine."

I touch my clit with my thumb. The sensation makes me gasp. I'm so close it isn't funny.

How does he do this to me every time?

"It's yours," I tell him.

"Say the words. Be dirty. I want to hear it."

His hand speeds up. His chest rises and falls rapidly. I roll my hips as I mimic his rhythm with my own fingers, wishing he was here with me.

"You own my body, Liam," I say. "My pussy is yours."

He groans and his hand stills. I watch as he surges, come spilling out of him, over his hand and stomach. A moment later I follow him into oblivion, my own body pulsing around my fingers as the pleasure uncoils in me, my hips lifting from the sofa as I let out a low sigh.

And when I open my eyes he's staring intently at me. I stare back, waiting for the embarrassment to come. Because it should. I just touched myself in front of a guy I'm trying to not fall for. And I watched him come on his stomach, wishing I was there to lick it off.

"Put your fingers in your mouth," he tells me, as though he can read my mind. "Let me watch you taste yourself."

I don't think I've ever been this openly sexual with a man before. Certainly not on Facetime. But I do as he says, sliding my fingers between my lips, my tongue fluttering on them.

And he groans again.

"Next time that'll be my cock."

"Next time?" I say.

"Yep. I'm flying home tomorrow night."

I frown. "I thought you had meetings in New York all week."

"I do. I'll fly back to New York the next morning."

I wait for him to laugh. To tell me he's just kidding. Why the hell would he fly from New York just for one night?

To see me. The thought of it is a thrill I can't ignore.

And then I remember the stupid submission I need to do. I'm going to have to work on it every evening this week and next if I'm going to finish on time."

"I can't," I say. "I have to do some work."

He's holding the phone so I can only see his face. He's completely composed now. If I didn't know he just came so hard he covered his stomach, I would barely believe it.

"Are you saying that because you don't want to see me or because you actually have work to do?" he asks.

"I do want to see you," I admit. "But I have this stupid submission thing to write. It has to be done by next week. I'm going to be working on it every evening. I'll have to work on it when we finish watching this episode."

"Tell me about it," he says.

"You'd be bored. It's nothing interesting."

"Everything you do is interesting to me. So tell me."

He listens carefully as I explain the plan for regional hubs, and the fact that Michael wants me to write our submission.

"I don't like that guy," he says.

I wrinkle my nose. "I know, but hopefully this will get me more exposure. Maybe even a promotion so he's not my boss anymore."

He nods. "So it's important. I understand."

A mess of emotions wash through me. He knows my job is important to me, and even though I earn a fraction of what he does, and have so much less power, it doesn't seem to faze him. I like that a lot.

But that respect he has for my work means I'm not going to see him tomorrow. And I'm so disappointed.

"I'll be to yours by eight," he says. "We can work on it together. I've written more proposals than I care to think about."

I blink. "You're still coming?"

He laughs. "I've no idea. It depends on how much progress we make on your work. But you'll be coming. I'll make sure of that."

"I didn't mean that." I roll my eyes.

"I know." He smirks. "But I did. Shall we watch the rest of Grey's now?"

"Um, yeah," I say, my heart hammering against my rib cage.

He's flying back to see me. And I'm stupidly excited about that.

CHAPTER
TWENTY

SOPHIE

When I walk into the office the next morning the biggest bouquet of flowers I've ever seen is obscuring my computer screen. Lisa is standing in front of them, a white card in her hand.

"From L again," she says, looking completely unembarrassed at the fact she opened the card intended for me. She lifts her brows. "From LaClasse."

LaClasse is a gorgeous flower boutique in the historic district of Charleston. It's hugely expensive which means I've never used it, but I've been to a few weddings where they've been responsible for the décor.

And they always hit it out of the park.

I pluck the card from Lisa's fingers and lift a brow as I read the words there.

Sophie, I asked the shop to give you the

most beautiful flowers they have. But they'll still pale in comparison to you. Tonight. L.

"Can you imagine the shop owner having to write that out?" Lisa asks, amused. "They must be pissed, right? He's dissing their flowers."

I laugh, because I guess she's right. "He's just being sweet."

"So are you going to tell us who *he* is?" she asks.

I open my mouth but close it firmly again as Michael walks into the room. There's no way I'm telling him anything about my private life.

"What are those flowers doing there?" he asks, his gaze flickering over to my desk.

"They're from a friend." My tone screams that I'm not interested in having a conversation about this.

"Oh." Luckily he's not interested either. To him I'm just the person he pushes all of his work onto. "How's the submission going?" he asks and I try not to smirk because he really is that predictable.

"Fine. I worked on it all last night and I'll do the same tonight."

"We need to have it in by next Friday," he reminds me, as if I don't already know. "Donald already asked me to give him an update. He wants it done right."

"It will be. I'll have it ready." It takes a lot of effort not to roll my eyes. Luckily he's distracted by his phone pinging. Ignoring me completely, he pulls it out of his pocket.

"Gotta go," Lisa says to me, shooting Michael's back a murderous look. "Let's grab a coffee after the lunchtime news? Catch up on things?"

"If I get the chance." I look balefully at Michael.

"I'll be in the café." She winks. "In the back booth." The one where other people can't overhear. She wants to grill me about Liam, that much is obvious.

She lifts a hand to wave goodbye and I move the huge-ass bouquet of flowers onto the filing cabinet next to my desk so I can actually get some work done today. And I pocket the card because I don't want Michael seeing it.

———

I arrive at the café a little late, because I had to stay behind to record a new forecast for the website. There's a storm pattern forming and our viewers love it when we give them the heads up, so I tell them as though it's a secret between us.

"It might or might not happen," I tell them. "But as always, the weather team at WVFY will keep you updated with the latest developments. Keep checking the page and we'll make sure you don't get wet."

People love a change in weather pattern, especially something disruptive like a storm. And the station loves it because it increases our viewership and our website visits – which increases the amount they can charge for advertising.

Lisa sees me as soon as I walk in and points at the table to let me know she's already bought my coffee. As I walk over, I pull my phone out to check any missed messages. There's a kiss from Liam in reply to my text thanking him for the flowers and giving him his daily forecast. After that is a message from Lauren asking why I've gone silent since Sunday, and one from Ava with an attachment of Charlie gurgling at a stuffie I bought him. I remind myself to message my friends later. I miss them. Ava's hugely busy with work and Charlie, and Lauren's always overrun at the bakery, but we've never not found time for each other.

I slide into the booth and smile at Lisa. "Thank you for the coffee."

"I got you a pastry, too," she says, sliding a Danish across to me. "Thought it might loosen your tongue."

I laugh. "You don't need to bribe me. There's not that much to tell. He's just a friend right now."

"Friends don't send you lunch one day then flowers the next."

"I think he wants to be more than friends," I admit.

"Of course he does." She claps her hands together. "Tell me more."

I tell her as quickly as possible about Liam, skirting over the physical stuff because that's private, and as much as I like Lisa I'd hate to tell her about this before I tell Ava. She'd be hurt if she found out, and I'd hate that. So nobody gets all the gossip before she and Lauren do.

Just as soon as I'm ready to tell them. Which I'm not. Yet.

"Yep," Lisa says when I finish speaking. "Definitely not just a friend. That guy is into you."

"Do you think he might just want what he can't have?" I ask her. This idea is still playing on my mind. I don't think he'd be doing it on purpose, but he's an alpha male. A high achiever who always gets what he wants.

But when he gets me? Because it's definitely a when, not an if. What happens then?

There's every chance he'll get bored of me. And that thought makes my chest hurt. Because as much as I've been trying not to, it's obvious I'm falling for this man.

"No. He's been watching Grey's with you," Lisa says, as though that explains everything. "Men don't do that if they're only after one thing."

"Are you sure?" I frown.

"He's wooing you. Can't you see that? The guy's got it bad." She grins. "The only question is, how do you feel?"

My chest tightens. "I like him," I admit.

"Of course you do. He's hot." She staring at her phone. I can't believe she's already googled him. "I can't believe he's flying back from New York just for tonight. That's so romantic."

Yeah it is. I exhale heavily.

"I don't get it," Lisa says, looking up at me. "Why aren't you bouncing off the ceiling? I would be if a guy wanted me as much as he wants you."

She's right. I should be. And part of me is. The romantic part that believes in Fairytales and Prince Charming and Happily Ever Afters. Liam was right all along. I do want those things. But can he give them to me?

Because when did Prince Charming ever say he didn't sleep with a woman more than once because he didn't want her to get the wrong idea?

"He's not good at commitment," I finally tell her. "And I'm not good at getting my heart broken."

She looks at me for a moment. I've sat with her through enough breakups for her to understand this sentiment. "The problem is," she says. "I think you'll be heartbroken if you walk away from him. But that'll be self-imposed."

Her words land like a thud in my brain. She's right, I'm not sure I can walk away from him if I tried.

And if I'm honest, I don't want to try.

I want him to come see me tonight. I want him to want me so bad he can't stay away. And I want to see where this goes.

It's a leap in the dark. But maybe those are the best kind of leaps. The ones that send your heart racing as you jettison yourself off the edge.

I just hope he's there to catch me on the other side.

LIAM

. . .

"So I'll be at yours by seven," Eli says. I'm only half-paying attention to him because I have a pile of reports to read before I head to the airport and I need to be prepared for my meetings tomorrow. But this last sentence cuts through. I lift my gaze from the numbers on the paper.

"What?" I ask.

Eli laughs. "Did you listen to a word I just said? I'm driving up to New York now. I have a meeting with a sponsor in the morning. I'm staying at your place and we're going out. Did that sink in this time?"

"I can't. I'm flying to Charleston tonight."

"You said you were in New York all week." Eli sounds genuinely confused.

"I'll be back in New York tomorrow," I tell him.

"Wait a minute," Eli says. "So you're flying to Charleston tonight and back to New York tomorrow? Why the hell are you doing that? You can't possibly have a business meeting in the middle of the night."

"There's somebody I need to see."

"Who?" he asks. I can hear the confusion in his voice.

"Sophie."

There's a pause. Then a cough. "Sophie as in Ava's Sophie? The one night woman? The one you want to avoid?"

"Yes," I say calmly. "That Sophie."

"But... but... you just called me for advice on how to avoid her. You didn't want to get involved, remember?"

My mouth twitches. That feels like a lifetime ago. Before I realized what I'd been fighting for so long.

That I wasn't just attracted to her. I was in love with her. It all makes sense now as I look back. "By the way, I never spent the night with her. That was a lie."

"What?"

"She lied to me. We didn't have sex." I'm kind of amused by that whole situation.

"But why did she do that? I'm so confused, man."

"I'd like to explain but it's going to take a while. Can we discuss it at dinner tomorrow?" I ask him. "I need to get some things done before I head to the airport."

He lets out a sigh. "Yes we can, but I need to be elsewhere tomorrow. I'm back in New York next Tuesday. Can we meet then?"

"Sure." I don't want to, if I'm being perfectly honest. I want to be in my bed Facetiming with Sophie. But this is Eli and I do have some loyalty. "I'll book a restaurant for us."

"I suppose there's no point in suggesting we go out to a club after dinner?"

"No there isn't." I'm trying to prove to Sophie that I'm the man she doesn't think I can be. I don't want to give her a reason to doubt me. Plus we have sixteen more seasons of *Grey's Anatomy* to watch.

And yes, I said I had loyalty to my brother but it only extends to dinner. I'd rather be in my room watching a decade old show with her than prowling a club with Eli. That's how much of a hold this woman has on me.

"First Myles, now you. I'm gonna call Holden. He can go out with me."

"Good idea," I say warmly. "I'll ask my assistant to book a table for three, then the two of you can go do whatever it is you like." While I go home. To call Sophie.

"Hmph. Whatever. I'll book a VIP table at Silk's in case you change your mind."

"I won't," I say, feeling smug because I don't even feel like I'm missing out. "Talk to you later."

"Can I still sleep at your place tonight, even if you're not there?" he asks quickly. "I haven't booked a hotel room."

"Sure," I say magnanimously, even though Eli can be a bit of a slob when it comes to taking care of my things. "I'll ask the concierge to let you in."

I hang up and check my phone for the time. There's a

message from Sophie, and like a sap my heart does this little weird twist in my chest.

> Hi! Was just wondering if you're still getting here by eight. I'll cook for you if you'd like. – Sophie.

Yeah, I do like. I mean I love cooking but I like being cooked for, too. By Sophie at least.

I start to type out that I'm hoping she'll be naked when she opens the door but I delete it. Fucking baby steps, Salinger.

Don't scare her now.

I start again.

> I'll be there by eight. No need to cook if you don't want to. I can bring something, or eat on the plane. – Liam x

> Don't be silly. You'll be tired. I'd like to cook for you. I owe you one after all. ;) – Sophie.

> Are we still talking about dinner? – Liam. x

> Maybe… – Sophie.

A soppy grin pulls at my mouth.

CHAPTER
TWENTY-ONE

SOPHIE

There's half an hour until Liam's due to arrive at my apartment, and there's something I need to do that I've been putting off all afternoon. So I pull up my contacts and scroll down to the S section. I'm surprised at just how many Salingers I have in there now, as I click the one that I need to speak to.

Liam's mom answers within two rings.

"Sophie, how lovely to hear from you." That's the thing about Linda Salinger. She always makes you feel like you're the person she's been dying to talk to all day. Ava always says Myles gets his charisma from his dad, but as far as I'm concerned his mom is pretty charming, too. "How are you?" she asks.

"I'm good, and you?"

"Oh you know, busy." She laughs. "But then what woman isn't busy? And it's all self-imposed. Are you still able to come to the party next Saturday?"

"Of course. I'm looking forward to it," I tell her. "Thank you again for the invitation."

"Are you driving over with Ava and Myles?" she asks. And again it feels like she genuinely wants to know. Maybe I have a mom fixation.

"No, I think they're planning to stay. I'll drive over on Saturday afternoon then home that evening." I wrinkle my nose. It's a hell of a drive from here. Maybe I should look at booking a hotel room and stay the night.

"It's such a long drive. I'll be worried about you on those country roads late at night."

"Honestly, I'll be fine. I'm used to driving at night. I'll make sure I'm safe." And then I swallow because there's some news I need to share. "Also, um, there might be some rain next Saturday. We're monitoring a storm system, and it's too early to say if it'll hit or not, but I wanted you to be aware." I don't try to explain that it's a mesoscale storm that we noticed forming in the radars today. Most people get bored when I try to get technical. But if we're right it's a series of thunderstorms that could last up to six hours if it hits badly.

I'm hoping we're wrong though.

"Oh dear." Her voice lowers. "Do you know how much rain?"

"Not yet. It's looking like a summer thunderstorm," I try to reassure her. "One of those that passes on after a few hours. I'm so sorry to be the bearer of bad news. I can't give you an accurate time estimate yet, but we'll be keeping a close eye on it over the next week."

"Oh sweetie, don't sound so sad," Linda says. "The weather isn't your fault. And it's better to be forewarned, right? I'll make sure that we have a contingency to move inside if the weather doesn't hold."

"Thank you for being so understanding."

"Thank you for giving me the heads up," she says. "And if

there's a possibility of rain, then that settles it. You'll have to stay with us at the house overnight. I'm not having you drive home in a storm."

"It might not even happen," I tell her. "And if it does there's every likelihood it will pass over by evening. It shouldn't cause any problems with my drive home."

"Nonsense, I won't hear of it. Even if there's a possibility of bad weather you shouldn't drive alone at night. Please stay, I insist."

I need to talk to Liam about this. I don't want him thinking… I've no idea what I don't want him thinking. But it feels like I'm getting cozy with his family when he might not like that. "Let me just check my plans," I tell her.

"Of course. But there's a room for you if you need one."

"Thank you."

It's funny because Linda doesn't actually live at Misty Lakes anymore. It belongs to her ex-husband, Rupert, and he lives there with his third wife, Julia, and their baby. And yet there's this whole family vibe going on. Linda, and Rupert's other ex wife, Deandra, are best friends and they're close with Julia, too.

Whenever there's a family party they're always together. And if I'm being honest, I'm a little bit envious of their big family. Being an only child and having lost my mom, it's so nice to watch them all come together and have fun.

We end the conversation and I put my phone down, walking into the kitchen to check on dinner. I agonized over what to make. I'm not as good of a cook as Liam but I'm also not terrible like Ava. I can follow a recipe but I can't add any flair.

And yet there's still a part of me that's excited to cook for him. I don't often get to do this for anybody other than my dad. So I check on the chicken and potatoes and quickly set the table in my little kitchen, adding two wine glasses because I think I might need some Dutch courage.

It's two minutes before eight when the intercom buzzes. I walk to the hall and check my appearance in the mirror – passable – then press the intercom button.

"Hello?"

"It's me."

My muscles do a weird clench. I hit the door release. "Come on up."

It takes less than a minute for him to take the elevator up to the third floor and knock on my door.

When I pull open the door, he looks even better than I remember. He's wearing a gray suit and a white shirt, no tie, and his hair is mussed like he's been raking his fingers through it. His eyes catch mine and he smiles.

And I know I'm done for.

"Hi," I whisper.

"Hi." His smile widens. "Are you gonna let me in or would you prefer that I stay in the hallway?"

Oh God, what a way to start. I step aside and invite him in, and the smell of his cologne fills my senses.

"How was your flight?" I ask him.

"It was passable. I managed to get some work done." He watches as I close the door before he cups my face with his warm palm. "You look beautiful." He leans down to give me the briefest of kisses. Little more than a feather of his lips against mine.

And yet it sets me on fire.

"You look pretty good, too," I tell him, tipping my head so he follows me to the kitchen. "No bag?"

"Hmm?"

"Didn't you pack a suitcase for tonight?" I grab the wine from the refrigerator. I splurged on this one, knowing that Liam is used to the best.

"I brought a carry on. It's in the car."

Oh. So he's not staying. I try to hide my dismay. "I guess you won't want any wine then."

He curls his fingers around my chin and tips my head until I'm looking at him. His brows knit. "Are you upset that I'm not staying?"

"No." I shake my head. "I just… I don't know. Assumed you would."

He nods. "And I didn't want to assume. My bag is in my car, Sophie. If I need it I'll get it, okay?"

My chest feels full. Like I've breathed in way too much air and have no way of exhaling it. "I want you to get it," I tell him. He's still holding my chin, his thumb caressing my jawline.

"Thank you," he says.

"What for?"

"For saying what you want. For being honest. I needed that tonight." The oven beeps and I remember the chicken.

"I need to…" I gesture at the oven.

"Of course. Do I have time to get my bag now or shall I wait until after dinner?"

"Get it now," I tell him, because I need it settled. He gives me the sweetest of smiles before he heads out to get it.

And a few minutes later we're sitting at my kitchen table, his case standing sentry in the hallway like a soldier ready for action. I cut my chicken, breathing a sigh of relief when I see it's cooked through, because when he cooked for me it was perfect.

"I spoke to your mom earlier," I tell him when I've swallowed a mouthful.

"I know."

"How?" I ask. "It was like twenty minutes ago."

"I'm on a group chat with her and my brothers. She's throwing Eli out of his cabin and making him share with Holden for the night of the party so you'll have somewhere to stay."

My eyes widen. "Oh no."

"It's fine. Eli's used to sleeping wherever he's told. He

travels a lot."

"I guess he does." I've spoken to Eli a few times. He seems very chill. "But I can't let him lose his cabin."

"I could tell them you'll stay in mine," he says, sliding a potato into his mouth.

"Nooo."

He tips his head to the side. "Why not?"

"Because then they'll know about us."

His lips curls. "I like it when you say us."

"You know what I mean," I tell him, trying not to smile. He makes it impossible to frown when he's around.

He puts his fork down on his plate and lifts his head. "Why wouldn't you want them to know about us?"

"Because I don't know what *us* is," I tell him. "And maybe it's too early for there to be an us at all."

His eyes don't leave mine. "There is an us. I think the past few weeks have proven that."

"But what if you decide you only want one night after all?" I ask him. "What if we're not sexually compatible?" My cheeks are burning. I'm overthinking but that's just my thing.

"I have no fucking doubt we're sexually compatible, Sophie." His stare is dark and I swallow hard, remembering how easily he can arouse me. "What are you really afraid of?" he asks.

"You," I say simply. "I'm afraid of falling for you and getting hurt."

"Now we're getting somewhere." He nods approvingly. And damn if I don't feel that little thrill again. I have no idea why I want his approval so much. "Okay then, there's only one option."

"What?" I ask, bemused.

"We'll have to get married."

I start to laugh, only trailing off when I realize he isn't laughing, too. Wait, is he serious? He can't be. He's the play-boy, the lothario, the one-night-only man.

"You can't go around proposing just because you need to prove something," I tell him. I shift in my chair. "That's just..." I trail off because I don't even have the words for it. "You just can't."

He doesn't look embarrassed. Or regretful. Just amused. "Isn't that what marriage is? Proving to the world that you're together? If people were just proving it to themselves they wouldn't have the lavish ceremony or the dinner and party. It's all about showing the world that you're taken."

"Liam, we haven't even slept together. You can't start talking about commitment."

"Technically, we slept together that first night. We woke up in the same bed, remember? And we did it again recently."

"You know what I mean," I say pointedly.

"Okay, we'll stop talking about marriage. For now. But I have no idea how to get you to trust me. I've never done this before." He looks pensive. "I wish I could change my past. I wish I could go back in time and not be that guy you described. Hell, I wish I could go back in time and treat you the way you deserved from the beginning. Even then I think I knew you were the one. I just fought against it because I was scared."

He reaches across the table, taking my hand in his. And I'm so aware of the irony of this situation. I'm the one who wants commitment. Who doesn't want to be another notch on somebody else's bedpost.

And now that he's offering it, I'm petrified.

"Tell me who hurt you," he says softly.

"What?" I blink at the sudden change in direction.

"What makes you so afraid of relationships?"

"I'm not afraid of them," I tell him. "You're the one who avoids relationships."

"And yet you're the one putting obstacles in our way. And I don't think it's because you don't want me. The chemistry between us is unbelievable. And I don't think it's because you think I'm lying either. It's because of you. Something in here." He touches his chest over his heart. "And I want to know because we can't let it stop us."

"This is not how I saw tonight going," I admit to him.

He tips his head to the side. "What did you think we'd be doing?"

"Having hot sex as soon as you walked in the door."

His jaw twitches. "That was on my mind, too."

Our gazes clash. I feel heat suffusing my skin.

"But I'm not here just for sex, Sophie. I'm here because I like you. I enjoy spending time with you."

"I know," I tell him. "And I want that, too. I just don't know how to stop this feeling inside of me." I touch my own chest. It's so tight.

"How about we take it slow?" he says softly. "Let's clear the table, put on some music, and we can take a look at the work you talked about.

The submission. I can't believe I forgot about that. "You remembered." Thank goodness somebody did.

"Of course I did. It's important to you."

I feel another rock in the wall between us crumbling. The wall I built because I wanted to protect myself. There are a few gaps now. Created by his kind words. His flowers, his lunches, his reactions to Derek still being married while sleeping with Meredith.

He's so right. I'm the one who's fighting this when I thought it would always be him. I want to believe him. I need to.

It's just going to take time.

"I'll make us coffee," I suggest. "Then we can work here at the table if that's okay?"

"That's more than okay," he says. "And I'll make the coffee. It's the least I can do to thank you for dinner."

CHAPTER
TWENTY-TWO

SOPHIE

I get to see another side of Liam tonight. First of all, he wears reading glasses – something I never knew about him. And damn if he doesn't look hot as hell with them on the bridge of his nose as he leans over the report I've printed out.

He's taken off his jacket and rolled up his sleeves so I keep sneaking glances at his strong forearms. Who knew I'd have a thing for those too?

He also can't stop touching me. He'll be talking about profit and loss one moment, then he'll cup my jaw and lean forward to kiss my brow the next. Then he'll take my hand, turning it over so he can trace the vein on my wrist, his fingers circling the inside of my elbow which apparently is a huge erotic zone.

Or at least it is for me.

I'm turned on like crazy and trying to concentrate on this submission because I need to get it done as quickly as possible. Luckily he doesn't seem phased by my gasping response to his every touch.

He's all businessman and somehow that makes me want him more.

"If you move that paragraph up it will have more impact," he tells me, leaning across to point at the screen of my laptop. "Remember, they'll make their mind up before they read the substance. They want you to persuade them that you're the best choice on the first page. It makes their life easier."

"Do you make your mind up on the first page?" I ask him, interested.

He gives me a crooked smile. "No. But I'm unusual, I've come to learn that. I need the substance before I can visualize whether something is going to work. I don't trust what I see on the surface."

He's standing behind me now, leaning over my chair so he can point out more things to change about my submission. If it was anybody else I'd probably be annoyed, but this doesn't feel like micromanagement. Every suggestion he gives makes my words look better. And by the time eleven o'clock rolls around I'm actually feeling like I might finish it before the deadline.

"It's late," I say to him. "What time do you need to leave in the morning?"

"I have an eight o'clock flight."

My eyes widen. "That's like nine hours away. And you'll have to leave here at six. You need some sleep." I push closed my laptop, feeling guilty that we've spent most of the night on my work. "We didn't even get to watch Grey's."

"That's not why I'm here." He takes my hand and I stand, turning to face him. He lifts it to his lips, kissing the inside of my wrist.

My thighs clench.

"I'm not here for that either," he says as though he can read my mind.

"Then why are you here?" I ask him, my voice low.

"Because I can't stay away from you. You're like a magnet.

I'll be in a meeting about derivatives and then I'll picture the way your lips curl when you smile and I forget what the hell I'm supposed to be talking about. Or I'll be out on a run and all I want to do is keep fucking running to wherever you are." He pushes a stray hair from my face. "And yeah, I keep imagining what it's like to be inside of you, too. Mostly because I want to know how you feel on me when you come. I want to swallow your gasps. I want to see your skin flush. I want to smell you all over me."

"You're so intense," I breathe.

His lip quirks. "I know. And if my brothers could hear me now they'd laugh." His brow dips. "Well, Eli kind of knows."

"He does?" I'm intrigued.

He runs a finger down my shoulder, pulling me close with his other hand, his palm cupping my waist. "I didn't understand this pull you have over me. I needed to talk to somebody about it. I hope you don't mind."

"What did he tell you to do about me?" I ask him.

"I couldn't understand why I was still so attracted to you. Why I couldn't push you out of my thoughts. Of course now I understand. It wasn't just sexual attraction. It was *more*. But back then..." He shakes his head. "I just wanted to stop wanting you." He pulls me even closer, until our bodies touch. Then he lowers his face. "He thought I could get over you. He was wrong."

I lift my head up to look at him. There's the strangest look on his face. Like he's not quite sure he can believe he's here. I'm not sure I can either. It's hard to remember the man who drove me crazy with his jabs, and teasing, and one-upmanship. This man is completely different.

Maybe that's why I feel so insecure about this.

"Did he tell you to talk to me?" I whisper.

Liam shakes his head. "He told me to sleep with somebody else."

I suddenly feel sick. "And did you?" The words can barely

escape my mouth. I don't want to know, yet I do. He's a grown man and at that point he didn't owe me anything. He could do what he wanted with whoever he wanted.

And yet I'm completely consumed with jealousy.

"No." He shakes his head. "I haven't slept with anybody. Not in a very long time."

I must look skeptical because he starts to laugh.

"I'm not lying. I know you all think I'm this sex addict who constantly needs to be surrounded by women. But after that morning when I woke up with you and couldn't remember a thing..." He takes a deep breath. "Something changed."

"Wait." I put my hand on his chest. "You haven't slept with anybody since then?"

He shakes his head. "No."

"But that was months ago. Like almost a year."

"I know." His gaze softens. "I've done the math."

"I haven't slept with anybody either," I whisper. "It's been... a while."

He nods slowly. "It's wrong to say I'm pleased about that, but I am." He slides the hand that was holding my waist around to my back, his fingers caressing my spine. "Shall we go to bed?" he asks.

I nod silently. He smiles and takes my hand, leading me down the hallway to my room. I push open the door and pull him inside, glad that I had enough time to change the sheets and tidy up when I got home. I redecorated this room as soon as I moved in and I love the pinks and golds.

"I like your room," he says, and I flush because I still love it when he compliments me.

"Thank you. Do you want to use the bathroom first?" I ask. "It's over there." I point at the door on the far side of the room.

"Why don't you go first? I need to get my bag, I left it in the hallway."

"Sure." I nod. "Sounds good."

I walk into my bathroom and close the door, leaning heavily on it. This whole evening has felt strangely domesticated. He came home from work, I cooked dinner for us, and then we spent the evening working on my report. If you ignore the fact he also flew for hours to see me, we could be a long established couple.

And we haven't even had sex yet.

My core clenches at the thought. Has he really not been with anybody in all these months? It's almost unbelievable that a man as sexual as Liam Salinger can abstain for that amount of time and yet…

It makes my legs feel weak, too. Because he's not the only one who's falling here.

I brush my teeth and jump in the shower because there's no way I'm sleeping with Liam Salinger without being freshly shaved. But I don't wash my hair because it takes too long to dry – I'll do it in the morning before work. Finally I rub my wrinkle cream and moisturizer into my face and check my appearance in the mirror.

"It's okay," I whisper to my reflection who looks as nervous as I feel. "You've got this."

When I walk out of the bathroom Liam is leaning over his bag. He's unbuttoned his shirt so it kind of flares out, and when he turns to look at me I can see his bare chest, his taut stomach, and the beginning of his hips as they disappear into his gray pants.

He's absolutely perfect. I think I make a sound like a cat. A kind of a meow that makes him grin.

"You look petrified," he tells me.

"I think I am." Why is this man-god obsessed by me? I'm worried he's going to find me out. Discover I'm just not that interesting. And by then I'll be in way too deep.

He walks over to me and cups my cheeks with his hands.

"We don't have to do anything tonight," he says. "Just let me hold you."

"But I want to," I tell him. The thought of him leaving in the morning and not having felt him inside of me is too much. "I want you."

"Let me shower first," he tells me. "I'm sweaty."

"I don't know that I can wait," I tell him honestly.

He laughs, looking gratified. "You look beautiful." He trails his finger along the towel where I've wrapped it around my chest. "Flushed. Clean. Warm." He kisses my lips. A sweet kiss, yet it still sets me on fire. "Give me five minutes. I'll be back before you know it."

I sit on the bed as he disappears into the bathroom. It's only a few seconds before I hear the running of the tap and I imagine him stepping naked into my shower. Then I think about last night, about the way he touched himself. My breath stutters.

When he walks out, he has one of my white towels wrapped around his hips and nothing else. His hair is damp, his body as flushed as mine.

"I think that's the first time I've showered without playing with jimmy and the girls in about a year," he tells me.

I laugh because he knows how to diffuse every awkward situation. I like the way he's so open, so funny, so real.

I like him. Too much. But I'll just have to come to terms with that. And to distract myself from that thought, I stand and pull off my towel until I'm naked in front of him.

"Fuck." His eyes roam my body, and suddenly it's me who feels like a god. "You really don't want me to get any sleep tonight, do you?" He walks toward me, his eyes dark, his jaw tight, then to my surprise he drops to his knees.

And breathes me in.

"You're bare." His voice is a strangled whisper as his nose presses against the apex of my legs.

"Yes," I tell him. "For you."

"Jesus." He inhales me again, and it doesn't feel weird like it probably should. He looks transfixed, like I'm a drug to him. His nose brushes my clit and my thighs automatically clench.

When he stands, his erection grazes my leg. "I feel like a kid in a candy shop," he tells me. "I've no idea which part of you to kiss first."

"You could try my lips."

"Old fashioned," he murmurs. "I like it." And then he does just that, brushing his mouth against mine, his hand steadies my neck as his lips start to move. I kiss him back, letting out a sigh as my breasts press against his chest, the scant hair stimulating my nipples. He slides his tongue against mine, a growl in his throat, before he pushes me back on the bed until my body meets the mattress.

He leans over me, kissing my mouth, my throat, the swell of my breasts. He's tracing my skin and telling me how beautiful I am and how he's dreamed about my body. He's wetting my nipples with his tongue, then scraping his teeth against them, and I have to clutch his shoulders to hang on.

When his mouth reaches my stomach, his chest between my thighs, I realize something. Being bare is different. It makes everything more sensitive. Even his chest grazing my thighs is making me heat up to boiling point.

And when he runs his tongue along my seam, I almost buck off the bed. He puts his hands on my pelvis to steady me, still kissing me there. Then his fingers join his tongue, teasing the pleasure from me, my hips pushing against his face as I call out his name.

When he slides his fingers inside of me I'm gone. Stars explode behind my eyes, breath pushes out of my lungs, and my thighs contract until I think my body might hit the ceiling. He keeps licking me, touching me, making the most sensitive part of me tighten again and again. I pull at his hair until he looks up, his face glistening from me.

"I need you," I whisper. And he knows what I mean because I hear the snap of a condom before he crawls over my body. His expression is strangely tender as I open my thighs for him, the heavy weight of his body a welcome pressure to my sensitive skin. I cup his face, not afraid of tasting myself on his mouth, and kiss him until we're both breathless.

"Now," I tell him.

He answers me with a surge of his hips, stretching me so wide I have to take a deep breath to get used to it.

His eyes catch mine. "Okay?" he asks me.

"More," I reply, and he gives me just that. Another rock of his body against mine and I'm so full of him that I'm not sure where he begins and I end. He stills as though he knows I need time to adjust.

His hand cups my face. "I'm never gonna stop wanting you."

"Fuck me," I tell him.

And he does. Sliding his hand down my thigh he hitches my leg over his shoulder, the other still wrapped around his waist. The angle makes my eyes widen, as his hips slam into mine, making pleasure coil in every muscle. My breath is escaping in pants as I start to see those stars again.

"Liam…" I cry out, my fingers digging into his shoulders. My breath is ragged, my body moving so fast with his.

"That's it," he whispers. "Come on my cock."

His words make me clench around him and he lets out a long, strangled groan. He tips his hips slightly, so every movement hits me right there, and within a heartbeat I'm clenching him again, but this time it doesn't stop as I call out his name and fly over the edge.

He stops moving for a moment, then I feel him surging inside of me, and he calls out my name before he kisses me hard. I'm still coming and so is he, and for a moment I wonder if we're ever going to stop.

It takes a while, I have to admit. And then I'm too sated to move.

His lips press against my throat, then move up to my mouth. "You're mine," he whispers, then he kisses me.

Yes I am. Truth be told, I think I've been his since the day we met. We've been fighting against this for so long.

And now we're together and it's perfect. And dammit, I start to cry.

"Are you hurt?" he whispers. "Jesus, did I hurt you?"

I shake my head. "I'm just feeling emotional."

"I can deal with emotions." He kisses away my tears then kisses my lips again. "Tell me how you feel."

"Sated. Overwhelmed. Scared…"

"Always scared." He looks almost sad. "We're gonna have to work on that one." He gently pulls out of me, holding the condom in place. "I'll be back," he tells me, climbing off the bed and disappearing into the bathroom. When he comes back I've already burrowed beneath the sheets because I feel too exposed.

"Come here," he whispers, climbing in next to me. He pulls me against him so my face is on his chest. "There's no need to be scared," he tells me. "I'm not going to hurt you." He kisses the top of my head and it so sweet the tears threaten again. "I'm going to take care of you. I wasn't lying when I told you that you're mine. You think I'm going to hurt something that belongs to me? It'd be like hurting myself."

I look up at him. There's so much sincerity in his voice, in his face. And I think I fall a little more. "Thank you," I whisper, because this man seems to understand me.

"I'm the one who should thank you." He strokes my hair tenderly, "Now go to sleep. You look exhausted."

"You're the one who has to catch a plane at a stupid time in the morning."

He gives me the softest of smiles. "I don't care. It was worth it to sleep with you in my arms."

CHAPTER
TWENTY-THREE

LIAM

The next week I walk out of the shiny skyscraper that houses Salinger Enterprises and into the humid New York evening. It's almost too warm to be walking outside, but I can't be bothered to take a car to the restaurant where I've arranged to meet Eli and Holden. It's only a few blocks and I can call Sophie as I walk.

We've spent the last week together, even if it's mostly been virtual. We've also gotten to season three of *Grey's Anatomy*, but don't ask me what's happened because I have no damn idea. I'm too busy staring at her.

Or telling her to touch herself.

She's fucking mesmerizing and I feel like I'm walking around with a permanent hard-on just thinking about her.

"Hi," she says as she picks up after the third ring. "Are you going to keep calling me every two hours forever?" She sounds happy and I like that.

"Yep," I tell her, because she needs to get used to me. "How was your day?"

"Long. But I'm home now, so…"

"What are you doing? I ask, picturing her apartment. I liked it a lot. It was like Sophie in real estate form. Pretty yet classic, and completely comfortable to be inside.

My mouth twitches at the memory of her clenching around me. We woke up twice more that first night. Or more specifically, I kind of woke her up because I couldn't stop touching her. It's a burden I have to carry.

But each time she'd pull me to her and we'd make love. The first time she lay on top of me, her body lazily sliding over mine. I think I came harder than I ever have in my life.

The second time she insisted on blowing me first. Her warm mouth was velvety and welcoming.

And this is how it ends. Death by orgasm. Or more specifically, death by Sophie West. And you know what? I'm okay with that.

"I'm cooking dinner and making those changes we talked about on the report," she tells me, bringing me out of my sex-induced memories. "Thank you for looking it over again."

She's been working on it for a week. I'm impressed by her diligence. And I showed her so over the weekend when I got down on my knees and worshipped her as she worked.

I'd gotten her to send it to me this morning and spent most of my flight marking up pieces that I thought could be tightened up. At first I was worried she'd be insulted by me changing her wording around but she couldn't be happier.

And that makes me happy.

"You think you'll make your deadline?" I ask her.

"Yes," she says cheerily. "I'll be able to send it over tomorrow afternoon. Then I can relax. At least it'll get Michael off my back."

I try not to let out a growl because I dislike that guy a lot. "We can celebrate over the weekend, You're still coming to Misty Lakes, right?"

She'd better be. Going to my mom's birthday party at my

dad's estate isn't exactly how I'd like to spend this weekend. But the fact she'll be there will make the party more bearable.

"Yes. I'm going to drive there on Saturday morning. What time are you planning on getting there?"

I feel a hard slap on my back. Being in New York I immediately fear the worst, spinning around to confront my attacker. If they have a knife I'll fucking run, but if they don't I'll hit back.

But instead of a glowering criminal I'm greeted by my brother's grinning face.

"Jesus Christ, Eli. I was about to hit you in the gut."

Eli's grin doesn't waver. "You wouldn't dare."

"Are you talking to Eli?" Sophie asks.

"Yes. I'm meeting him and Holden for dinner." A few years ago Myles would have been here, too.

"Have a lovely time," she tells me.

"I'm heading back to my place afterward," I tell her. "Can I call you then?"

Eli rolls his eyes. I send him a withering look.

"Of course." She sounds happier, thank God. "Have a good dinner."

"You too, sweetheart."

"Sweetheart?" Eli mouths.

"Fuck off," I mouth back.

I end the call right as we walk around the corner to the block where the restaurant sits. Holden is walking toward us from the other direction. He looks harassed, but then Holden always looks harassed. When he told us he wanted to be a doctor we'd all warned him that his life would never be his own. He works at Hamilton General, a public hospital uptown.

We're proud as hell of him. But he's the only one of us that isn't paid what he's worth.

"Hey." He goes to bump my fist but Eli body tackles him into the wall.

"Dude," he says. "Good to see you." Eli and Holden have always been close, the same way Myles and I are. And I guess Brooks and Linc, too, though their closeness borders on violence.

"You too." Holden's voice is muffled. "Can you let me go now?"

Eli laughs and releases him and the three of us walk into the restaurant, Holden regaling us with a story from today's surgery as we wait for the Maître D' to seat us.

We order three beers and look over the menu as Holden asks us if we're all ready for the party this weekend.

"It's gonna be good," Eli says. "Apart from the fact that I have to give up my fucking cabin." He gives Holden a pointed look. "You better give me the bedroom."

"Not happening," Holden tells Eli. "You get the sofa bed."

Eli groans.

"It's *my* cabin," Holden reminds him.

"Yeah, but I'm not there voluntarily," Eli points out. "I'm being forced out of my own place so Liam's girlfriend has a room to sleep in."

"You have a girlfriend?" Holden asks me, shocked.

"Sophie's a friend," I say, because I know she's still jittery and I can't call her my girlfriend yet. "I'm working on the rest."

Holden lets out a low whistle. "Wow. Never thought I'd see the day."

"She won't last," Eli says. "She's just a novelty, that's all. Somebody who said no to him."

"Shut the fuck up," I tell him. "And you better not say that to Sophie."

He rolls his eyes. "I'm not going to say that to her. And if I'm wrong then great. I'm happy for you. I just know you better than you think."

I give him a sour smile. I love Eli, I really do. He's the

nicest of people, would do anything for anybody. But he also says what he thinks way too often.

"What does Myles think about this?" Holden asks. And that sour taste in my mouth increases.

"He said the same thing as Eli," I admit. "That I want her because I can't have her. But he's wrong, too."

Holden nods, his expression serious. "Yeah, I think he is."

"You do?" I lift a brow.

"I always knew you'd fall like an idiot someday. Just thought it might take you a little longer."

I blink, unsure how to detangle the support from the jibe. "Thank you, I think."

"So are we driving to Misty Lakes together or what?" Eli asks. "We might as well leave here on Friday afternoon, right?"

"I'm going back to Charleston first," I say. "So I'll meet you there."

"Why the hell would you do that?" Eli frowns. "It'll take half the time to go from here."

"He wants to take Sophie," Holden says.

I shrug. "There are a few reasons I need to go there first."

"Name them." Eli folds his hands over his chest.

I look at him until he has the good grace to blush.

"He's right though," Holden says quietly. "You'd be better to go from here."

"Why?" I ask him.

"Because, and I'm saying this with the best of intentions, flying back to Charleston just to drive this woman to Virginia makes you look like an intense motherfucker."

Eli muffles a laugh.

"And since I've only just discovered that this thing between you and Sophie exists, I'm gonna assume it's new. Which means you being that intense motherfucker can be scary. I get it, you like her. But give her some space, man."

Eli types something on his phone while Holden talks. A moment later it lights up as a reply lands.

"Yep, as I thought," he says. "Sophie is driving herself."

"Are you messaging her?" A weird sensation takes over me. Jesus, is this what jealousy feels like? All twisted in my stomach and tight muscles and wanting to punch my brother?

Damn.

"No. I'm messaging Ava. Just asking what everybody's plans are. And those are Sophie's. So let's travel together, okay?"

"Whatever." I just want this conversation to end.

"Can I drive your car?" Eli asks. He has a thing for my cars. Here in New York, I have two parked in the underground lot.

"No. You can sit in the back," I tell him.

"Fuck that. Shotgun." He lifts a brow.

"Sounds good to me," Holden agrees. "I can sleep in the backseat the whole way."

———

SOPHIE

I hit send and watch as the email on my screen flickers and disappears, a sent icon appearing next to it. Attached to it is the final report. My mind is full of excitement about the weekend and getting to see Liam again.

Michael, on the other hand, is getting worked up about the potential storm.

"It's gonna hit on Saturday afternoon," he tells me. "I'll be here in case it's worse than it looks."

Normally, I'd be annoyed because severe weather events are our glory opportunities. Any other storm and I'd be tracking it in real time all weekend, writing updates for the website and our social media and getting excited about barometer readings. But instead I'll be seeing it from the other side. As a guest at a party that might get rained on.

"You remember I'm away this weekend, right?" I ask him.

"Yep. If you could just be in early Monday morning that'll be great. I'll take the late shift and Madison is working the socials."

"Cool." I turn back to my laptop, determined to get my work finished on time. And I do, despite the fact that I had to record some extra slots for the weekend's web coverage. They are explainer videos. About how storms form and how we track and monitor them. It's pretty dry stuff but the producer assures me he's going to intersperse the video with images from real storm events and the aftermath so hopefully it won't be as dull as I think.

At five I pack up my bag, including the chocolates that Liam sent over today. He should be en route to Misty Lakes now. He called last night and told me about Eli and Holden traveling with him, and though he sounded grumpy about it I think he was pleased, too.

His brothers are his best friends, I've learned that much from being around him and Myles. And everybody needs their best friends.

Which reminds me. I have to type out a message to Lauren, one long overdue. I promised her an update and I haven't had the chance to do it. To save time, I decide to voice record, hitting send as I walk down the sidewalk toward the historic district, where I'm meeting my dad for dinner.

This is the first time I'm seeing him since our embarrassing encounter, although we've spoken on the phone. It still feels awkward but he's my dad and we need to get over this. I need to see him fully clothed and he probably needs to see me unembarrassed.

"Sweetheart." He's early, as usual, and when I walk into

Ray's Steakhouse he stands and embraces me. "Thank you for meeting me."

He looks tired. And suddenly old. Maybe it's the lighting in here, I'm not sure. I hug him back and we both take a seat.

"Sophie…" he begins, just as I blurt out, "I'm sorry."

We both laugh and then I gesture at him to go first.

"Darling," he says. "I should have warned you about Jenny. I wasn't expecting you two to meet that way."

"It's okay," I reassure him. "You're an adult. You're both single, what you do is your business."

The waiter arrives to take our orders and we give them quickly. We've been coming to this steakhouse since I was tiny. Every birthday was celebrated here growing up. I used to go crazy for their milkshakes. Now I'm ordering a cocktail to give myself some Dutch courage to talk to my dad.

"It has something to do with you, too," he says. "You're my daughter. And it doesn't matter how old you are, you'll always miss your mom."

My throat goes tight. He's right, I do. Every day. I miss her warmth, her soft hugs, the way she smelled.

"I miss her, too," he tells me. "So much."

I blink away the tears. "I know."

"And Jenny, she's a fine woman. But she'll never replace her." He reaches across the table to squeeze my hand. "I need you to know that."

"I didn't think she would. But it's okay that you have a girlfriend. Mom's been gone a while." And he's been so lonely. I've hated seeing him that way.

"I'd like to say that your mom would have liked her," he says. "But I'm not sure she would." He leans forward like he's about to confess. "Your mom hated 'new age mumbo jumbo'." He crooks his fingers into mock quotation marks.

I bark out a laugh. "She did," I agree.

"And Jenny is really into crystals. And she's a good woman. And she seems to like me."

"Of course she does. Why wouldn't she?" I squeeze his fingers. "You're a catch. She seemed nice, from what I could see of her." I widen my eyes and it's his turn to laugh. And somehow that awkwardness between us melts away.

The waiter brings over our drinks – a beer for dad and an espresso martini for me, and we clink them together the way we used to when I was a kid.

"And you like her, right?" I ask him.

He nods. "She makes me laugh. And we keep each other company."

"Maybe I can meet her again under better circumstances," I suggest gently. I don't want to push it, especially if he's not in that space, but I want him to know I'm okay with what he does.

He nods happily. "I'd like that. And so would she. She was so embarrassed."

"Let's arrange something soon," I tell him, taking a sip of my cocktail. I'm only going to drink one tonight. They make them strong here, and I have an early morning to make my way to Misty Lakes tomorrow. Luckily the waiter brings our appetizers over fairly quickly. We've opted for a plate to share like we always do. Potato skins and chicken wings plus some cut up vegetables to dip into the blue cheese sauce.

It's so bad for you but it tastes so good.

"So are you going to tell me why Liam Salinger was with you?" he asks.

I shift in my seat. "We were just spending some time together," I tell him. "It's a new thing. We're just…" I reach for the right words to describe what's going on between us but they don't exist.

I don't want to tell my dad about Liam's sudden change of heart, or the fact that he is so into me I don't know what to do about it. My face flushes as I remember the way he took me again and again in my bed the other night.

I take a deep breath. "We're just seeing where things go."

"I like him," Dad says. "He seems like a good man."

I nod. "He is."

"And he cares for you, yes?"

I look up at him. "I think so," I whisper.

"So why do you look so sad?" he asks me.

"I'm not sad. I'm contemplative. As I said, it's early. Anything could happen."

His brows knit. "That's not good, being defeatist about it. This is supposed to be the fun part. You're supposed to be enjoying it."

"I am." I relax my features because I'm aware of how tense they are. "It's just he has a bit of a reputation. For not settling down."

"Ah." Dad nods as though he understands. Thank God he doesn't know the specifics. "So you don't trust him to settle down with you either?"

"I don't know," I say honestly. I can't remember the last time Dad and I were so open with each other. Maybe right after Mom died and we tried to help each other in our despair. But I like this. It feels like we're equals.

"Him not settling down until he meets the right woman isn't unusual," he continues. I lean in because he might actually have some insight into Liam's thoughts. "I saw it happen to a lot of my friends when I was younger. They'd insist they'd never want to have a long term relationship, let alone get married, but as soon as they met the one woman who knocked them off their feet they changed their tune immediately."

"You think I've knocked him off his feet?"

He smiles. "You'd knock any man off his feet. But yes, I think that man would do anything for you. He kept looking at you during the Christening when he knew you couldn't see him."

I don't bother correcting him that at the Christening we still hated each other.

"And then when you came to my house on Sunday." He shifts because there'll always be a slight embarrassment to that situation. "His eyes kept drifting to your face. He wants to take care of you. I could tell. And as a father I'm okay with that." A smile pulls at his lips. "It was the same for me. The moment I saw your mother I knew that I was a goner. I'd fight wars for her, sail seas for her. I knew she was the one, though she took a little longer to be persuaded. She was like you in that way," he says approvingly. "And I gotta tell you, it made me want her more."

"Do you feel that way about Jenny?" I ask him.

He pauses for a moment, considering my question. "No," he eventually says. "And she doesn't have the same fireworks with me that she had with her late husband. He died a few months before your mom did. But we're friends and we make each other laugh and at my age I'm damn grateful for that."

"I am too," I tell him. And I really am.

He winks and spears the last chicken wing, putting it on the small plate that came with our appetizers. "Then bring him along when you come to meet Jenny. We might as well kill two birds with one stone."

And there he is. My practical dad. "Okay," I agree. "That sounds good."

He finishes the wing and wipes his fingers. "Look at us moving on," he says. "Taking the future by the balls."

I laugh because I don't think I've ever heard him use the word 'balls' before. "We're kicking future's ass," I tell him.

"I'll drink to that." He lifts his beer, and clinks it against my cocktail. "Cheers, sweetheart."

"Cheers, Dad." And I smile because things are finally coming together. The submission is in, my dad and I have cleared the air, and tomorrow I see Liam.

Who wouldn't want to smile about that?

CHAPTER
TWENTY-FOUR

SOPHIE

The sky is overcast as I begin the drive to Misty Lakes. Liam's dad's estate is on the other side of the state line, in Virginia, and I'm thankful for my car's GPS because I have no sense of direction at all. Liam called me early this morning – he arrived at his father's place with his brothers late last night. When I told him I should be there in the early afternoon he sounded pleased.

I don't know why I ever thought I'd be able to do this trip there and back in a day. It's not exactly short. And as I get closer to Virginia, the clouds darken ominously, reminding me that later on there's almost certainly going to be a deluge.

When I make the turn onto a graveled road, the tree canopy above casts a dark shadow on the path ahead. Ava told me that there was a kind of forest between the road and Misty Lakes. Liam's dad likes his privacy and they provide a welcome barrier.

I'm starting to wonder if this forest will ever end when I

finally drive out of the other side, and in the distance I see the main house sitting on the top of one of the rolling green hills. The road meanders and then ascends up the hill, and I get the most gorgeous view of the lakes that the estate is named after. They don't sparkle because there's no sun to reflect off them, but they look tranquil and beautiful.

When I reach the house the driveway is filled with cars. There are three men wearing yellow vests over their white shirts and black pants and one of them walks forward. "Miss West?"

"Yes." I nod. Impressive, Liam must have given them my car details.

"If you'd like to go up to the house we'll park your car and take your luggage down to your cabin," he tells me.

So I climb out and grab my bag and phone, as well as the paper bag that has Linda's birthday gift inside, and I walk up to the steps, taking a deep breath because I'm going to be seeing him again.

And then he's opening the impressive oak front door, his expression unreadable as he walks down the steps to meet me.

"Sophie." He kisses my cheek. "How was your drive?"

"It was good," I say breathlessly because this man has such an effect on me.

"I'm glad."

I'm a little perplexed by his reaction to me. I'd envisioned him sweeping me off my feet, kissing me until I couldn't regain control of my muscles. But instead he's being cool. Almost aloof.

And then I look over his shoulder and I see his mother and stepmothers, plus his father and brothers, all standing at the door.

"I don't know how you want to play this," he whispers in my ear. "Are you okay with everyone knowing about us?"

I take a deep breath, remembering my dad's words from last night. It's about the future. And I don't want to be afraid of that.

"Yeah, I am," I tell him.

"Thank Christ for that." Before I can say another word, he spins me around and pulls me against him, his mouth warm against mine as he kisses me.

I curl my arms around his neck, rolling onto my toes to try to get a little bit higher, loving the way he holds me so tight. His tongue slides against mine and there's a low rumble in his throat that sends pleasure straight to my thighs.

Somebody lets out a whistle and Liam pulls back, his smile huge.

"Hello," he tells me, as though we're starting over. "I missed you."

"I missed you," I tell him honestly.

He slides his fingers through mine, taking the gift bag out of my other hand, and leads me up the stairs to the door. Eli lifts a brow at him and Myles looks at me and mouths, "You okay?"

And I know he's asking me if I'm okay with this. With Liam outing us. I nod at Myles and he smiles. The next moment, Ava is putting Charlie into his arms and pulling me away from Liam, hugging me tight.

"You and I have a lot to talk about," she tells me.

"I know. And I'm sorry." I should have warned her about this.

"Don't be. I'm just happy for you both. Come on in, I'll get you a drink." She slides her arm through mine.

The noise levels reach a high point as we walk inside. Liam's brothers are teasing him, but he seems to be taking it in good humor. His dad is there, too, but his mom and Deandra along with Julia – his dad's other ex-wife and his current one, who is carrying their little girl – walk ahead with Ava and I.

"Thank you so much for giving me the storm warning," Linda says, sliding her arm through mine. The hallway is so large it can easily allow us to walk three abreast. "I would have panicked when I woke up this morning if I hadn't already made contingency plans."

"I just wish I could have chased the storm away," I tell her.

"Ah well. Maybe next time." She leads us into the kitchen, a huge room with windows that look out over the hills and lake. There's a patio right outside, filled with tables and chairs, and a path that winds down the hill past beautiful flowering bushes and ornamental trees until it reaches the lake.

A pair of arms encircle me. I smile and lean my head back on Liam's chest. "I'll take you down to your cabin," he tells me. "Help you get settled in."

From the hard ridge pressing against my bottom I'm pretty sure that's not all he has planned.

"Can you wait for ten minutes?" Linda asks. "Ria will be here with her girls. I'm putting Ariel in the cabin with Sophie, and Ria and Claire will share the last room in here."

Liam stiffens, but not in a good way. "What?"

"You'll like Ariel," Linda says, ignoring his pissed tone. "Ria's my oldest friend. Ariel and Claire are her daughters. They practically grew up with my boys."

"Give them all Eli's cabin," he says to his mom, his voice louder this time. "Sophie can share with me."

"That won't work," Linda tells him. "Linc and Brooks need to go in with you. Their cabin flooded this morning, didn't they tell you?"

From the look on Liam's face, I'm guessing they didn't.

"It's too short notice to get the plumber out. They'll just bring some sleeping bags and hunker down on your floor for the night," Linda continues. "Which leaves Ariel needing somewhere and there's a spare room in Eli's cabin."

"Won't Ariel want to be with Claire?" Deandra – Liam's stepmom – asks.

"No, Claire needs solid electricity for her machine." Linda glances at me. "She has sleep apnea so she and Ria will share the last room in here. But Ariel's very much looking forward to meeting you, Sophie."

I nod. "I'm looking forward to it, too. I'm just grateful you've found somewhere I can stay."

"Well of course." Linda smiles. "You're part of the family now."

Ava pours me a lemonade and drags me over to one of the tables on the deck. Myles is still holding Charlie and from the corner of my eye I can see Liam walk over and tickle Charlie's chin. His expression still looks like thunder.

"Uhoh," Ava says as soon as we're out on the patio. "Somebody's mad."

Liam turns and looks at me, his gaze unwavering. I feel myself blush. "We haven't seen each other for a couple of days," I murmur.

"Oh, I remember those days. That was Myles and I when we came here for his dad and Julia's vow renewal. There was so much sexual tension I thought I might explode."

"Do you know Ariel?" I ask her. "This woman I'm sharing the cabin with?"

"No. I only know that Linda's best friend is from London. They met when she was studying for a year in New York when they were both students. Her husband was a diplomat, I think, so they've lived all over the world."

That should be interesting. I love hearing about different countries and cultures.

"So you and Liam, huh?" Ava grins. "I knew it. You two were way too invested in one-upping each other for there not to be sexual attraction between you."

"You didn't say anything," I remind her.

"I know. Part of me wondered if it was wishful thinking, hoping my best friend would fall in love with my brother-in-law."

"Who said anything about love?" I ask her.

She lifts a brow. "I know you. You don't give yourself lightly. And I already know he's head over heels in love with you."

"You do? How?"

She tells me about his coming to see her and Myles that Sunday for help. And my chest twists a little more.

"Oh."

"Yeah, he's smitten. And he should be. Oh I'm so happy right now." She claps her hands together.

"Which is more than I can say for Liam." I can see him still scowling in the kitchen. He's trying to talk to his mom but she's shaking her head. And Eli and Holden are grinning at him. His other brothers – Linc and Brooks, are waving at me through the window.

I wave back. And Liam scowls a little more.

"I think he thought we'd be able to spend more time together," I say to Ava, who's smiling at his obvious annoyance.

"Well you can after the party. You'll just have to go to his cabin."

"That's what he said, but that's rude. I can't leave Ariel to sleep alone, can I?"

"I guess not." Ava wrinkles her nose. "But where there's a will there's a way." She grins at me. "I think this place has some magic about it. It's where Myles and I first admitted we felt something for each other."

As though he knows he's being talked about, Myles walks out to join us on the patio, carrying Charlie. I jump up and kiss his round, sticky cheek. Charlie's that is. Myles' cheek is more stubbled than sticky as I discover when I kiss him, too.

"I need to change his diaper," he tells us. "I'm going to take him down to the cabin and let him have a nap, too."

"I'll join you in a minute," Ava says smiling at him. He nods but there's some unspoken words there. She's already told me they have the best sex when Charlie is napping. Apparently, the time limit really concentrates Myles' mind.

"Hey," Liam says, walking out to the patio. He's managed to regain his composure and is looking his usual happy-go-lucky self. "Let's go for a walk after you settle into the cabin," he says. "I'll show you around the place."

"I bet you will." Ava grins.

"I'm forty fucking years old and I can't even be alone with my girlfriend for the weekend," he tells her, lifting a brow. "So don't push me."

Okay, so he's still annoyed. And it's kind of hot if I'm honest. I stand and turn toward him, sliding my hand onto his face. His jaw is so tight I could bounce a ball off it.

"We can go for lots of walks," I tell him. "Until our legs fall off."

The ghost of a smile passes his lips. "That sounds like a challenge."

"And I'm out." Ava grins at us. "I need to go before Myles falls asleep."

"Don't you mean Charlie?" I ask her.

"Sadly not." She grins. "I'll see you in a while."

"Sure."

She follows the same path as Myles and Charlie did, and before long she disappears into the tree line that leads to the cabins. She's already told me that they were built by the Salinger brothers themselves, each of them designing them to their own needs. They're not huge and luxurious but they reflect their personalities.

I'm looking forward to seeing them.

Now that we're alone, I slide my arms around Liam's

waist and rest my head against his chest. "I'm sorry the plans have changed," I tell him.

He puts one hand on my back, the other in my hair. "It's not your fault."

"I know. But you're annoyed."

"I just wish people would think, you know? *Oh maybe Liam might want a bit of fucking privacy with the woman who turned his world upside down.*"

I smile against his chest because he's so damn cute. "I turned your world upside down?"

"You know you have."

Lifting my head up, I trace the line of his jaw. "You've turned mine upside down, too."

He kisses me. And then there's a whoop from the kitchen.

"Fuck my life," he whispers.

"I'd like to," I tell him. "If I get the chance."

His gaze softens. He kisses my brow and my nose. "Remind me again why we're here and not having sex in a hotel room until neither of us can walk?"

"Because it's your mom's birthday," I tell him. "And you love spending time with your family."

"I'm reassessing that situation."

I squeeze his hand. "We have plenty of time for hotel rooms later."

His gaze dips to my mouth. "I like the sound of that."

"So let's just get through this weekend, okay? It's been a long few weeks and we've both been so busy. Let's kick back and have some fun."

"I like the sound of that, too," he murmurs. He's relaxed again. He leans down and kisses me, and this time it's so sweet it makes my chest ache.

This man. He could own me if I give him the chance.

My breath catches at the thought.

"Liam, honey?" Linda calls out. He pulls back and raises a brow at me. There's a promise in his stare. This isn't over.

At some point he's going to get me alone and I'm here for that.

"Yes, Mom?" he asks patiently, looking over my shoulder at her.

"Ria and the girls are here. Can you come help your brothers with their luggage?"

CHAPTER
TWENTY-FIVE

SOPHIE

"Are you sure you don't mind us stealing your cabin?" Ariel asks Eli, as he and Liam walk us inside.

"You're all good," Eli tells her. "Holden and I are going to shoot hoops for the bedroom in his place."

"No we're not," Holden says, joining us in the cabin's small living area. It's actually sweetly cozy in here. I walk over to Liam and slide my arm around his waist. "Is your cabin the same as this?"

"My living area is bigger. Eli wanted two bedrooms but I only have one. It's more like Myles'."

"So Linc and Brooks really are sleeping on the floor in your living room tonight?"

"They'll duke it out for the sofa I expect." He looks around this cabin. "They could always take your room."

"Oh God, don't leave me with those two," Ariel says, wrinkling her nose. "It'd be like sleeping with a pair of rutting stags."

"I know," Liam says, deadpan. "I'm so excited that I get to have a sleepover with them."

Ariel takes my hand, pulling me away from Liam. She's very lovely. Tall and slender with glossy dark hair and an accent that belongs somewhere in the mid-Atlantic. Walking down to the cabin she told me all about the apartment she's currently living in on the 8th Arondissement in Paris. It's within walking distance of so many beautiful galleries and museums, and as she describes them I almost feel like I'm there.

"Which room do you want?" she asks, pulling me into the first bedroom. "This one's bigger, but it's also Eli's. Which means whoever sleeps in here will have to put up with the sweaty jock smell."

"Hey," Eli protests, following us in. "I don't smell of sweaty jock."

Ariel blows him a kiss. He shakes his head and walks out again.

"The other bedroom is smaller," she says. We only have to take two steps down the living area to get to it. "But it's sweat free."

"Sophie will take that one," Liam says.

I look at him, surprised. He just shrugs.

"Yeah, because I don't want you two having dirty sex in my bed, thank you very much," Eli says.

Ariel shoots me an interested look. "You and Liam?"

I nod.

"Oh. Okay." She gives me the sweetest of smiles. "So you're happy with this room?"

"It works for me."

Liam carries my bag in from where the valets left it outside, and Ariel wanders back to her room. As soon as she steps out, Liam closes the door with the sole of his shoe then walks over to me. Wordlessly, he pulls me into his arms and lets out a groan.

"I've never wished harder that I was an only child," he tells me.

"Stop it, you love your brothers."

"I do, but I'd like them all to disappear right now." He slides his hand down my neck, his palm warm against my skin. "Leave the window open tonight. I'll come here to be with you."

I try not to laugh at the thought of Liam trying to get his large frame through the tiniest of windows. I'm not sure it's physically possible.

"But Ariel…"

"Gave you this room for a reason," he finishes for me. "She's okay, really."

"She seems more than okay. She's lovely. You all grew up together?"

"Not really. Ria would come visit mom most summers. Sometimes they'd come here while we were staying with dad. You know, happy families." He lifts a brow.

"So she's your age?" That can't be true. Ariel looks like she's closer to twenty than forty."

"Two years younger."

"Wow. I need to find out what brand of moisturizer she uses."

Liam laughs softly. "You're perfect just the way you are." And that makes me melt a little. I kiss his jaw and he closes his eyes for a moment. And then a loud clap of thunder pierces the air in the cabin, making me jump.

"Did you see any lightning?" I ask Liam, my heart picking up a pace. "I should check the maps again for your mom. I wasn't expecting it to hit this soon."

"You two decent?" A hand slams on the door. Before we can answer, Eli walks in. "We should all head up to the house before it really starts to rain, or Mom will throw a fit." He inclines his head at the window. Storm clouds loom above the main house, making it look almost ghostly.

Specifically, it's a cumulonimbus arcus formation. The kind that feels close to the ground, with a steel gray color. An arcus – a shelf like lower cloud that hangs the lowest, is at the front of the storm. And Eli's right, it's heading this way.

"How long did you say it was going to storm again?" Liam asks, resting his chin on my head as I stare out at the sky.

"An hour or two." Like most summer storms, it will pass fairly quickly. It's the result of a cold front mixed in with the humidity, and the unstable air pattern means it explodes then moves on.

"Okay then. I guess we walk later," he says, his lip curling.

"I guess we will."

———

LIAM

The rain starts as we're all walking back into the house. I'm holding Sophie's hand because right now it's the only physical contact I can have with her. It's not enough but I'll get over it.

Once we're inside, my mom corners Sophie, asking her about the weather and if she thinks people will be able to make it this evening, when her birthday party is due to begin. Sophie opens her phone, and she and mom sit down in the living room and Sophie talks her through the storm maps. I listen in because I'm nuts about this woman and her fascination for the weather fascinates me.

But then Holden comes along to ask for my help with setting up the chairs in the big ballroom where the party will be held if we can't be outside, so I slink off with a promise that I'll be back.

When everything's finally set up I go back to the living

room but Sophie isn't there. My mom's in the corner, picking up some empty glasses people must have left there earlier.

When she sees me in the doorway, her face splits into a smile.

"Darling, come in." She moves her hand in a beckoning gesture.

"Where's Sophie?" I ask her.

"She's gone to help Deandra and Julia with some food. All the girls are in the kitchen, apart from me." She smiles. "Your younger brothers need to learn how to clean up after themselves."

I walk into the room and take the glasses from her. "You shouldn't be cleaning up on your birthday," I tell her.

"Apparently I'm not allowed to cook either." She rolls her eyes. "I don't know what I'm supposed to do between now and when the party starts."

"Sit down. Relax. Enjoy yourself."

"I'm not very good at sitting still."

"I know that feeling." I get it from her. Always having to be on the move. Doing the next thing. Never taking time to smell the roses.

"Sit with me for a moment," she suggests, sitting on the sofa and tapping the seat next to her. Part of me wants to take these glasses to the kitchen and see my girl, but this is my mom and she's always happier when we're with her.

"Okay." I put the glasses down on the table and sit next to her. She takes my hand and squeezes it.

"Sophie is lovely," she says softly. "I'm so happy for you both."

"It's still new, Mom," I warn her.

"I know it is. But the way you look at her, darling, I never thought I'd live to see the day. Are you happy? Tell me you're happy."

I lift a brow. "I'm very happy."

She lets out a contented sigh. "So am I. First Myles and

now you. I've waited for you both to find contentment for so long."

"Don't go marrying me off yet," I warn her.

"I don't need to," Mom says. "I think you'll do that all by yourself. I know you, Liam. Better than all your brothers do. And I know you put on this happy face and make everybody feel good, but deep inside there's been something missing for the longest time."

My throat tightens. "Mom…"

"I know." She nods. "And I won't go there. But you and I both know that Sophie's been a long time coming."

Yeah, she has. The woman I never knew I wanted. And by some major miracle she actually wants me.

Now if I could just get her alone and *show* her how much I want her that would be good, thank you.

"Look at you," Mom says smiling. "You can't wait to see her, can you?"

I roll my eyes but her fond expression doesn't waver. "Go," she tells me. "You've humored me enough."

Love for my mom rushes through me. She's been through a lot in her life. Back when dad left her we wondered if she would ever smile again. Hell, we wondered if she'd ever get out of bed again. I remember Myles and I having to cook dinner for the five of us. He'd make sure Holden and Eli were fed and I'd tiptoe upstairs and force mom to take some mouthfuls of whatever godawful thing we'd cooked.

My chest twinges. That was the first time I learned that love could hurt. It took a long time for us to forgive our dad for that. And maybe we haven't completely. Myles hasn't, that's for sure.

We love him. He's our dad. But do we trust him?

Nope.

My mom though, she's always been there. And though she's fallible, she also shows us unwavering support. I'll never truly understand how she and Deandra got so close, or how they both are happy to spend time with Dad, but part of me wonders if it's for us.

She wants us to be happy, so she'll do whatever it takes. And that's true love.

The kind of love that would sacrifice anything.

I lean forward and hug her. She lets out a warm, contented sigh, her face resting against my chest. I can remember the first time I realized how tiny she was. I was twelve years old and had reached the same height as her. A few weeks later I was taller, and she was asking me to reach things on shelves for her.

And now she's about a foot and a half shorter than me. Doesn't make her any less fierce though.

"You're a good man," she whispers against my chest. "You keep holding onto that happiness, okay? Don't let it go."

"I won't," I promise her. And it's a promise I intend to keep. I'm not going to hurt Sophie the way my dad hurt my mom. I want to protect her. Keep her happy. Make her feel safe in my arms.

If it takes a goddamned lifetime I'm going to prove to her that she can trust me.

I stand and grab the glasses I left on the table and wink at my mom. She grins back as I walk out of the living room and head to the kitchen. I hear the sound of dishes being put on counters and laughter and the familiar pitch of female voices. When I walk inside I spot her immediately, talking to Julia as she stirs a pot with a large wooden spoon.

Julia says something that makes Sophie laugh just as the clouds part for a shaft of sun to break through them. It hits the glass doors that lead out to the patio and the hills beyond, casting a halo over Sophie's golden hair.

And then she looks up at me.

Her lips part and her eyes light up and all I can think is that I want her.

No, I *need* her. Now.

And I don't give a shit about who's sleeping in whose cabin or the fact that despite the break in the clouds it's still pouring outside. Or that this room is filled with people who are all watching the silent interaction between me and my girl, who's still staring at me as though I could part the oceans for her.

Sophie's stopped stirring the pot of whatever's cooking in front of her. Julia notices and takes the spoon, gently moving Sophie to the left.

"I need to speak to you," I tell her.

She runs her tongue over her bottom lip and nods. I hold my hand out to her and she walks toward me, not caring that everybody's watching us.

When her fingers slide into mine it feels like the sun is coming out. And I don't give a shit if everybody knows I'm about to drag her to whatever private place I can find and bury my face in her body until I'm about to suffocate. Or that I want to feel her convulse around me again and again until she can't remember what day it is.

The only person I care about is this woman staring up at me.

"Ready?" I ask her softly.

"Yes." She nods and I pull her out of the kitchen. As soon as we're gone they all start to talk at once.

"Oh. My. God."

"Did you see the way he looked at her?"

"Is anybody else having a hot flash right now?"

"I don't know about you, but I'm gonna need to open some windows."

CHAPTER
TWENTY-SIX

SOPHIE

Liam touches me everywhere. No part of me goes unstroked, unkissed, unadmired. From the sole of my feet to the dip of my back right above my behind. He can't get enough of me and it makes me feel like a goddess.

When his attention reaches my thighs, I'm already so close to the edge. My breath is ragged, my fingers curled into his hair – still damp from our dash from the house to his cabin – and when I groan out his name it doesn't sound like my voice at all.

It's too deep. Too desperate. But it makes him smile against my skin.

We're both naked, our clothes like a breadcrumb trail from the front door of his cabin into his room. If Brooks or Linc came in now they'd have no doubt about what's going on.

And yet I don't care. I need this as much as he does. I need Liam, all over me, inside me. I need the connection because I know that this is right.

When his tongue slides against me I scream out his name.

Another glide of it and I'm begging for more. He pushes his fingers inside, knowing just how much I need to feel full of him. But it's still not enough.

"I need you," I tell him.

"You've got me." He kisses my thigh.

"Inside me, now. Please, Liam."

It takes him less than ten seconds to snap on a condom. He's thick and hard against my thigh, and I roll my hips to get closer to him. My lizard brain has taken over, seeking nothing but sensation. His mouth covers mine, taking, giving. I wrap my legs around him, our bodies sliding together until I feel him right where I need him.

But instead of sliding inside he rolls over, pulling me with him until his back is on the bed and my body is straddling his. "Ride me," he tells me, his voice thick. "I want to watch you."

I slowly slide down on him, the sensation of absolute fullness making my mouth drop open.

"You've never looked more beautiful than you do right now," he says. He takes my hands, letting me lean against him as my hips begin to move in a rhythm as old as time. It's deeper this way. More personal, too, because I feel his gaze wash over me as I lift and fall against him.

My face flushes, my hair falls over my shoulders, and still his hands hold mine, the same way his gaze does. There's a half smile on his face, and the intimacy between us makes my heart ache.

He was right. I needed this. I just didn't know how much.

It's like my world is turning upside down and inside out. Those last bricks of the wall I built around me are crumbling, leaving me exposed and raw. This man has broken me down then built me up again.

And I love him.

The heat builds between us, our breathing ragged and rapid and our bodies slick with sweat. My thighs clench his hips, my body slams against him, and still he watches me, his beautiful lips parted.

"Liam…"

He nods as though he knows. "Use me," he urges. "Ride me. Make yourself come on me."

And I do in a glorious explosion of cries and clenching and fireworks behind my eyes. It makes my muscles go weak, enough for him to release his hold on my hands and grasp my waist, holding me upright as I shatter into pieces above him.

He follows me into oblivion with a grunt of my name, still holding me, his eyes unwavering. And when I collapse on him he kisses me softly, our bodies still riding the wave of pleasure, until finally we drift to the shore, clinging closely to each other.

His touch is gentle as he sweeps the hair from my face. Our brows are touching. It takes a long, long moment for us to catch our breaths.

And when we do he laughs.

"What?" I ask, my brows knitting.

"I just…" He shakes his head. "Every time I think life is perfect, it just gets a little better."

I roll my eyes at him. "It won't be so perfect when we go back to the house and everybody knows what we've been doing." And yeah, I'm starting to worry about that.

"Fuck them."

"No thanks. There's only one Salinger I want," I say.

His smile widens. "That's good. Because I don't feel like beating anybody up today."

"We should go back, shouldn't we?" I ask reluctantly. Because let's face it, I'd so much rather be in his arms.

"I guess…" He gently lifts me off him, securing the condom. Then he rolls over and puts his feet on the floor. "In ten minutes, maybe."

"Twenty," I tell him. I need to shower.

"Half an hour. And it's not even party time yet," he says. He gets up and disappears for a moment, presumably to clean himself up. But when he walks back in he's carrying a glass of water and a pastry.

My stomach growls in anticipation. "Where did you get that?" I ask him.

He smiles and looks so pleased with himself that I want to hug him. "I bought some supplies on the way here yesterday." He passes me the water and I gulp thirstily. "I just realized you hadn't eaten since you arrived. I'm sorry, I should take care of you better. When we get up to the house I'll make you a proper lunch."

"It's almost dinner time," I point out. "And this will do fine." I'm so eager I almost snatch the pastry from him. He watches, amused, as I devour it. When I've taken another mouthful of water I fall back on the bed, completely sated. Liam climbs onto the mattress next to me, his arms around me, and I breathe him in.

I could get used to this. In fact, I think I already am.

———

Nobody notices us when we sneak back into the house. Everybody is too busy. Wait staff fly around readying the kitchen and the ballroom, a band is setting up on a temporary stage, and all the doors have been flung open to the large patio beyond, the storm having passed.

By the time Liam's made us a late lunch of soup and bread – having charmed the catering company to let him do his thing in the kitchen – we all head back to our cabins to get ready.

It's fun being in there with Ariel. She has a dry sense of humor and clearly adores all the Salingers. She regales me with stories about their annual Olympics – where the brothers would compete for the prize of being top Salinger –

and how they would get into physical fights over who was the best.

"Holden would fight?" I ask her. He seems the calmest of the six of them. Maybe it's because he's a doctor – his aim is to preserve life, not endanger it.

"Yep, even Holden," Ariel says. "I like the way you've done your hair. How do you get it to twist like that?"

I demonstrate it for her and she claps her hands. "I'm going to try that next time I go out," she says, and even if she's just humoring me I feel gratified that the sophisticated Parisian likes how I look.

We disappear into our rooms to put on our dresses and she walks back out looking absolutely stunning. Her dress is a silver sheath that clings to her perfect curves and I still can't believe she's almost forty.

"You look fabulous," I tell her.

"And so do you."

We walk out of the cabin together as we see the Salinger men approaching. Ariel slides her arm through Eli's and Liam walks over to me.

"Beautiful," he murmurs, his face serious. "Shall we just go back to the cabin again?"

"No way," Linc says, huffing behind us. "Try to keep it in your pants for at least the next few hours, bro."

Liam rolls his eyes. "You have an exquisite turn of phrase, Lincoln."

Myles and Ava join us a few moments later. They've dressed Charlie in the world's smallest tuxedo and we all coo over how adorable he looks.

But Liam's the one he reaches for, his hands clinging onto the lapels of his tuxedo. Reluctantly, Myles passes him over and Liam whispers in Charlie's ear.

And he gives the most delightful laugh. We all stared, rapt. Even Lincoln looks a little broody.

"What did you say to him?" Ava asks, smiling.

Liam lifts a brow. "Just a little uncle nephew thing."

"I heard what he said." Myles stares at Liam. "And thank you for telling my son you've been getting jiggy."

Eli coughs out a laugh. I'm stuck somewhere between mortification and amusement. And Liam just shrugs because that's what Liam does.

When Ava tries to take Charlie back, he clings tighter to Liam's jacket. So he carries him up to the house, his big hand cradling Charlie's head, and I have to send an SOS to my ovaries to calm the heck down.

When we reach the house, Linda and Deandra walk out to greet us, Julia and Rupert behind them. Everybody hugs everybody but before we can walk inside, the doorbell rings and the guests begin to arrive. Liam slides his hand around my waist and kisses my brow.

"Okay?" he asks.

"I'm more than all right."

His eyes are soft. "That's good. Because as soon as this party's over we're going back to your cabin."

I lift a brow, secretly pleased that he wants to be alone with me. "What about Ariel?"

"Holden's going to give her his room. I've made him an offer he can't refuse."

"What kind of offer?" I'm intrigued now.

"Probably best not to share specifics," Liam says. "But believe me when I say you're more than worth it."

CHAPTER
TWENTY-SEVEN

SOPHIE

The party is in full swing by ten that evening. The music is pumping and the weather has improved enough for the party to spill out onto the patio. Liam has been cornered by an old family friend who I gather from their conversation is also an investor, so I leave them to talk shop and head for the bathroom. They actually have separate ladies' and men's' bathrooms, with two stalls and two sinks. I guess they host a lot and it made sense.

I'm reapplying my lipstick when my phone vibrates in my purse and I pull it out, seeing my dad's name on the screen.

"Hey Dad," I say, putting the lid back onto the lipstick and sliding it into my purse. "You okay?"

"I just wanted to let you know I'm fine," he says. "Despite the storm."

My stomach drops. "Did something happen?"

"The roof tiles slipped. One of them shattered at my feet as I was trying to stop the trash cans from rolling down the hill."

I grimace. "It hit Charleston bad, huh?"

"For a while. Imagine my surprise when it started." Uhoh he sounds annoyed. "If only I had a daughter who could have warned me."

I wrinkle my nose. "Did I not tell you last night?" I run my mind back over our conversation. Surely I would have told him to secure everything.

"Nope. Not a word."

Oops. I think I was pretty distracted by the thought of seeing Liam.

"But you saw the weather forecast, right?"

"No. Just knew it was storming when it hit."

I let out a sigh. "I'm sorry. I'll buy you a new trashcan." He's usually the first person I call when there's a weather event coming. I feel terrible.

"It's fine. I just wanted to check on you. Did you get there safely? Did you avoid the rain?"

"Yes and yes." The bathroom door opens and Ariel walks in. She notices I'm on the phone and gives me a nod. I step into the hallway to give her privacy because nobody wants an audience when they have to go.

"And there's no more rain due tomorrow?" he asks.

"No." I can say that for certain. "It's going to be a beautiful day. No rain, just sunshine. Almost too hot again probably."

"Well you drive safely when you head home. And call me, I want to hear all the details about the party."

"I will, Dad. Sorry again. I've been a bit distracted."

He gives a little chuckle. "I know. I love you, honey."

"I love you, too." I hang up and for some reason decide to check my messages. And when I do it's like I've been hit in the chest by a ten ton truck.

There are five texts from Michael. Each one more irate than the last. All basically saying the same thing.

> Sophie, can you please answer my damn
> calls? Your report was never submitted.
> We've missed the deadline. THIS IS BIG
> SHIT!!! – Michael.

What? That's not true. I remember sending it on Friday. It doesn't stop my hands from shaking as I pull up Michael's number and hit the call button.

As soon as he answers he lets out a huff. "Finally."

"Michael? The report, I sent it." My throat feels tight. "I remember sending it. I hit the button."

"No, you didn't. They called me about five hours ago and said they were surprised we didn't put in a bid. I told them we had but they have no emails from you at all."

My heart starts slamming against my chest. "I have a send receipt. Let me find it. The email should be in my sent folder."

He sighs again. "Call me back when you do. I'm going to have to tell Donald about this. I fucking promised him we would do this, Sophie. I gave him my word."

"Okay," I say quickly. "I will."

I hang up and open my email app, but it doesn't load properly. I only have a single bar of signal on my 4G. I hadn't bothered asking for the internet password when we arrived since I wasn't planning on needing the internet much while here.

A couple push past me, laughing and drinking champagne. I step back but my back hits the wall. Then the band gets louder and I can't think properly. I keep hitting refresh but nothing happens.

Ariel walks out of the bathroom and spots me jabbing at my phone.

"Is everything okay?" she asks.

I blink. "It's fine. Just a work thing." I'm too anxious to actually talk about this. I just want to prove I sent the damn thing. "I might just go back to the cabin." My laptop is there, and I know Eli has his own WIFI code on the wall. It'll be quicker to log on there and pull my email account up on the laptop.

"Want me to come with you?" she asks, still looking concerned. "Or get Liam?"

"No, it's okay." He doesn't need to know about this. I don't want to spoil his mom's party.

"Okay," she says, still looking at me. "I hope you manage to sort it out."

I nod and turn on my heel, making my way out of the front door so nobody sees me. It's rude to leave mid-party, but hopefully nobody will notice if I do this quickly then head back. My mind is full of anxious thoughts as I almost run down the lit path toward the cabins, having to hold my dress up with one hand as I clasp my purse with the other. The lights outside Eli's cabin are on so I can easily see as I hurry up the steps and slide my key into the lock. Throwing my purse onto the table next to the door, I head for my room and grab my laptop.

It takes longer than it should to key in the WIFI code, mostly because my hands are shaking. Finally, it connects and I use my finger on the mouse pad to open up my work email app, and slowly it loads in front of me.

The first thing I do is click on the sent emails. There are a few there from Friday so I have to scroll down but then I see it. My email.

And then I see what's wrong. The email address. I put in the wrong email address. Instead of sending it to NTV – our parent network – I sent it to our rivals, BTV.

No. Please tell me I didn't press B instead of N. I feel sick as I realize how close together they are on my laptop keyboard and how harassed I was the day I sent the submission

Gritting my teeth, I open it up and read the email address again and my sanity starts to waver as I see BTV.tv in the 'to' box. I'm toast. Not only did I send it to the wrong email address but I sent it to a competitor.

What the hell is wrong with me? Why didn't I check it? I'm close to hyperventilating when my phone starts to ring again.

"Michael," I say, my hands shaking as I accept the call.

"Did you find it?"

"Yes." I take a deep breath. "I sent it to the wrong address."

"For fuck's sake!" he thunders. "Why the hell didn't you check?"

"I don't know…" My voice wavers.

"Why didn't you call to make sure it arrived?"

I was so sure it had gone off properly. I remember feeling a sense of relief and maybe even victory. And if I'm being honest, I was distracted. By meeting my dad. By coming here this weekend.

By Liam.

"I don't know what I was thinking." I'm hyperventilating now. I never do this. I always double check everything. "I, um, need to tell you something else."

There's silence for a moment. Then he finally speaks. "What is it?" he says, his voice low.

"I sent it to BTV."

"*What?*"

I squeeze my eyes shut, mortified by my own incompetence. "I know. I'm an idiot. I thought I typed the right address." They're our competitors. They shouldn't even know that the Network is planning to reorganize its weather offering. "It might not even get to them, right?" I say, hoping I'm right.

"I don't know," he says. "I need to think. You're in deep shit, Sophie." He sounds almost jubilant about that fact. "I need to call our legal team. That submission was confidential. It had all the plans for the hubs."

"I know," I say, trying to keep it together. "I should be the one to talk to legal."

"Yes, but you're not here, are you?" It's almost a taunt.

"No."

"And it can't wait, Sophie. Not when there's intellectual property involved. We need to talk to Donald and legal and then call New York."

"Can it wait until Monday?" I ask vainly.

"What, so you can finish partying before we sort out the mess you made?" He gives a laugh that has no mirth behind it. "No, it can't. I need to talk to people now. Just go and… do whatever. I'll let you know how it goes."

"I'm sorry," I say again because I have no idea what else to do. I'm going to throw up, I think.

"Be in first thing on Monday. Donald will want to see you."

I know he will. He'll want me to explain. And I don't know if I can.

I just wish I had a time machine.

Michael doesn't bother saying goodbye. I say his name but there's no response and that's when I know there's a dead connection. I stare at the black screen. I've messed up so badly and there's nothing I can do.

That's when I run to the bathroom to vomit up my dinner.

———

"Sophie?"

I hear Ariel's voice from where I'm still leaning over the toilet in the bathroom. Slowly I pull myself up from the floor and turn on the faucet, rinsing my mouth out as much as I can.

I'm not sure how long I've been in here. It feels like a lifetime. I keep going through things in my mind. How could I have been so stupid?

"Are you in here?" Ariel calls out, banging on the bathroom door. "Are you okay?"

She's not going to go away, I can tell that from the tone of her voice. I take a look at my smudged make up and red eyes and think at least it isn't Liam or Ava.

I can't face either of them. I definitely can't tell them about this. I'm too ashamed about my own incompetence.

When I open the door Ariel stumbles, as though she's had her ear to the door. "Oh God, you look terrible. Let me get Liam," she says.

I shake my head and grab her arm. "No, please don't."

"Are you ill?"

"No. I just..." I exhale heavily. "It's that work thing I told you about. I need to do something about it."

Relief softens her expression. "Oh, Thank God. I thought it might be something terrible. Let me get you some water." She walks over to the tiny kitchen area and grabs a glass out of the cupboard, filling it with water from the refrigerator. "Here," she says, handing it to me. "Drink."

So I do, and though it's refreshing it doesn't make me feel any better. I'm going to get fired. I know I am. And everybody will know why.

"Okay?" Ariel asks softly when I stop drinking.

I nod, but I'm far from okay.

"Please let me get Liam. He'd want to be here."

I shake my head. "It's his mom's birthday. He should be with her." I'm so embarrassed. He's a smart businessman. He doesn't make mistakes like this. He'll think I'm an amateur.

I just can't deal with seeing his face when I tell him.

She pulls her lip between her teeth and she looks so awkward I feel sorry for her. "You can go back to the party," I tell her. "I'll just stay here for a while. But I'd be really grateful if you don't tell anybody." Eventually Liam will realize that I've disappeared. But by then maybe I'll have worked out how to face him.

"He adores you," she says, as though she knows I'm thinking about him. "Which is wonderful. We never thought he'd be like this again."

"Again?" I frown. That's a weird way of putting it.

"After Marie," she says, nodding as though I should know what she's talking about. "He changed so much after her. But now he's back to the Liam we all remember."

"Marie?" I try to say it casually, like I know what she's talking about. "His..." I trail off, trying to think. "His girlfriend?"

"Yes," she says. "Or his fiancée, I guess. They were engaged, right?"

"Right." My hands start to shake. "When was that again?"

"Through college." She gives me a strange look. "He did tell you about her, didn't he?"

"I think so. Yes, Marie." I nod. "I can't remember who ended the engagement though."

Her mouth drops open and I know she knows I'm lying. I'm still terrible at it. I shouldn't have started this whole conversation.

"Neither of them broke it off," she almost whispers. "Marie died. Twenty years ago. And he's never been the same since."

CHAPTER
TWENTY-EIGHT

SOPHIE

Ariel is absolutely mortified. I can tell from the way her shoulders droop. I want to hug her but I know I must smell terrible. And I'm not sure she wants a hug from me.

Liam was engaged. He was in love. There was another woman who captured his heart.

And then she died and he never got over it. Which makes me, what? His Jenny?

She's a fine woman but she'll never replace your mom. She was the love of my life.

Of course she was. For a moment I see Liam, years younger and carefree, kissing a bride who's staring up at him adoringly.

A bride who isn't me. The woman who broke him so badly he couldn't commit again.

Until he met me and realized we were compatible and maybe that was enough.

Oh God, I'm going to be sick again.

"Sophie?"

"I just…"

I want to cry. I want to hide. I want to be at home.

I want my mom.

More than anything, I don't want to be here. I can't think. It's like my head is full of thick, wiry wool. I consider banging it against the wall.

"You're freaking me out," Ariel whispers.

"I'm sorry," I tell her, forcing myself to smile. "I didn't mean to scare you. There's just this important thing happening at work and they need me to help with it."

She nods as though she understands. "You work at a TV station, right?"

"Yes," I tell her. "In West Virginia. I need to go there now."

"It's a Saturday night." She frowns.

"I know, but it's open twenty-four-seven. And if I get back now I might be able to sort out this problem they're having." I have to get out of here. I can't let them see me break down. I hardly know his family, they'll all think I'm a drama queen.

Maybe I am.

"Haven't you been drinking?"

No, thank God. "I had a mimosa about four hours ago but that's it." I take her hand. "The thing is, I need your help."

"What can I do?" she asks me.

"I need you to not tell Liam about this. Or that I've gone. Not until the party is over. He'll want to come with me and that's not fair to Linda." Or he'll want to stop me from going at all and I can't deal with that now.

I can't deal with him, more to the point.

"I don't know…" She pulls at her skirt. "I don't want to lie to him."

"I get that." I nod quickly. "I'll write him a note. You can give it to him when the party ends. I'll explain that it isn't your fault."

She looks hugely uncomfortable.

"I'm sorry," I tell her. "I wish you hadn't come down here."

"I shouldn't have told you about Marie," she whispers. "It's not my place."

"This isn't your fault. None of it is. Just please… help me. Please."

She lets out a long breath and nods. "Okay. But he's going to kill me."

"Thank you." I hug her. "Thank you so much."

It takes me five minutes to change into a pair of jeans and a t-shirt. Another minute to write a note to Liam and fold it into little pieces. Ariel takes it from me and frowns. "Are you sure you're okay to drive? Even if you haven't drunk anything you're upset and it's dark."

"I know. But I'll be fine. I'm calm now." I hold my hand out and it's stable. To be honest, it's true. All the fear and anxiety have been replaced by some sort of tranquil knowledge that at least I can do something about all this if I'm in Charleston. And yes I'll arrive in the middle of the night but it's still better than being here. I'll call Michael on the way and ask if we can meet first thing.

I take my bag and we walk up the path. She heads back to the party and I skulk around on the grass so nobody sees me heading toward the driveway. When I get to the front, the men in yellow jackets are still there, and I give one of them my name. He points at my car, on the far side of the driveway, and carries my bag over there for me.

Then I get in and start up the ignition. Liam's going to be hurt. Ava's going to kill me. But I know I'm doing the right thing leaving like this.

It's my mess and my job to solve it. They don't need to get involved.

———

LIAM

"Have you seen Sophie?" I ask Ava, a frown pulling at my brow. I've been looking for her since I managed to extricate myself from my mom's aunt.

Ava's sitting in the living room feeding Charlie. I feel bad for interrupting her, but I really thought I'd find Sophie with her.

"No." She frowns. "I haven't seen her for a while. Did you check the cabin?"

"Why would she be in the cabin?" I ask.

"I don't know." Ava shrugs. "It's just a thought."

I grab my phone from my pocket. "I'll call her."

But when the phone connects it rings to her voicemail without her answering at all.

"Everything okay?" Myles walks in and frowns when he sees me watching his wife breastfeed.

"Liam has lost Sophie."

Myles smiles. "That's careless."

"Have you seen her?" I ask him, sighing.

"Maybe she realized what an idiot you are and ran off," he says, still grinning.

"Shut up." I walk out and leave them to it, heading to the kitchen to see if she's there.

After five minutes, I'm actually starting to get worried. Maybe Ava's right, I should go and check the cabin. Pulling the kitchen door open, I walk onto the patio. Guests are still milling around in the warm night time air. You wouldn't believe we'd even had a storm.

I spot Ariel and Clare in the corner, sitting at a table with their mom. I haven't had a chance to talk with Ria yet, but I will once I find Sophie.

"Hey, have any of you seen Sophie?" I ask them, leaning down to kiss Ria's cheek.

"Is that your girlfriend?" Ria asks.

"You know it is, Mom." Clare rolls her eyes. "Sorry, Liam, I haven't seen her for a while."

Ariel shifts in her seat but says nothing.

"Guess I'm going to head to the cabin. See if she's there."

She nods and looks away.

I'm halfway down the path when I hear my name being called. I turn to see Ariel running – or doing her best in those heels she's wearing. She's holding up the hem of her dress and she looks distinctly out of breath.

"Liam," she says, puffing out a mouthful of air. "There's something you need to know."

"What?" I smile at her. "Hey, take a breath or two. We don't want any fatalities at this party."

She doesn't smile back. In fact, she can barely bring herself to look at me. "Ariel? Is everything okay?"

"Sophie's gone."

"Huh?" I wrinkle my nose. "What are you talking about?"

"She left. There's a problem at work she had to get back for."

"That's not right. She's not working this weekend. She's probably in the cabin."

Ariel puts her hand on my shoulder. "Liam, she's gone. She left a note." She scrambles through the silver purse that's hanging on a chain from her shoulder. "Here." She passes me a piece of paper folded into four.

Liam,

I'm so sorry, I have to go. Don't blame Ariel. This isn't her fault. I just asked her to cover for me. I'll explain when... I don't know. I just need to make things right.

I'm sorry, I'm sorry, I'm sorry.
Sophie

I stare at her words for a moment. It doesn't even sound like her. "What's going on?" I ask softly, looking up at Ariel.

She shifts her feet. "She was really upset. Something happened but she wouldn't tell me what. I wanted to get you but she begged me not to."

"Why wouldn't she want me?" I try to ignore the tightness in my chest.

"I don't know." Ariel grimaces. "But there is something else I have to tell you."

I don't say anything. Just lift a brow. I think she knows I'm getting pissed.

"I'm so sorry, Liam, but I told her about Marie." She reaches out for my hand. "I didn't realize she didn't know about her. I thought…" She trails off, shaking her head. "I opened my mouth and it just came out."

Fuck. "What did you say?" I ask, my voice gritty. "Tell me exactly."

"That we never thought you'd love somebody again. But I was so glad you'd found each other. It was good stuff, Liam. Nothing awful. But her face…"

"What about her face?"

"She just looked so upset. And I think she threw up."

"And you let her drive in that condition?" I thunder, because what the hell is going on here? "You really thought that was a good idea?" I tug at my hair, trying to work out what to do. She could be in a ditch somewhere, hurt or worse. No, I can't think like that. I pull my phone out but once again when I call her it goes straight to voicemail.

"I'm so sorry. I didn't want her to go. She made me

promise not to tell you. She was so upset. I just wanted to make it all okay." Her face is crumpled as she looks at me and I feel like a piece of shit.

"It's okay," I tell her, putting my hand on her arm. "I know this isn't your fault. I'm just worried." That's an understatement. "How long ago did she leave?"

"About half an hour," Ariel says, her voice full of misery. "I made sure she hadn't been drinking. And she seemed a lot calmer once she'd made a plan." Her eyes meet mine. "She'll be all right, won't she?"

"What's going on?" We both turn to see Myles walking toward us, lit only by the soft glare of the moon. "I heard shouting."

I feel bad because I never should have shouted at Ariel. "Sophie's left and gone back to Charleston."

Myles blinks. "Why? Did you do something to her?"

"No." I can't even be bothered to play this game right now. "She's having some work issues."

"At the station?"

"Apparently," I say, my voice tight.

"And she didn't come to see you before she left?" Myles looks confused. "Why wouldn't she?"

"She was upset and didn't want to ruin the party," Ariel tells him. "I promised I'd tell you all afterward."

"So she'll be driving for hours in the middle of the night?" Myles' eyes are clouded with thoughts. I'm kind of gratified that he sounds as worried as I do. "Have you called her?" he asks me.

"Yes." But I try again anyway. And again it goes straight to voicemail. "I need to follow her. I can probably catch up with her if I leave now."

"You can't drive," Ariel tells me. "I definitely saw you drinking earlier."

Two beers with my brothers. And some champagne. Shit. "Have you been drinking?" I ask her.

"Yes."

I look at Myles and he shrugs. I know for sure that our other brothers aren't fit to drive either. And there's no way I can ask any of the guests to give me a ride for four hours just to find my girlfriend.

"I'll call a taxi," I say.

"In the middle of nowhere at this time of night?" Myles shakes his head. "That's not going to happen."

He's right. I kick the dirt with my polished shoe, frustrated. "Should I call somebody in Charleston?" I ask him. "Her dad or Lauren?"

"Not now. You'll panic them for no reason. Wait until morning, then you can leave first thing."

"That's too much time to wait," I tell him. I can't stand the thought of her driving out there alone.

"What choice do you have?" he asks. "I'll come with you in the morning. You were there for me when I needed you." I know he's referring to the night he thought he'd lost Ava. But he never really had.

He hadn't lied to her. Hadn't hidden a dead fiancée from her. Christ, what was I thinking?

Ariel takes my hand again. "He's right, Liam. I know it's hard. We can keep calling her until then."

I nod because there's no other way. And Myles is right, no car service would get here before morning at the very least. So I call Sophie one more time and actually leave a message this time.

"It's me. Please let me know when you get back to Charleston safely. It doesn't matter what time it is, I just need to know you're okay." I end the call and look at them both. "I'm going to head back to the cabin." The last thing I feel like doing is socializing.

Myles nods. "Of course. I'll cover for you at the party. I don't think it's going to last much longer anyway. Let me know if you hear from her. Ava's going to go apeshit and I'd like to be able to reassure her."

"I will," I tell him. "And thank you."

He nods for a second, but then he steps closer and hugs me. I blink, surprised, but hug him back anyway.

"I love you," Myles tells me. I must look more upset than I thought. "And Sophie does, too. I hope you know that."

CHAPTER
TWENTY-NINE

SOPHIE

The drive back to Charleston takes longer than I'd planned. Mostly because it's so dark and even with my high beams on I can barely see the twists and turns ahead of me. I'm also shaking, and my head is so messed up with thoughts of my mistakes, of Liam's fiancée, of just being a complete failure, that I have to drive slowly to make sure I don't crash.

A couple of hours in, I have to stop in a rest area. The soft drinks I had earlier have caught up with me, so I wander into the building and visit the bathroom before I find a vending machine that serves coffee.

It's suitably disgusting, but I hope the caffeine kicks in soon.

When I'm back in the car I finally check my phone. There are no more messages from Michael, so I have no idea whether he will be meeting with legal in a few hours' time. But there are voicemails from Liam. My stomach contracts as I consider not listening to it.

Ariel must have told him I left. He'll be annoyed even though I did the right thing.

As soon as I connect to my voicemail I hit one to listen to his message.

"What the hell is going on? Call me. Please. You said you trusted me."

My heart clenches. I did. I do…

Do I? I blink, unsure who I trust. Maybe not even myself.

It's the middle of the night and I have no idea if he's asleep or not. I mean, he should be, everybody should be. It gives me an excuse not to call him.

So instead I send a message.

> I'm sorry. I messed up. I'm an idiot. I'll explain tomorrow if you're still talking to me. – Sophie

I've barely hit send before my phone starts to ring, his name on the screen. With shaking hands, I accept it.

"Hello." My heart is racing. I don't feel good.

"Why did you leave without telling me?" His voice sounds wrong. Like he's almost broken.

"There's a work problem," I tell him, still hedging around the facts. "I need to be in Charleston."

"That doesn't explain why you didn't find me and tell me," he says hoarsely. "I would have gone with you."

"It's your mom's birthday. You couldn't have done that. And you didn't need to, this is my problem."

He's silent for a moment. I can hear the blood rushing through my ears. "You still don't trust me, do you?"

I swallow hard. "I do…"

"No, you don't. If you trusted me you would have found me. We would have been a team, facing this together. You ran, Sophie. You ran because you're scared."

"I *am* scared," I whisper. "I'm scared of losing my job."

"You should have told me!"

I try to answer him, but he's right. I should have. I should have done a lot of things. "I'm sorry," I say again, because my heart is starting to hurt.

"Ariel told me you know about Marie."

I can't talk about this. Not now. "It doesn't matter," I tell him. "That's not why I left."

Not even if you loved her more than you could ever love me. Not if she got the best of you. The Liam who was young and carefree.

"It's part of it though, isn't it?" he asks. It's like he's reading my mind. "It confirmed to you that you're on your own. That we're not in this together."

"Liam…" I can't think of what to say. I can't think of anything. "I'm so sorry."

"Where are you right now?" he asks.

"At a rest stop about an hour from Charleston." Probably two at the rate I'm driving.

"You're at a rest stop on your own?"

"Yes, I needed a break."

"Do you have no fucking sense of self-preservation?" he asks me. "It's not safe there. You need to get home."

"Liam, we need to talk."

He laughs but there's no mirth there. "Oh, now you want to talk? No. You need to drive."

"Can we talk tomorrow?" I ask him, feeling desperate.

"Just go do whatever you need to do," he says, and there's pain in his voice. "Don't worry about me."

"I do worry—" I stop talking when I realize he's ended the call. My heart feels like it's about to burst. Like it's too big for my chest, rattling against my ribcage. It takes a concerted effort to breathe.

Broken. That's how he sounded. And it's my fault. He's right, I should have trusted him. But I didn't. I couldn't.

I thought he was the one who needed to change, but maybe it was me all along.

That thought bounces around my head for the rest of the drive home.

————

It's eerily quiet when I walk into the station stupidly early the next morning, having gone home only to shower and put on my work clothes. Even the security guard looks bored. We run on a skeleton crew overnight, making sure the networked shows broadcast smoothly. But there are still a few people in the news office and the sports room, getting a head start for the first broadcast of the day.

Michael looks up when I walk in. "I thought you were in Virginia," he says, frowning.

"I came back. To sort things out," I tell him.

"There's nothing you can do," he says. "Donald is coming in at ten to meet with legal. They'll take it from there."

"Can I come to the meeting?" I ask.

He lets out a huff. "No. It's a management meeting. If we need your input we'll ask for it."

"But it's about me. I should be there to explain exactly what happened," I tell him. I need to be in that meeting. I don't trust him to stand up for me.

"Don't you think you've done enough damage?" he snaps. "I need to get ready for the morning news. If you're staying here – which is without pay by the way – do me a favor and load up the forecast on the website."

I nod because at least it'll give me something to do while I wait.

I spend two hours messing around on the website and kicking my heels, counting down until the meeting. At half-past five, Michael knots his tie and pulls on his sports jacket and checks himself in the little mirror at the side of our office, then heads out to the studio without even saying goodbye.

I look up at the monitor we always have running. The

credits roll and then Dan comes on, his mouth moving though the television is on silent so I can't hear what he says.

The camera switches to Michael. He gives an all-American grin to the screen as though he hasn't a care in the world. Ugh, I hate him. He hasn't had much more sleep than me but he looks so much better. I swear he's running on pure venom right now.

Half an hour later, my phone starts to ring. It's a group call and I see Ava and Lauren's name at the top.

"Hey." I put it on speaker because there's nobody else here.

"Don't hey me," Ava says. "I'm angry with you." Her voice softens. "No, I'm not really that angry. I'm worried. Why did you leave without telling me?"

I blink. I'm not going to cry again. I've already used up way too many tears. "I messed up," I tell them. "I think I might lose my job."

"What happened?" Lauren asks. I can hear the noise of her bakery behind her.

"Shouldn't you be opening up?" I ask her.

"I have twenty minutes. And even if I didn't my best friend comes first. So spill. Tell us everything."

So I do. I let it all go, embarrassed as I am. I don't sugar-coat it because these are my best friends.

"Oh sweetie," Ava says. "I wish you'd come to me last night."

"I wasn't thinking straight. I panicked and thought I needed to be here at the station. I need to explain everything to Donald. Face to face."

"And have you?" Lauren asks.

"He's not here yet," I tell them. "And Michael won't let me come to the meeting he's scheduled for ten this morning."

"Ugh he's a rat bastard. You want me to put a hit on him?" Lauren asks. She sounds vaguely serious.

"No, I just want to be able to plead my case."

"Have you heard from Liam?" Ava asks.

"I spoke to him a few hours ago. He was angry." I bite my lip. "I shouldn't have walked out on him either."

"No you shouldn't," Ava says. "But you were upset. Did you talk to him about Marie?"

"Who's Marie?" Lauren asks.

I let out a lungful of air. "Liam's dead fiancée."

"What?" she shouts.

"I'm as surprised as you are," I say softly. "Ava, did you know about her?"

"No. Apparently they don't really talk about her. Liam moved on and that was that. But I know now. Myles spilled the beans when I threatened to chop his balls off."

"What did he tell you?" I ask her.

"Don't you think you should let Liam explain?" Ava asks softly. "It's not really my place to tell you."

She's right. But it hurts my heart to think about Liam having to tell me this. Not just because it's something he's hidden from me, but because I hate that it must have hurt him so badly.

Enough to make him swear off relationships. To become this happy guy on the surface but underneath he must have been in so much pain.

I love him. And yet there's a side of him he's hidden from me. That hurts, too.

"He's a good guy," Lauren says. "He obviously adores you."

"He does," Ava agrees. "He was in pieces when you left last night."

Guilt washes over me. I need to talk to him. To apologize. To explain the panic I had when I saw where I sent that email. The knowledge that Michael would use it to screw me over.

The fact that I was afraid of losing him. So I ran.

"I need to go," I say softly, because it's getting hard to breathe. "There's so much to do."

"Of course," Ava says. "Call us once that meeting is over and you know the results. We're here for you, honey."

"And if you need me I can be there in ten minutes," Lauren tells me.

"You have a bakery to run," I remind her.

"Bakery shmakery. You're my friend, you come first. Always."

I'm so lucky to have them. "Thank you," I whisper, because if I say anymore I might cry.

"Hang in there," Ava says. "It's going to be okay."

The problem is, I'm not so sure it will be.

———

From: SophieWest@WVFY.tv
    To: LiamSalinger@SalingerEnterprises.com
    Subject: Your weather forecast

Dear Liam,

The sun will shine all day in both West Virginia and in Misty Lakes. Temperatures will top out at the mid-eighties and the humidity is moderate for this time of year.

There's no rain in the forecast and tomorrow is shaping up to be just as glorious.

And I'm sorry.

So sorry.

. . .

I know you don't want to talk to me right now. But I need to talk to you. Please call me when you get a chance.

Be safe.
    Sophie

I hit send, making damn sure I've sent it to the right email address, and then I turn to the satellite maps, jotting down notes about the weather direction for the next few days. I'm working on autopilot, loading up today's social media updates so Michael doesn't have to. And because if I sit here doing nothing I'll go out of my mind.

He hasn't come back from the studio, even though the broadcast finished a while ago. I can't help but feel jumpy at what he might be up to.

Just after eight, Lisa puts her head around the door, blinking when she sees me sitting at my desk. "What are you doing here?" she asks. She's carrying a venti coffee in a Styrofoam cup and has a huge rucksack slung over her shoulder. "Michael said you were in Virginia."

"I came back." I'm not sure if I'm supposed to say anything about the email. Or whether they'll try to hush it. "There are a few things I need to do."

"Michael said you were refusing to come back. That you were leaving him to clean everything up."

"What?" I frown. Lisa walks inside the office, slinging her rucksack on the floor and perching on the corner of my desk.

"He was raging late last night," she told me. "Ranting about how irresponsible you were. Said he had to call in legal and they were demanding a meeting with you but you wouldn't come back from your weekend away."

"That's a lie. He told me not to come back."

She blinks. "But you came."

"I didn't know what to do." I look up at her. She's sipping at her coffee but it's obviously too hot, as she winces when it hits her tongue. "Did he tell you what happened?"

Her expression softens. "He told the whole damn station." She must notice my face fall because she hurriedly adds, "not that there were many of us here last night. You know what it's like on a Saturday night. Skeleton crew."

Yeah, but that means everybody will know by tomorrow. "I'm going to lose my job," I tell her. I'm blinking back tears again. I know that a job isn't supposed to define who you are, but I've been here for so long that I think mine does. At least to some extent. An image of my dad's proud face flashes into my mind.

He's going to be devastated when he finds out. And I don't want him to be. I don't want anybody to be.

"You won't. If anybody should lose their job, it's Michael. He's your boss, he's the one who was supposed to be doing that report. If he wasn't such a lazy bastard none of this would have happened." She puts her cup down on my desk and reaches for my hand. "We're all on your side. You know that."

I glance at the clock. It's only five minutes past eight. I should still be in bed. With Liam. In Eli's cabin. The way he'd arranged it because he couldn't bear to be apart from me for one night.

I should have gone to him. I should have told him. There was no excuse for not doing that.

"Sophie?"

For one moment the male voice sends a shot of hope through my body. But it's not Liam, it's Donald. He's looking as surprised as Lisa did, and I'm starting to realize that Michael's been waiting for this opportunity to screw me over.

"Hello." My voice wavers as I stand. Lisa conveniently

walks over to the filing cabinets and pretends to look through one. "I know Michael told you what happened. I'm so sorry. This is all my fault. I didn't check the email address and I should have—"

He puts up his hand. "You can explain it at the meeting. In the board room. Nine o'clock."

"I thought it was at ten." And that I'm not invited.

Donald shakes his head. "No, it's definitely at nine."

Michael. Again. Part of me wants to walk into the studio and scream at him.

But he couldn't have been able to do this if I hadn't messed up. I have to take my fair share of responsibility for that.

"I'll be there," I tell him.

"I should think so." He turns and walks out, and Lisa puts her arm around me.

"It's just an email address," she says. "You didn't kill anybody. Try to not look so scared. Listen, I have to go and do the sports update on the website, but I'll be around. Come find me after the meeting. No matter what happens."

I nod. "Okay."

She's silent for a moment, and then she squeezes me tight. "It's going to be okay."

It's funny how she's using the same words Ava did. Neither of them fill me with hope. They're the kind of words I'd use if I was comforting somebody. And yeah, eventually I will be okay. Maybe.

But right now it doesn't feel that way. I've messed everything up. I can't believe I left Liam without saying a word.

When she leaves I pull out my phone, checking my messages, my texts, my emails. There's nothing from him. The last message I sent doesn't have a read tick next to it. And there's no read receipt from the email either.

That's when I make the decision. Whatever happens at this meeting I'm going to leave straight after. Head back to

Virginia to explain to him. I just need to see him, to tell him I'm sorry.

Because I'm starting to realize something. The thing I should have known all along.

That losing my job would be terrible. But I could recover from it.

But to lose him? That would be pure and utter devastation.

CHAPTER
THIRTY

SOPHIE

I try calling Liam before I have to go to the boardroom but he doesn't pick up. Like the meeting room, the boardroom is on the top floor of the television station, but I take the stairs rather than take the elevator, mostly because the exercise will stop me from thinking too much.

Donald is already there, next to two men who are wearing almost identical dark suits and gray ties. Michael is on his right, looking annoyed as I walk in.

"Ah, Sophie. Take a seat, please." Donald nods to the seat next to his assistant, Rhian. I don't know her very well because she looks permanently harassed, but I nod at her and she does the same.

I wonder if she knows how much my job is in the balance. Probably she does, because next to her is Monica from HR. My chest constricts. HR never gets called into a meeting unless something is extremely wrong.

"Let me introduce you," Donald says. "Sophie West. She works for Michael as our meteorologist. Sophie, you know

Monica and Rhian, I believe. And next to me is Charles Faulkener of Faulkener and Spring. And Robert here is his associate."

Both men nod at me. We're too small a station to have a permanent legal department, so it's outsourced to a local company.

"Hello," I whisper as I situate myself.

"Well I think we all know why we are here," Donald says. "Sophie, maybe you can explain to us exactly what happened."

I take a deep breath and tell them about the report. About the email. About not realizing until last night that I'd sent it to our competitor. Rhian is scribbling down everything I say on her notepad, while Monica from HR is shaking her head.

"When did you become aware of it?" Donald asks Michael.

"Well, I found out yesterday that the report hadn't been submitted," Michael says, his voice even. "And then Sophie told me it had been sent to the wrong address when I called her. Obviously I realized it was a catastrophe of the highest order, and with Sophie being away I took the initiative and called you." He looks pleased with himself.

Donald nods and looks at me. "Did you raise the alarm as soon as you realized your error?"

"Yes I did."

"But it doesn't alter the fact that our competitor now knows what happened," Michael points out. Rhian lifts a brow.

The lawyers nod.

"I have requested a call back from the network's legal team," Charles Faulkener says. "That should be taking place right after this meeting. We'll then agree on an approach to the competitor's team."

"I've also got a call in to the CEO," Donald says. "Sophie,

we're going to have to ask you to stay away from the station for the next few days."

I blink. "I'm suspended?"

"We need to show the network that we're taking this seriously. I understand it was human error, but the effect could be catastrophic." He looks at Monica from HR. "Could you escort Sophie out?"

"But..." My heart is racing. "Michael can't run the weather desk alone."

"Madison can help me," Michael points out. "I'll be fine."

"The weather team isn't your concern right now," Donald tells me. "Please just do as I ask."

Monica stands and gives me a sympathetic smile. I follow her out, and as the door closes I hear the conversation begin again. Without speaking, Monica hits the button for the elevator, and when it arrives we both step inside.

"Do you have things to pick up from your desk?" she asks softly.

"My bag. And my laptop." I frown. "Should I leave that here for now?"

"I'll take the laptop. You just take your personal things."

It sounds like the end. "Okay."

When the elevator opens onto my floor, we step out and Monica walks slightly ahead of me. The sound of our shoes hitting the tiled floor echoes in the hallway. Lisa walks out of the sports office and frowns when she sees us.

"How did it go?" she asks.

I shake my head because I think I might cry if I speak.

"What's happening?" She follows the two of us into the weather office. I unplug the laptop and hand it to Monica.

"Oh no," Lisa says. "They fired you?"

"Suspended," I say, my voice thick.

"This isn't fair," she tells Monica. "Sophie's been working every free moment to finish that submission. She's overworked and underpaid and has been covering for Michael for months."

"She's not being fired," Monica says. "If that's a possibility she'll have the opportunity to defend herself."

Lisa stands with me as I pack my things into my bag. Monica watches us from next to the door, my laptop in her arms.

"Is that everything?" she asks me.

I nod.

"I'll walk you out then."

"No," Lisa says. "I'll walk her. The last thing she needs is everybody staring at her because she's being escorted out by HR."

There's not many people here to stare but I appreciate Lisa's sentiment.

"Okay." Monica nods. "I'll just need your badge."

I unclip my ID badge and hand it to her. Lisa slides her hand into mine. "This isn't right," she mutters as we walk out of the office and down the corridor. We pass one or two people who give me a strange look.

And then we walk through the front entrance. Like I'd forecasted, the sun is bright, the air is warm. The kind of Sunday for sitting in the park with friends. My heart aches.

"Do you want to grab a coffee?" Lisa asks.

I shake my head. "I just want to go home." So we start to walk to my car.

And that's when I see him. Striding toward us, the sun behind him lighting up his hair. Liam's wearing a pair of light jeans and a gray t-shirt and he looks exhausted and annoyed.

But he still looks wonderful to me. And that's when I start to cry.

———

LIAM

• • •

She's crying and it's killing me. A woman walks next to her, patting her arm, but I only have eyes for Sophie.

I don't care that I'm supposed to be pissed that she drove home while upset, or that I'm also pissed at myself for being an asshole to her when she called – because I can't stand to see her in pain.

"Come here." I pull her into my arms and she almost melts into them.

The woman with her looks up at me with interest. "Hey, you're the auction guy."

"Liam Salinger." I nod at her over the top of Sophie's head. Her face is against my chest and I can already feel the dampness of my t-shirt where she's crying.

"Lisa." She pulls her lip between her teeth and looks at Sophie again. "You want me to drive you home?"

Sophie pulls her head from my chest. "No. I can do it. Thank you, for everything."

"What's happened?" I ask her. "What's going on?"

And I know there are things we need to talk about. I know there's one big almighty fuck up I need to explain. But right now I need to know what happened and what I can do to help.

"I've been suspended from my job," Sophie says. "While they investigate my errors."

My first inclination is to go into the TV station and talk to Donald Regan. I'm pretty sure I can get her back in there in two seconds.

"Tell me everything, please." I slide my arm around her shoulders. She feels frail, but I need to hear this from her. I'm good at solving problems but only if I know what the hell the problems are.

Her friend goes back into the building after kissing Sophie's wet cheek. She's still leaning on me and I'm here for that.

I'm here for *her*. She needs to understand she can't push

me away.

"I'm sorry," she finally says. "For leaving without telling you."

"We'll talk about that later," I tell her, because there's a lot I need to talk about, too. "But first let's deal with this. I'll drive you home. My place or yours?"

"Mine. But I have my car…"

"Leave it. I'll get somebody to pick it up." I wait for her to protest because I know she hates causing extra work. But she doesn't and it makes me realize just how upset she is.

She's tearful the whole way home. There are no huge gasping sobs, but tiny little ones that stutter every now and then like she can't quite catch her breath. They wreck me more than any screaming sob could. She's so fucking restrained, even when she's upset.

Somehow I manage to get most of the story out of her. And I'm even more pissed when I find out why she's been pushed out of the building.

"Because of an email address? Seriously?" I shake my head. I wonder if I can buy the damn station.

But she'd hate that. And I love her so I won't. Dammit.

"It's a competitor."

"That email might not even exist at the competitor. There's no proof that it even arrived there."

"You know how email servers work," she says, her lip trembling. "It'll go there anyway, especially since it didn't bounce back. If the right person reads it then they'll know all about the weather hub plans."

"But they shouldn't send you out of the building until they know for sure." And yet there's part of me that knows I'd do the same. I have a ruthless streak when it comes to most things.

"They did anyway," she says wanly. "And they're right, it is my fault. I should have checked that email. I always double check things. I was just…" She sighs. "Stupid, I guess."

Guilt pulls at my stomach. I distracted her. And I couldn't even tell her the truth about my life. We pull into her apartment's parking lot and climb out, walking silently into the lobby. She pushes the button for the elevator, then leans against me. I take it because dammit I need the connection.

When we're inside I make her coffee and insist she actually eats something because I know for sure that she won't if given the choice. My own stomach is growling so I make us both a sandwich. She manages three bites before she gives up.

"I love you," I tell her, because I need her to know she isn't alone.

She nods. "I love you, too."

"I could make this all go away," I say, because it needs to be said out loud. "I know the right people. Just tell me to call them and I will."

She blinks. "No. I don't want…"

Of course she doesn't. That wouldn't be my girl. She's gotten to where she is thanks to sheer hard work and grit.

But it's killing me to see her like this.

"I think I'm going to take a shower," she says. "And then maybe try to sleep. It's been a long few hours."

"That's a good idea," I tell her.

"Do you want to go home? There's not much you can do here."

"I'm not going anywhere."

She gives me the smallest of smiles then walks to her bedroom, leaving the door open. A moment later I hear the shower running and I clean up the kitchen and then grab my phone.

I call Ava and Myles to let them know I'm with her. I call my mom and my dad to explain why I left in such a hurry. They're all worried about her and insist that I do something to help.

So then I call Sam, my assistant, because she's the only one

I know who can do what I need right now.

And when I explain she laughs softly. "Only you would ask me to do that."

"I know. And I'm going to put it in writing because if there's any blowback it falls on me, not you." She's a single mom. I'd never let her do anything that risks her family's security.

"Okay. I'm on it. But it may take a little while. And I can't promise anything."

"I understand," I tell her. It's a shot in the dark. "But if you pull it off I'm going to give you the mothership of all pay rises."

"That's music to my ears, boss."

Ending the call, I walk into Sophie's bedroom. She's curled up on the bed, her wet hair splayed out on the pillow, a white towel wrapped around her. I climb in beside her and pull her against me, and after a couple of minutes I feel her relax, enough for her breath to even out and her eyes to flutter shut.

I stay with her while she sleeps because I want her to know she's not alone. Even if it's only a subconscious feeling.

CHAPTER
THIRTY-ONE

When I open my eyes I'm disoriented. It takes me a moment to realize that Liam's holding me, tight against him, my back against his front, his strong arms wrapped around my chest.

He's asleep, I can tell that from his steady breathing and the heaviness of his arms on me. It's no surprise, he probably got as little rest as I did last night. I manage to twist in his arms so I can look at him. Asleep he looks younger, carefree. Like the almost-man who was probably in love with Marie.

And again I feel my heart ache for him. I don't care that he loved somebody else. I'll be his Jenny. I'll take him however I can get him because nothing makes sense without this man.

He came to save me. *Again.* And this time I want him to.

I lift my head to softly kiss Liam's lips. They're warm and soft. Then I kiss his jaw, his cheek, the soft skin beneath his ear where his hairline ends and his beard line hasn't yet begun.

He sighs softly and slowly his eyes open.

"Hi," he murmurs, his gaze wary.

I hate that he has to be guarded around me. "Hi."

He pulls his arm from around me and cups my face. "Did you sleep?" he asks.

"A little." I take a deep breath. "I'm sorry I left without telling you."

"I'm sorry you had to find out about Marie in that way. Ariel's devastated." He looks concerned as he strokes my cheek softly.

I feel bad about Ariel, too. I'll have to call her. But right now Liam and I need to talk.

"Tell me about Marie," I ask him.

He takes a deep breath, his worried eyes not leaving mine. "Okay." So he does, his hand still cupping my face, his voice soft as he tells me about his second year of college. Meeting a freshman who had moved in with a friend of a friend.

"We got along," he tells me. "We had fun. I was a kid and I wanted that person, you know? Like in *Grey's Anatomy*."

"You wanted your Meredith." I smile softly because I wanted that, too. The fact we're both here means we never got what we wanted.

"And for a year it worked out pretty well."

"And then?" This is where it's going to turn. Where she dies and his heart is broken. Where he loses his person and is never the same.

I need to hear it but it still hurts. Because I know it hurts him.

"Then I realized I didn't want to be with her anymore."

My eyes widen. "What?" This is not what I was expecting. "But..."

"I was a fucking punk. I didn't want to be the bad guy. The one to break it off. So I hung around hoping she'd notice and be the one to end things. But she didn't because she couldn't read minds. And also because she was starting to feel sick. Turns out she'd been feeling bad for a while but figured it was due to having too much school work. I went with her for testing, and that's when she found out she had colon cancer. It was rare for somebody her age but pretty advanced."

My heart aches for him. "Poor Marie."

"Yeah." He exhales heavily. "I knew then that I couldn't tell her I'd fallen out of love with her. So I did the opposite. I asked her to marry me. And she said yes."

"You made her happy," I whisper.

"I tried. I tried so fucking hard. More than I've tried at anything in my life. We planned the wedding, she bought a dress. I asked Myles to be my best man. But then she got sicker and it was obvious she couldn't get married like that. So we agreed that we'd postpone the wedding until she was better again."

"But she didn't get better," I whisper.

"No. She got worse. It happened mercifully quickly after that."

"Oh Liam." I cup his face. "You lied but you made her happy."

"I hope so."

Tears prick at my eyes. "I know you did." Because I know how Liam loves. Furiously. That's the best way to describe it. And even if he'd fallen out of love with her, he'd still have the memory of it.

He'd still care enough to do whatever he could to make things right.

"And after she died I made myself a promise to not hurt anybody else the way I could have hurt her."

"But you didn't hurt her."

He blows out a mouthful of air. "At the very end she told me she knew I didn't feel the same about her. That she'd pretended I did because she didn't want to be alone. That she wanted to die feeling loved." He pulls his gaze away from mine. "I fucked everything up. That's when I realized me and relationships didn't work."

"But they do," I whisper. "You're here with me now."

His lip curls. "Yeah, I am." When he lifts his head up his eyes are a maelstrom of emotions. "I tried," he tells me. "I tried so hard to not fall in love with you."

This time my smile is stronger. "Ditto. And yet here we are."

"Thank God," he says, stroking my face. "Thank God you're here."

"Thank God for you," I say. And that's when I realize that nothing else matters. If I lose my job it'll hurt but I'll pick myself up and carry on. If I lose this apartment I'd find somewhere to live – even if it meant moving in with Dad for a while.

Everything could end and it would still be okay.

He cups my face with his hands, tipping my head until our mouths are a breath away from each other. There's such warmth in his eyes. Such need. It makes everything inside me tingle.

"I love you," I tell him.

"Don't run away from me again. Don't ever do that," he tells me.

"I won't." It's the truth. A promise I can keep. I've learned a lot about myself these past twenty-four hours.

That I can survive no matter what. That I can love so deeply it hurts my soul when I think the other person is hurt.

That I don't want to be without this, strong yet vulnerable man beside me.

"Good," he whispers. "Because I love you, too. Now please let me call your boss and tell him to give you your job back."

I laugh and it feels good. Genuine. "No. Don't do that."

"It'd only take one phone call."

"I know. But I need to hold my head high."

"You'll do that no matter what. You deserve that job."

"You're the sweetest," I tell him. "I love how frustrated you look right now."

"I just want to make you happy." He brushes the tip of my nose with his lips. "It annoys me that I could do that if you'd let me."

"You do make me happy. And I'll keep on letting you," I promise. "But you calling my boss' boss' boss would make me feel uncomfortable."

He lifts a brow. "You're going to have to get used to me taking care of you."

I smile at him. "And you're going to have to use to me wanting to be independent."

"We're going to need to find a middle ground," he murmurs. His lips catch mine, leaving me breathless. "I think it's probably right about here." His mouth parts and his tongue flickers against mine and suddenly I'm soft in his arms. If taking care of me means kissing me like this I'm all for it.

His throat rumbles as he rolls me onto my back, still kissing me as he cages me with his arms. He holds his body over mine, keeping some of his weight off me, but I can still feel parts of his chest and stomach as they press against my curves.

And then my phone rings.

He groans and rolls off. My heart starts to hammer against my chest because this could be it. The truth of my future.

Donald Regan may have decided my fate.

But it's Lauren's name that fills my screen, requesting a video call. "You may want to roll over," I tell Liam. "You're about to be on camera."

He doesn't move an inch. Okay then.

"Hey," I say when the screen flickers to life.

"What happened to my phone call?" she asks. "You were supposed to update us."

Oh I was. Damn.

Then she laughs at my expression. "It's okay, Liam called me."

I glance over at him. He shrugs.

"He did?" I ask her.

"Yeah. But that's not what I want to talk about. Are you watching your television right now?"

"No."

"Turn it on."

"What channel?" I ask her.

"WVFY, of course."

Grabbing my remote, I press the on button and my television slowly warms up.

"Are you watching?" Lauren asks.

"No. It's an old set. It's slow."

She lets out a sigh and tells me to watch the phone. She'd switched the camera view because her television set fills the screen.

And in front of it is an image of our television studios.

There are a group of people outside, and even though the screen is small and the image is a little blurred, I recognize them all anyway.

"Well, it's not often we get to give you a story about our own television station," the reporter, Joanna, says, smiling into the camera. She's standing outside with the crowd. "But today our news and sports team walked out in support of a member of staff who they feel has been treated badly. Dan Keyes is here to tell us more."

The camera cuts to Dan. He's in jeans and a college football sweatshirt – far from his usual business attire. It's like he's dropped over on his way to a game.

"Good afternoon, Joanna. And I'd like to say I'm reporting on behalf of my friend, Sophie West, and not on behalf of WVFY. I'm not being paid for this report." He has this way of capturing you on camera. "Many of you know Sophie West. She's one half of our superb weather team, and an excellent meteorologist. WVFY is extremely lucky to have her. But today she was accused of something she didn't do, and we're all out here to support her. And I have to tell you that this will be the last time you'll see me on camera until Sophie is reinstated."

"Oh my God."

"They're all there for you," Lauren says, swapping the camera so I can see her face. "Did you see them all?"

My throat is tight. "I did." There are at least thirty people standing on the sidewalk. Most of them don't even work on the weekends. They haven't just walked out of the station, they've driven there to protest.

"I need to get over there," I say.

"Aren't you a little underdressed for that?" Lauren asks, looking amused. I glance down and realize I'm still wearing the towel I wrapped around myself after my shower hours ago.

"I'll make sure she looks decent first," Liam says.

"Good plan." She ends the call and I almost jump out of bed.

I can't believe they're doing this for me. My heart feels so full right now.

"Can we take a raincheck on that kiss?" I ask Liam.

"Yep." He nods, his gaze soft. "Now let's go."

CHAPTER
THIRTY-TWO

SOPHIE

On the way to the station my phone rings again. This time it's Donald.

"Ah, Sophie. We were wondering if you were free to come in to meet us," he asks.

"Actually, I'm on my way to the station right now."

"You are?" He sounds strangely happy about that. "Good, good. Come straight to the boardroom. We'll be waiting for you."

"Did you hear that?" I ask Liam. He looks strangely amused.

"I did."

"Did you call him?" I ask, suspicious. I know he was aching to.

And maybe I would have let him after a while. I certainly can't be angry at him for wanting to help me.

"I really didn't," he says. "I might have folded eventually, but I haven't yet."

At least he's being honest. He's also driving like a maniac

and manages to cover the distance between my apartment and the station way too quickly. He parks and we hurry over to the station entrance, where all my friends are waiting for me.

Madison and Lisa are there, along with Dan and Ray and Lorena. Nearly everybody I know at the studio is standing on the sidewalk.

Some of them have even painted banners. It brings tears to my eyes. They surround me, telling me they're on my side, that it isn't fair, that they'll protest for as long as it takes."

"I need to go see Donald," I tell Lisa, who's looking almost Amazonian in her anger. "He's asked me to meet with him in the boardroom."

"Hopefully to give you your job back," she says grimly. "Because otherwise he's going to lose this station."

I lean forward to hug her. "Thank you," I whisper. "I know you're responsible for this."

"Not just me. All of us. When I told them you'd been sent home we all agreed we had to do something."

The crowd parts and I walk inside, Liam holding my hand. "You want to stay here?" I ask him.

"I'll walk up there with you. Wait outside." The way his eyes are narrowed I'm almost certain somebody's going to get hurt. You can only push a man so far. "Okay, thank you." We take the elevator up to the top floor and I point at a chair he can sit in while I walk over to the boardroom and knock on the door.

"Sophie, come in." Donald stands this time as I walk inside. The lawyers are still there but no HR, Michael, or Rhian. There is a guy in a pair of jeans and a t-shirt that I think I recognize from our IT department.

"Please take a seat," Donald says, and a sense of déjà vu washes over me. I do as he says, and look at him expectantly.

"First of all, I want to tell you that your job is completely secure," Donald says. "I was, ah, a little rash sending you home earlier. Please accept my apologies."

I blink. "Okay." Surely Liam must have called him.

"This is Finn," he says, pointing at the man in jeans. "You may know him from our IT team."

"Hi," I say to Finn. "I think I've talked to you about the website before."

He nods back.

"Finn found something interesting when he went into our email servers a little while ago," Donald tells me. "Your email finally bounced back."

"What?" I ask, confused.

"Maybe Finn can explain," Donald suggests. I turn to look at him and he nods.

"There's ah… different kinds of bounces. Soft bounces and hard bounces," he says. "Hard bounces usually get sent back to the server right away. You've probably seen them before. You'll get an email undeliverable message in your inbox."

"Yes, I've had some of those. But I didn't get one for this," I tell him.

"No," he agrees. "Which is weird, because it's actually a hard bounce, but it came through like a soft bounce."

I've no idea what he's talking about or what this means for me, but I nod anyway, encouraging him to continue.

"A soft bounce happens when the recipient's inbox is full or the server is down. Either way, we get information explaining why something bounces." His eyes light up, as though he's talking about his very favorite thing. "It's called an SMTP reply but you probably don't need to know that." He smiles, embarrassed. "It tells us why something bounces, and then our servers can use that information to decide whether to resend or to block that email account."

"So my email bounced?" I say. "Does that mean that BTV never received it?"

"Pretty much." Finn nods. "But I'm still confused because it looks like a hard bounce acting like a soft bounce."

I'm still clueless. So is Donald and the legal team by the looks of it, but this is good news, right?

"Does that mean that BTV doesn't have the email?"

"That's correct," Finn says. "It's as though it never arrived. Which I guess it didn't if it's a hard bounce." He frowns. He's confusing himself.

"So what happens now?" I ask.

"Well obviously the email is deleted so our server will never try to resend," he says. "But BTV definitely has some kind of problem, because their email server is whacked. Emails shouldn't act like that."

I can't really bring myself to care about the competition's email server. Not when their failure means I haven't given any of our secrets away. "That's good news, right?"

"It's wonderful news," Donald says. "Obviously that means we'd like you back at work right away." He clears his throat. "And maybe you can let the crowd outside know that you still have your job."

I let out a mouthful of air. "So that's it?" I ask. "It's over?"

"Well, I've also managed to get ahold of the person responsible for receiving the weather hub submissions. They've agreed to look at ours if you email it over before the end of the day. Can you do that?"

"Yes I can." I nod. "I'll just need my laptop."

"Monica left it in your office. In your top drawer."

"Thank you," I say gruffly.

"Well that's it," Donald says, standing. "It's been a long day and I'm sure everybody would like to get home. Finn, Charles, Robert, thank you for your time." They shake my hand and file out, leaving me and Donald in the boardroom alone.

"Ah, while you're here, I've had some reports about the weather team being extremely understaffed," Donald says.

"I'm going to look into that tomorrow. I wonder if you'd be available to talk about that as well as a possible restructuring of the team?"

"Yes, of course."

"Good, good." He holds his hand out. "Thank you. And if you could make sure everybody comes inside before it's time for the evening broadcast I'd be very grateful."

He walks out and I follow him, but he comes to an abrupt halt when he sees Liam standing there.

"Well hello," Donald says jovially, shaking Liam's hand like he's his best friend. "What are you doing here?"

"Waiting for my girlfriend," Liam says.

Donald blinks, looking from Liam to me. "Sophie's your girlfriend? Why didn't you say? You could have come in with her for the meeting." He presses two fingers to his temple, looking distinctly uncomfortable. "Or you could have called me. We could have talked this through."

"Sophie prefers to fight her own battles," Liam murmurs, looking at me. "Is everything okay?"

I nod. "Everything's fine. More than fine."

"Sophie's a valued member of the station," Donald tells us. "I just wanted her to know that."

Liam's lips twitch.

"We should have lunch soon," Donald says to Liam.

"Sure," he replies smoothly, still looking at me. "Let's do that."

Donald nods and walks down the hall, leaving the two of us alone.

"So it's all okay?" Liam asks me, pulling me into his arms. I melt into his chest. This is my favorite place to be.

"The email bounced," I tell him. "From BTV's servers. It's like it never got sent."

"Is that right?" he asks mildly. "That's good."

I step back, giving him a quizzical look. This time he

won't quite catch my eye. "Did you have something to do with it?" I ask.

He lifts a brow. "Something to do with the server of one company bouncing an email back to another company, neither of which I have anything to do with?" he asks.

I notice he doesn't say no.

————

LIAM

It feels like a minor victory that I could do one thing for her to make it better. She's going to have to learn to accept help but I'm a patient man. I can wait.

Decades if I need to.

I linger back as she walks outside to tell her friends about her reinstatement and the email and that they really should come inside and get back to work. This is her victory and she deserves it.

And I want her to realize I'm not the only one on her side. They all are. Every one of them with the exception of Michael, her boss. And I'm kind of certain he's not going to be her boss for much longer.

I'm almost certain she's going to grill me about the email later. And I'm here for that. I'll be honest with her, the way I'm always going to be honest with her.

And maybe she'll meet me in the middle occasionally. Let me help her, protect her, not tell her everything because I know she feels uncomfortable in gray areas.

It all boils down to one thing. She needs to trust me. And I need to earn it.

The door opens and Sophie walks back in, followed by her friends and colleagues. Her face is glowing and when she sees me waiting for her she gives me the sweetest smile.

And I know I need to get her home and soon. I want the making up part right now.

"I'll be five minutes," she tells me. "I just need to go get my laptop and send that email."

"Double check the address," I advise her. She rolls her eyes at me.

And I'm here for that, too.

They walk into the hallway that leads to the offices and I follow them idly, deciding that she might not be in such a hurry if she can see that I'm happy waiting. I still feel guilty about that email. She was crazy busy that Friday thanks to my late nights with her and having to get away for my mom's party.

When she reaches the office with *Weather Dept* written in blue lettering above the door my teeth grit because I can see her boss in there. He doesn't move despite her attempt to duck around him.

My fists curl. Don't push me, asshole.

"You got lucky," he tells her. "If that email hadn't bounced you'd be out of a job by now."

My jaw tightens.

"Don't be stupid," she tells him. "It was a mistake. A genuine one. And I don't appreciate the way you seemed to be enjoying my pain."

She gives him a look of disdain and pushes past him, causing his arm to bang against the door jamb.

"Hey, that hurt."

She ignores him.

The problem is that *I* can't. I want to. For her sake mostly because I know she doesn't like confrontation. But I love her and I want to protect her and this asshole is hurting what's mine.

So I walk over to him and grab him by the collar, then I pull him out of the damn doorway and into the hall. I must take him by surprise because he doesn't resist, just moves those tiny shiny feet until I push him against the wall.

"Remember our last talk?" I say to him.

"Um… yes?"

"That's funny," I tell him. "Because you're not acting like you remember it at all. Lucky for you I do. Every word. And I think I told you that if you talked to Sophie like that again you'd lose your job." My lips curl. "Oh and that I'd hit you." I can't do it, I know that. But I want to.

He blanches. "You can't do that. I'd sue."

From the corner of my eye I see Sophie's friends watching us. I think about hitting him anyway, but it wouldn't be a fair fight.

And I like my right hand. Although I'm hoping it will get a bit less use in the future.

"Let me just say this," I say, leaning forward until he can feel the heat of my breath on his face. He tries to cower back but I don't let go of his collar.

"You're hurting me," he complains.

"I'm not going to threaten you with violence this time," I tell him. "Or your job. Because I don't think you're going to have it for much longer anyway."

His bottom lip starts to tremble.

"You're all seeing this, right?" he calls out to the people behind me.

"Seeing what?" Sophie's friend, Lisa asks. "Does anybody see anything here?"

"Nope," the guy next to her says.

"Me either," the female news anchor whose name escapes me adds. "Actually, I think I see Michael Rimmer being a bully to his staff. Maybe we should report that."

I let go of his collar and step back. He keeps himself pinned against the wall like he's unable to move.

"We've got this," Lisa says. "Haven't we, guys?"

"She's safe here always," a mountain of a guy standing

next to her says. "He steps out of line and he's toast." He walks forward and shakes my hand. "I'm Ray and if you want to send more shellfish in for lunch I won't complain."

I grin. "I'll remember that."

"Thank you."

Sophie walks out and sees us all standing there. Her brows knit for a moment. She shoots me a 'do I want to know about this' look and I shake my head.

I'll tell her later. Hopefully, much later.

"You good?" I ask her.

"Yep. All done." She bites into her juicy bottom lip and I hold my hand out for her. She takes it and I immediately feel grounded.

"Come on then," I say to her. "Let me take you home."

"Your home or mine?" she asks, her eyes on mine.

"Both are home to me." It's the truth. Home is where she is. It's where I want to be. And I know I need to prove myself even more to her. I need to show her she can trust me. Even if it takes the rest of my life I'm okay with that.

Her expression softens. She steps closer, placing her hands on my shoulder. "I'm sorry I left," she whispers. "I won't do it again."

"Good," I tell her. "But even if you did I'll always follow you."

Her lips curl. "I'm counting on that." She moves her hands up, until her fingers are curled around the back of my neck. She's on her tiptoes and I automatically reach down to hold her hips to keep her steady.

"You know the good thing about both our homes?" she asks me.

"What?" I tip my head to the side, feeling so damn lucky to have this girl.

"They're empty. No family, no friends. Just us."

"Hallefuckingluhah," I say, because even though yesterday feels like forever ago, the need to be alone with this woman is still coursing through my veins. I love her. I adore her. I'll cross oceans and climb mountains for her.

Hell, I'll do morally dubious server raids, or at least ask my right hand woman to do so, just to save this beautiful girl's ass.

"I love you," she tells me, as though she can read my mind.

"The feeling is mutual, West," I say, my throat tight. "I love you, too."

"Then take me home."

And I do.

EPILOGUE

LIAM

It's been six weeks since I chased her back to Charleston and I'm starting to wonder if moving in together is a good idea. She's bent over a box in the kitchen, her skirt pulled up to reveal her smooth, tan thighs, and I've got a boner the size of Brooklyn as I imagine walking behind her and sliding those pretty panties aside.

There's every possibility that I'm going to fuck her until we both die of exhaustion. The only time I don't think about sex is when we're both at work, or when I'm playing racquetball with Myles. I thought I'd get used to it by now but moving in together has only made me hornier.

I'm imagining christening each room with her. Multiple times. Bending her over the bath, pushing her against the tiled wall in the shower, eating her for breakfast on the counter.

"Did you find the coffee pot?" her dad asks, walking in with a tray of cookies. I immediately deflate which is a very good thing.

"Yep, it's here." Sophie stands and holds it up like she's won a prize. Then she sees me skulking there like the dirty stalker I am.

"Oh hey," she says. "When did you get here?"

"Five minutes ago." And yes, I've been watching her the whole time. She's my girl. Sue me. "Everything's finished with your apartment. I handed the key back."

I first saw this house before Sophie and I were officially together. Even then I could picture her in it perfectly. It has a skylight that spans the length of the kitchen and she loves looking up and watching the clouds.

And I love watching her do it, so we both win.

"Do you want some coffee?" she asks.

"Yes, please," Myles says, carrying in a box. We've pretty much enlisted the whole family. Eli's driving his truck – yep, he's actually driving his own vehicle – which has most of my things from Myles and Ava's bungalow. I'm kind of sad to say goodbye to that place because it means I'll see less of Charlie.

Although we have a room here that's perfect for him if he ever wants to sleep over. Or more importantly, if Myles and Ava ever let him. I know they trust Sophie but me…

I'm working on it.

Sophie makes the coffee and her dad hands out the cookies and then I call a local pizza delivery joint and arrange for enough food to arrive to keep my brothers from bitching about being hungry. Even Holden's here, having gotten a few days off from work. And Linc and Brooks have actually been helpful, setting up the beds in all the rooms and putting together the furniture Sophie and I bought.

I love them all. But I'm damn happy when they all leave a few hours later and it's just the two of us. When I close the door after Eli, the last out, I turn around and let out a sigh before walking through the house to find her.

This house is big. Probably too big for just us. But it's only a few minutes away from Myles and Ava and within easy distance of work for Sophie. Plus it has a great office I can work from when I'm here.

I've still kept my apartment in New York. I'll have to fly there once a week, at least for the foreseeable future. But I have a plan.

Sam's gotten a well-deserved promotion. She's more than good at what she does. She's also hungry for more. And I trust her.

Plus she's already a hit with our clients. They love her. Between us we're keeping them happy which keeps me happy because I get to spend more time with my girl. If she keeps doing that I can see her becoming the head of our New York operations in no time.

Sophie's currently in the bathroom, taking off her makeup. I walk into our bedroom hoping for a quick view of her stepping into the shower, but the door is closed. I frown and wonder if it's too much to open it, but then I see a note on the bed.

Along with a piece of black fabric. A mask. One of those ones you wear when you can't sleep at night.

Picking up the note I read her words.

Put this mask on and shout 'ready'.

This isn't like her. I'm the one who makes the demands. She's my good girl. And yet I kind of like this. It's kinky and I'm here for it.

Shrugging, I pull the mask over my eyes. It takes a minute to adjust the elastic because it's clearly made for a woman's smaller head, but eventually it doesn't feel like it's cutting off the blood flow to my ears.

And then I call out to her. "Ready." Or at least I think I am.

I hear the creak of the bathroom door and the thud of bare

feet against the floor. "Do you trust me?" she asks, her voice throaty as hell.

I ask her that all the time. I'm happy to report her answer is always yes these days. She trusts me and it's like I've won the damn lottery.

"Always, baby," I tell her honestly.

"Good. Take my hand," she says, sliding her palm into mine. "We just need to go somewhere."

A smile plays at my lips as I let her lead me out of the bedroom and into the hallway. We turn left, which means we're heading toward the living room that opens up to our beautiful backyard.

"I'm hoping you're naked right now," I tell her.

Sophie laughs softly. "Stand there," she whispers, so I do. I stand and try to ignore the throbbing in my dick because even smelling and touching this woman makes me hard.

I hear a shuffle. A click of a lock and a sudden cool breeze. She must have opened the back doors. "Are we outside?" I ask. I picture her naked on the grass, her hair splayed out, her eyes wide as she stares up at me.

"Yes, we are. You can take the mask off now," she says, her voice more distant than I thought it would be. I reach up and pull it over my hair, my eyes eager to see her naked in our yard.

But what I see is even better.

She's fully clothed. Kneeling on the grass in front of a huge lit up sign.

Liam Salinger. I love you. Will you marry me?

"What the?" I walk all the way outside and she's still kneeling there, a dark blue box in her hands. It's open and nestled inside are two rings. A thick dark band and a thinner one.

"These are just temporary," she tells me. "If you say yes we can buy some new ones."

I fall down to my own knees in front of her. Some guys

would hate this. They'd want to be the one to do the asking. Maybe they'd even feel emasculated.

But not this guy. I didn't even know I needed this but I did. I needed to know she trusts me completely.

And these rings and her kneeling and that sign… yeah. I'm welling up.

"Will you?" she asks, her eyes shining.

I swallow because there's no way I'm crying even if my eyes are telling me different. "Yeah," I say my voice rough. "I'm going to marry the fuck out of you. Here in the backyard."

She laughs. "Is that a euphemism?"

"Kind of." I definitely want us to marry at our house. I can't imagine anywhere better. But yeah it's also a euphemism because I want her. *Now.*

So we slide the rings on, then I pull her into my arms and show her exactly how not emasculated I am. She's soft and smiling as I kiss her. Looping her arms around my neck, I pull her toward me until she's sitting on my thighs. I slide my lips down her neck and she lets out that little mewing sound that makes me harder than steel.

My feisty kitten. My girl. My future wife. How the hell did I get this lucky?

"We'll do it soon," I say, laying her down on the grass. "Get married." She looks almost exactly like my vision but with too many clothes on. I begin to rectify that, unbuttoning the front of her dress, pushing it open to reveal the flimsiest of lacy bras. Taking a moment to admire the sheer perfection of her body, I dip my head and scrape my teeth against her nipple.

"How soon?" she gasps.

"What you doing tomorrow?"

She laughs again as I stroke my tongue against her. "Working. As are you." She's spent most of the last few weeks recruiting new employees. Since Michael quit and headed west, she's been appointed head of the weather department. Her job is growing because her submission won and Charleston is now the regional weather hub, too.

She's killing it and I love that for her.

"Within the next two months." I kiss my way down her stomach. I like this dress, it buttons right down to the hem. So I unfasten the rest of them until it opens up like a gift in front of me.

Her panties match her bra. Lacy. Almost non-existent. I kiss the little bow at the front of them because it deserves a thank you.

Then I yank them down. She lifts her ass and her thighs to help me.

"Good girl."

She fucking glows. I'll never get tired of that.

I kiss her soft thighs, her jutting hips, the crease where her legs meet her torso. And then I give her one long, languorous lick right where she needs me.

"Liam," she gasps. "The neighbors…"

"They don't overlook us," I remind her. "And if you keep it quiet they'll never know." Another good thing about a big house like this is that it has a huge ass yard. The possibilities are pretty endless.

We can spend the rest of our lives trying them all.

Or maybe not. The kids might notice. We'll have to be more discreet. But I can work with that.

And kids? Yeah. We want a lot of them. A whole new Salinger dynasty. Or a West-Salinger dynasty.

Or Salinger-West dynasty. I blink because there are so many possibilities.

"Where have you gone?" she murmurs, stroking my hair.

"I was just thinking about our kids."

"Shall we get married first?" she asks. "I know it's old fashioned, but it'll make our families happy."

I nod, and kiss her right at her center, making her gasp. "And what will make you happy?" I ask her.

"You," she says simply, her fingers raking my scalp. "It's always you."

Want more of Strictly Pleasure?
If you're not quite ready to let Liam and Sophie go, get a glimpse of their happily ever after in this exclusive bonus epilogue.
Download It Using This URL:
https://dl.bookfunnel.com/4eqhrbs6aj

And if you enjoyed Liam's and Sophie's story, the next book in the Salinger Brother's series is STRICTLY FOR NOW - Eli's and Mackenzie's story.

DEAR READER

Thank you so much for reading Liam and Sophie's story. If you enjoyed it and you get a chance, I'd be so grateful if you can leave a review.

The next book in the series is Eli's story - find out what happens when he meets his match in Mackenzie Hunter in STRICTLY FOR NOW.

WANT TO KEEP UP TO DATE ON ALL MY NEWS?

Join me on my exclusive mailing list, where you'll be the first to hear about new releases, sales, and other book-related news.

To sign up put this web address into your browser: https://www.subscribepage.com/carrieelksas

I can't wait to share more stories with you.

Yours,

Carrie xx

ABOUT THE AUTHOR

Carrie Elks writes contemporary romance with a sizzling edge. Her first book, *Fix You*, has been translated into eight languages and made a surprise appearance on *Big Brother* in Brazil. Luckily for her, it wasn't voted out.

Carrie lives with her husband, two lovely children and a larger-than-life black pug called Plato. When she isn't writing or reading, she can be found baking, drinking an occasional (!) glass of wine, or chatting on social media.

You can find Carrie in all these places
www.carrieelks.com
carrie.elks@mail.com

ALSO BY CARRIE ELKS

THE SALINGER BROTHERS SERIES

A swoony romantic comedy series featuring six brothers and the strong and smart women who tame them.

Strictly Business

Strictly Pleasure

Strictly For Now (releases June 30th 2023)

THE WINTERVILLE SERIES

A gorgeously wintery small town romance series, featuring six cousins who fight to save the town their grandmother built.

Welcome to Winterville

Hearts In Winter

Leave Me Breathless

Memories Of Mistletoe

Every Shade of Winter (releases March 31st 2023)

ANGEL SANDS SERIES

A heartwarming small town beach series, full of best friends, hot guys and happily-ever-afters.

Let Me Burn

She's Like the Wind

Sweet Little Lies

Just A Kiss

Baby I'm Yours

Pieces Of Us

Chasing The Sun

Heart And Soul

Lost In Him

THE HEARTBREAK BROTHERS SERIES

A gorgeous small town series about four brothers and the women
who capture their hearts.

Take Me Home

Still The One

A Better Man

Somebody Like You

When We Touch

THE SHAKESPEARE SISTERS SERIES

An epic series about four strong yet vulnerable sisters, and the alpha
men who steal their hearts.

Summer's Lease

A Winter's Tale

Absent in the Spring

By Virtue Fall

THE LOVE IN LONDON SERIES

Three books about strong and sassy women finding love in the big
city.

Coming Down

Broken Chords

Canada Square

STANDALONE

Fix You

An epic romance that spans the decades. Breathtaking and angsty
and all the things in between.